RED TELEPHONE ALERT

"Uh-oh. Are you saying the Russians are attacking our space program? Oh, man," the President groaned. "I think I'd rather it be the Martians."

"There are no Martians," Dr. Harold Smith said testily.

"I wouldn't be so su Fox telecast when be from Washingto photographer off. W NSA—everyone. They all disavow sending any agents."

The President lowered his voice to a hoarse hush. "Before Rust was hauled off, he was talking about Men in Black."

"That term is not one I am familiar with," Smith admitted.

"Men in Black are these mysterious guys who go around confiscating UFO evidence. Some say they're CIA. Others that they're Air Force." The Chief Executive's voice dropped lower. "A lot of people think they're really space aliens."

"I trust you do not believe the latter theory," Smith said thinly.

"A smart President doesn't rule anything in or out when dealing with national security issues. Especially one who watches 'The X-Files' faithfully."

Created by
WARREN MURPHY
and RICHARD SAPIR

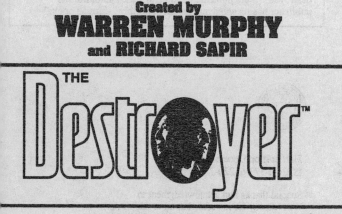

THE
Destroyer™

SCORCHED EARTH

A GOLD EAGLE BOOK FROM
WORLDWIDE.®

TORONTO • NEW YORK • LONDON
AMSTERDAM • PARIS • SYDNEY • HAMBURG
STOCKHOLM • ATHENS • TOKYO • MILAN
MADRID • WARSAW • BUDAPEST • AUCKLAND

First edition December 1996
ISBN 0-373-63220-7

Special thanks and acknowledgment to
Will Murray for his contribution to this work.

SCORCHED EARTH

For Jeanne Elizabeth Kilian—
not to be confused with Killian's Red,
even when she's at her reddest.
Happy first anniversary, with love.

And for the Glorious House of Sinanju,
P.O. Box 2505, Quincy, MA 02269

1

In the beginning, no one expected the BioBubble to burst.

Certainly not the national press, which hailed it as being in the vanguard of man's exploration of space—even though it wasn't part of the space program.

When the space program angle became old news, the press hailed it as the perfect tool for solving the global eco-crisis of the moment.

The eco-crisis of the moment changed from moment to moment, of course. Sometimes it changed from newspaper to news outlet.

On the same day, at opposite ends of the continental United States, the BioBubble—a three-acre honeycomb terrarium of thermopane glass supported by white-painted steel trusswork—was simultaneously hailed as the solution to the global-warming crisis and the jumping-off point for man's eventual relocation to a less polluted planet.

Thus claimed the *New York Times* and the *San Francisco Chronicle*, respectively.

After a while, the national press began seeing it differently. Even with the decline in readership and the spiraling cost of bulk newsprint eroding the page counts of most big-city dailies, the editors still had column inches to fill.

The first red glimmering of trouble came when to support the faltering project—no one at BioBubble Inc. would say why it was faltering, just that it was—the facility was opened to tourists. Only then was the first discouraging word heard.

"Tourists? Isn't the BioBubble hermetically sealed? With airlocks?" asked a reporter at an outdoor news conference at the BioBubble site with the eroded red-sandstone hills of Dodona, Arizona, shimmering in the background. The spot had been chosen for its resemblance to the landscape of Mars, according to the earliest press releases.

"Yes. To simulate every ecosystem on our fragile planet," said the director of information for Bio-Bubble Inc., Amos Bulla.

"If you let in tourists, won't that destroy the BioBubble's eco-integrity?" a second reporter pressed.

"Tourists will not be allowed in. Only to *look* in. Think of it as a zoo with people on both sides of the bars."

"What if someone throws a brick?"

"The glass is tempered and bulletproof. But no one would be so malicious," Bulla said sanctimoniously.

In truth, no one was. Unless one counted the press and their figurative cast stones called factoids.

There was a spate of editorials criticizing the project for stooping to the level of a scientific Disneyland. But another round of editorials from rival papers, insisting that scientific research needed to hack out uncleared paths, put a temporary halt to that line of criticism.

Then a Japanese tourist with a Nikon and a roll of Fuji Super D Plus film shot the half-chewed pizza crust sticking out from the compost heap on the other side of the sealed glass-and-steel honeycomb habitat.

He sold the shot to the *National Enquirer* for sixty thousand dollars, and the *Enquirer* ran it on the front page, with the headline BioBobble Revealed. Because the *Enquirer* was now a chief news source for the national press, the *Boston Globe* took it seriously and sent one of its photojournalists to investigate.

"The photos clearly showed a pizza crust in the compost heap," the journalist argued.

"I agree," Amos Bulla said forthrightly. "But not *our* compost heap."

"The photo definitely showed white-painted steel trusswork in the foreground."

"A clever fake. The BioBubble has been sealed for over a year now. All the food is grown organically, then recycled. There is no pizza being baked or grown in the BioBubble habitat."

"Then why did the *Enquirer* pay a Japanese tourist sixty grand for a snapshot?"

"To sell newspapers. Just like you're doing," retorted the director of information for BioBubble Inc.

After the pizza-crust crisis blew over, things settled down for a while. And so did publicity. With publicity off, the tourist flow dropped to a lazy, sporadic trickle.

"We need to pump up the volume on this thing," said the financier of the project by long-distance telephone.

"Last time, the whole thing was almost blown out of the water," Bulla told him. When not dealing with the press, he functioned as project director—a position neither demanding nor critical, inasmuch as the facility, once sealed, was supposed to be self-sustaining.

"Whose fault was that?"

"That won't happen again. I laid down the law. Next time we sneak in pizza, everybody eats their crust, too. We can't afford another PR problem."

"Maybe we can manufacture a crisis."

"What kind of crisis?" asked Bulla guardedly, thinking *I'm the front man so I'm the fall guy if anything goes wrong.*

"An eco-crisis. What else?"

A solemn press release was duly issued, alerting the nation and the universe at large that the BioBubble, the self-sustaining greenhouse that was itself a miniature Mother Earth, was mysteriously, inescapably losing oxygen.

"This may in some way mirror the loss of greenhouse gases our dear Mother Earth is currently experiencing," Bulla announced.

This was said at a press conference at the Dodona, Arizona, site of the BioBubble construct with the hot sun making the Dome resemble an otherworldly gem.

The press was there in substantial numbers. It was a slow news day.

"Do you have any reason to suspect leakage?" Bulla was asked.

"BioBubble integrity stands one hundred percent. There is some atmo imbalance occurring within the habitat. Or one of the ecosystems."

Someone wondered if there was excess methane in the air.

"As a matter of fact, that *is* one of the rising gases. Why do you ask?"

"Methane is released through intestinal gas. There's a theory that bovine methane emissions are responsible for the ozone-layer problem," said the stringer from *Mother Jones*.

"There are only a dozen cows in the BioBubble."

"People fart, too. Especially eco-pioneers living off beans and tofu."

This was said in all seriousness, but the assembled press rippled in raucous laughter.

The director of BioBubble information wasn't amused and did not join in the merriment.

"Methane is only one of the problematic ascendant gases," he added. "Nitrogen is up, too. As is carbon dioxide."

"Will you pump in fresh oxygen?"

"Absolutely not," Bulla said firmly. "BioBubble seals must remain intact until the current test period is over. Otherwise, the experiment will be contaminated, and we must start over."

"How about sabotage?"

"Impossible. Who in their right mind would want to sabotage the salvation of all mankind? It would constitute mass suicide for Spaceship Earth."

Because this made a great soundbite, no one questioned Amos Bulla further. They rushed to beat each other to the air or in print with it.

The story made the back pages, and the press and public forgot about the BioBubble until the next crisis: another photograph showing portable tanks pumping oxygen into the supposedly airtight dome.

This time it was a *National Enquirer* photographer assigned to the BioBubble beat who broke the story. It turned out their first story had raised circulation thirty thousand copies. The *Enquirer* wanted to hold on to their readers and their quarters.

When the *Enquirer* broke the oxygen story, the national press jumped on it with all four feet.

Director of Information Amos Bulla fielded new questions like a man before a firing squad dodging bullets. Badly and not at all. His neck kept jerking.

"Why wasn't this oxygen infusion announced?" he was asked.

"Our last announcement was barely covered by you people. We concluded there was no press interest."

"What about the public's right to know?"

"They know now. We are hiding nothing." Bulla spread his meaty palms in a gesture of abject innocence. Every camera caught the slick sheen on his perspiration-drenched palms.

"Is the habitat environment contaminated?" he was asked.

"No. Just refortified. It was either this or start over. Since oxygen is a pure and natural gas, we thought it acceptable to introduce a fresh supply. It's organic, you know."

"What about pizzas? Are you introducing more of those?"

"That story is a fraud," Bulla snapped indignantly.

In the end, the reputation of the BioBubble was tainted, and once the first blot had appeared, the press went scurrying for more.

They found plenty. Falsified résumés. Drug use. Financial diversions.

Despite the rain of discredit, the lame jokes and talk-show ridicule, and every attempt to expose the BioBubble as a glorified tourist trap, it refused to burst. It remained unburst for so long that people forgot their expectations.

The project lumbered on, and the press moved on to the O.J. story and never looked back.

Until the night the BioBubble became a smoking, stinking heap of blackish brown silicon-and-steel trusswork whose pristine white paint framework turned black and bubbly as hot tar.

Nobody saw it happen. Not exactly. The only witnesses were calcified by the tremendous heat that melted them inextricably into the viscous glass-and-steel bubble.

It was after sundown. There were no tourists. And no press.

The BioBubble sat in the red desert, burnished by silver moonlight and looking as dignified as a child's cluster of bubbles. The internal lights were off. The inhabitatants—as they were called—were fast asleep, from the tiniest songbird to Project Director Bulla in his mobile home a quarter mile away.

Only the cockroaches, imported from many parts of the globe to ingest vegetable waste, were awake. In the three years the BioBubble had been operating, they had managed to flourish, proving that the scientists who predicted cockroaches would one day inherit the earth were, for once, correct.

The roaches crawled along the inside of the tempered glass panes as if they owned the project. By night, they did. Nobody was brave enough to stay up after lights out.

No one witnessed the event because nighttime visitors were distinctly prohibited. The official reason was to allow the inhabitatants to get their proper rest. They went to bed at dusk and rose with the sun.

The unofficial reason was nighttime was when the catering truck usually arrived.

This was an off night. There was no catering truck.

So there were no witnesses other than the roaches and the inhabitants of the nearby artist's colony of Dodona, Arizona, some of whom later swore they saw a white-hot column of light sizzle down from the clear, star-dazzled sky for the briefest of seconds.

A crack like thunder sounded, waking others, who also swore they saw the beam of light once they understood it was a sure way to be interviewed on national TV. The pale mushroom cloud of moonlight-illuminated smoke was sighted by several people as it drifted and billowed up from the desert floor.

Since it sounded like the thunder accompanying a lightning strike, no one bothered to check the Bio-Bubble until the next morning.

That's when the brown slag heap of vitreous, rehardened glass and steel was discovered and people started to tell their stories—true or otherwise.

The first thing people realized was that the thunder followed a lightning strike. It never preceded it.

And no one had ever heard of lightning that could reduce a project the size of the BioBubble to slag, cooking all its eco-dwellers to burned pork chops.

This once, even the cockroaches didn't survive.

2

His name was Remo and he was trying to make liver pâté.

The trouble was the livers on the menu of the day were not being cooperative. Their owners wanted to keep them—preferably in their bodies and functioning normally.

Remo had other plans.

It was a simple assignment, as assignments went.

For two years now, the city of Minneapolis, Minnesota, had succumbed to a triple-digit annual homicide total, fueled by the simple mathematics of the drug trade. In the process, it acquired the disreputable nickname of "Moneyapolis."

At least, that's how Remo's employer, Dr. Harold W. Smith, explained it to him when Remo had blurted out, "Minneapolis?"

"An ounce of crack cocaine that sells for five dollars in Chicago and other cities fetches twenty on the streets of Minneapolis. This has attracted drug traffickers in unusually high numbers. Consequently there is a drug turf war going on."

"You want me in the middle of it?" asked Remo.

"No. I want you to neutralize the next round of players. A rising Mafia group, the D'Ambrosia crime family."

"Didn't I nail one of their soldiers a while back?"

"I do not keep track," Smith said with lemony disinterest. "They operate out of San Francisco. But they see an opportunity in Minneapolis. If we interdict them now, the D'Ambrosias may decide to remain in San Francisco, where local law-enforcement agencies can contain them without our intervention."

"Gotcha," said Remo, who was in a good mood because it had been over a year since he'd gotten a simple in-and-out assignment.

"The D'Ambrosia Family is convening a meeting with a local supplier at the Radisson South Hotel, adjacent to Twin Cities Airport," Smith continued. "See that their meeting adjourns permanently. Arrangements have been made for you to join the wait staff."

"Why do I have to go undercover for a simple massacre?" Remo wondered aloud.

"The usual reason—security," said Smith, then hung up.

Since he was in a good mood, Remo didn't rip out the pay telephone at Logan Airport. Instead, he went to catch his flight, knowing that the superefficient Smith had already booked him on the cheapest air carrier known to man.

Presenting himself at the Friendly Air reservations desk, Remo said, "I'm Remo. You have a ticket for me?"

The clerk looked him up on his monitor, and asked, "Remo Bozzone?"

"If that's what it says," said Remo, who often got his cover surname from people not in the loop. He had been Remo Williams most of his life. Until the electric chair.

"What was that?" asked the clerk.

"Remo Bozo. That's me."

"Bozzone."

"That's me, too," said Remo cheerfully, fishing out a driver's license at random and flashing it with his thumb over the last name.

The clerk saw that the face matched and the first name was the same, so he didn't push the issue. "Good news, sir," he said brightly.

"I have a crash-proof plane?"

"No. We're bumping you up to first class."

Remo's face fell. "No way. Stick me in coach."

"But there's more leg room in the first-class cabin."

"My legs fold just fine."

"It's free."

"I'm not paying for this. My employer is."

"Complimentary drinks," the clerk coaxed.

"I can get distilled water in coach. Alcohol and I parted company a million years ago."

Remo now had the bored reservation clerk's interest.

"What's wrong with first class?"

"The stewardesses have way too much time on their hands," said Remo with a straight face.

The clerk looked at Remo as if Remo was John Wayne Gacy come back from the grave. Remo looked back as if he were John Wayne come back from *his* grave to deal harshly with his namesake.

In the end, the clerk sniffed and said, "We have no seats available in coach. Will you take a later flight?"

"No time. Is there a place that sells luggage in this terminal?"

"Try the main concourse."

"Fine. Give me the ticket."

Boarding pass in hand, Remo went to a gift shop, picked through the luggage until he found a tan leather carryon with a tiny, keyed padlock and purchased it using his Remo Itri credit card.

"It's one of our finest bags," the gift-shop manager said, handing back the card and receipt.

"I only care about the lock," said Remo, taking the padlock and the tiny wire keyring with its two flat keys and walking out.

The manager called after Remo. "Sir, what about your bag?"

"Keep the change," said Remo.

Going to a men's room, Remo took the padlock hasp between two fingers and began rubbing it vigorously. After a moment, the metal began to thin and elongate until the U shape of the hasp was longer and thinner than manufacturer's specs. When it was long enough to do the job, Remo ran the end through the square hole in his zipper tongue and hooked it in an up position with his belt buckle. Then he locked it with a tinny snick.

Separating the keys, he slipped one in his Italian loafer under his bare foot and the other in one pocket of the tan chinos and hoped the metal detector wouldn't go off.

It didn't.

Already it was a good day.

The flight to Minneapolis had only one hitch. The usual. A stewardess with short russet hair and green eyes like happy emeralds rested her gaze on Remo's trim, 160-pound body, his overthick wrists and the strong planes of his not-too-handsome face and used a line Remo had been hearing from stewardesses for the best part of his adult life.

"Coffee, tea or me?"

This one smiled. Many didn't. Some wore pleading or hopeful expressions. Others actually wept. And one memorable bleached blonde turned their encounter into an unmistakable cry for help by jamming her TWA letter opener into her throbbing jugular and threatening to take her life right there in the center aisle if Remo was brute enough to give an ungentlemanly response.

"I don't drink any of those things," said Remo this time.

The redhead wasn't taking no for an answer. Redheads, Remo had long ago discovered, rarely did.

"But you don't know how I taste," she said plaintively.

"You taste like a redhead. I've tasted lots of redheads. And I'm in a stark, raving blonde mood today. Sorry."

Without missing a beat, the redhead whistled up an ash blond flight attendant from the back of the plane.

They huddled. The blonde, listening attentively, looked at Remo with eyes like small blue explosions of pleasure and nodded animatedly.

They stormed back, the redhead taking point.

"Can you come with us to the first-class galley, sir?" she asked with breathy politeness.

"Why?" Remo asked suspiciously.

"There's more room there."

"For what?"

"For you to jump Lynette here and me to watch."

"You just want to watch?"

"It's better than riding my vibrator to Minneapolis," the redhead said with resigned sincerity.

"There's nothing in the first-class galley I want," said Remo, folding his lean arms stubbornly.

"Well, I guess you'll just have to do him here," said the redhead to the blonde with an air of determination. "Scare me up a blanket, Lyn."

"Nothing doing," said Remo as the blonde hurried back to an aft storage bin.

"Sir, it's our duty as flight attendants to cater to your every need. You said blonde. So you're getting a blonde. And that's it," the redhead fumed, dropping into the empty seat beside Remo and reaching for his zipper.

"Let me make you comfortable." That's when her tapered fingers encountered the tiny luggage padlock and her glossy red mouth made a tasty O.

"What's this?"

"A simple precaution," said Remo.

"Where's the key?"

"In my luggage."

"Oh, my God. It's way down in the cargo hold by now."

"You could go get it," Remo suggested.

"I might miss the flight."

"If you don't get that key, you'll definitely miss the show."

"Don't let the plane take off without me."

"Never happen," said Remo, who watched the redhead scurry up the aisle, not at all hindered by the broken shoe heel lost when taking the turn to the main exit door at 2 G's.

When the ash blonde returned with a fluffy blue blanket, Remo put on an innocent face.

"Your friend just quit."

"Oh! Does that mean it's off?"

"Catch me on the return flight."

"I'll be there."

"But I won't," Remo murmured as the 727 backed out of the gate and taxied to the runway with the red-haired stewardess running in her nylons after them, waving her pumps.

When Remo gave her a little finger wave, she threw her shoes at the aircraft's tail assembly one at a time.

Later the blonde stewardess brought Remo a silver tray from the galley.

"I found you some liver pâté."

"Don't eat the stuff."

"Gentlemen who prefer blondes usually like liver pâté."

"I only said I like blondes to discourage the red-head. Actually I'm into brunettes this week."

"I'll be right back," the blonde said, rushing back to coach.

When she came back, with a zaftig brunette in tow, Remo had locked himself in the first-class rest room, and no amount of pounding, threats or promises would bring him out until the jet's turbines were spooling down at the Minneapolis gate.

Other than that, it wasn't a bad flight, and it did give Remo the idea for making liver pâté.

So when he wheeled the sterling service cart up to room 28-A of the Radisson South Hotel in his starched whites, a Chef Boyardee cap cocked on his head, Remo had his line of attack already planned out.

The door opened, and an overfed hair-bag in a sharkskin suit grunted, "You the guy with the steaks?"

"No, I'm the liver pâté chef."

"I don't want your liver," he snarled.

"But I want yours," said Remo, running the cart in despite the best attempts of the hair-bag to block his way. The hair-bag filled most of the doorway, so he was the most befuddled man in Minneapolis when Remo was suddenly behind him bringing the cart to a squeaky stop.

The hair-bag turned with all the lightning reflexes of a wooden totem pole. It took him six careful steps to get all the way around.

"I said we don't want your liver, jerk-ass!" he bellowed.

"And I said I want yours," returned Remo in an unperturbed tone.

By that time, the men in bad, tight-fitting suits with bunching unibrows over snarling eyes were getting out of their seats looking belligerent.

"What the fuck is this?" asked a black man who wore a gold chain that linked his earlobes, nostrils and nipples and possibly other portions of his anatomy beneath his white silk shirt and tight-fitting white vinyl pants.

"Liver-pâté chef," said Remo, taking the silver domes off six serving dishes.

The bodyguard stumped up, looked down, blinked three times real slow and announced the supremely obvious. "I see only fucking lettuce."

"Haven't pâtéd the livers yet," said Remo.

"We don't want none," the bodyguard growled. "Tell him, Mr. D."

Mr. D. looked all of thirty and as bright as a twenty-five-watt bulb. Remo pegged him for the D'Ambrosia honcho on the scene. That made the guy with all the chains the local supplier.

"Look, we ordered the steak and lobster. You got the wrong room," Mr. D. insisted.

The last dome clanged down, and Remo turned, smiled disarmingly and said, "You first."

"Me first what?"

"You first for liver pâté."

"I don't want—"

The man felt the dull pressure in his abdomen. Being a gangster for most of his short life, he assumed the worst—that the chef had stuck a knife in his gut. It felt like a knife. It punctured the fibrous abdominal walls like a knife, and made his lungs clutch up the way an inserted knife would.

But when he looked down, his eyes horrified, Mr. D. caught a glimpse of his liver, pinched between two hardly bloody fingers, emerging wetly through a round hole in his shirt.

The liver jumped up before his face, unfolded like a fat manta ray and the chef's two thick-wristed hands made some kind of prestidigitation. When the liver flopped down onto one of the service trays, it was a livid paste.

"That's my—" said the late Mr. D as the life oozed out of him through the hole in his 180-dollar silk shirt.

Not everyone had a clear view of what happened. Not everyone's comprehension skills were at their sharpest. Not with all the uncorked Chianti bottles lying around.

But these were men who had come up from the mean streets, and the thud of one of their own hitting the rug was enough to make them reach for assorted 9 mm artillery.

Remo started moving then.

To his superhumanly developed eyes and senses, the surviving five men were moving in slow motion.

A hand snaked out with a gun butt, and Remo's much quicker hand slapped the knuckles, unnerving the fingers. The gun dropped. While the hands, sensing emptiness, clutched for it, Remo's free hand slipped two chisel-stiff fingers into the man's abdominal cavity, located the liver, flopped it over like a fat, foldable steak and drew it out through the quarter-sized hole.

Splat. It landed on lettuce, a purply paste.

By that time, Remo was on to mafioso number three, who brandished a switchblade with an illegal-length blade. It went snick as it came out of his belt sheath, and Remo guided the blade so that it debuttoned the owner's sharkskin suit coat before bisecting the front of his white shirt.

The man's exposed hairy belly opened up like a bearded man smiling. And out spilled his lower intestinal tract.

Remo fished the throbbing liver out of the steaming mass of internal organs and slapped the liver between two hands, rolled it in a ball and tossed it casually over his shoulder.

It landed perfectly. By this time, slow brains were beginning to grasp hard reality.

"Get out of here!" the bodyguard started screaming. "It's a hit!"

Remo let him scream.

There was a bald guy with three rolls of fat at the back of his neck. He fumbled his 9 mm pistol out and was sweeping the room with it.

Remo stopped being a moving blur long enough to deal with him.

The gun snapped out shots, catching the body-guard across the front of his chest. Blood came out of the holes, including his gulping mouth, and he pitched forward as Remo moved in on the rolls of fat from the side.

The edge of Remo's palm connected with the doughy rolls, and the man's head all but jumped off the neck. The dislocation left him looking like a bro-ken-necked puppet, and Remo allowed him to fall dead while he attended to the final live gunman in the room. The local guy festooned with gold chain like some alternative-life-style Christmas tree.

This one had a wheelgun—a chrome-plated Colt Python. Remo handled it with a trick any ordinary man could pull off. He simply clamped the cylinder with his fingers and let the man try to pull the trigger. The trigger wouldn't pull. So Remo plucked the pistol from his hands and showed him a trick no ordi-nary man could perfect.

He crushed the wheelgun to metallic fragments with a single hard squeeze.

The goon goggled at the chrome bits dropping to the rug. "How'd you—?"

"Do that?" prompted Remo, spanking his hands clean of steel shavings.

"Yeah."

"Easy. I gave it a good squeeze."

"It's steel and you're not."

"I'm alive and you're not," countered Remo.

The "Huh" matched the gunman's dulled-by-shock expression, and Remo used his right index finger to hook the man's network of gold ropes. He gave a quick tug.

The chains were solidly anchored. They came loose, pulling off red pieces of nose, lips, earlobes, nipples and navel.

The belly button was especially well secured. It came out last, taking the twenty-four-carat gold stud and a big swatch of washboard musculature with it.

Remo got another flood of internal organs and caught the liver on its way down.

Quickly he collected the remaining livers of the dead and worked them into pâté, which filled the remaining serving dishes very nicely.

Recapping them, Remo smacked his hands together and surveyed the room. "Can I cook or what?"

And he walked away whistling.

3

It was Kwanzaa in the White House.

The traditional Christmas tree stood on the White House's sprawling North Lawn. A Douglas fir this year, festooned with traditional holiday lights and decorations.

It had been a tremendous relief to the President of the United States when the First Lady had announced that they were going traditional this year.

"Does that mean no Star of David on top?" he asked, recalling one memorable tree-lighting ceremony he'd rather turn into a repressed memory. Like the 103rd Congress.

"No Star of David," the First Lady had promised on the day after Thanksgiving, which was also celebrated in the traditional way, much to the Chief Executive's unbounded relief.

"No kachina dolls, Eskimo totems or voodoo saints?" the President asked, burping up the fresh taste of turkey.

"Red and green bulbs garnished with silver tinsel."

"Your fans are going to think I had you killed and replaced with a clone," the President said warily.

"I want to celebrate our fourth White House Christmas like Abraham Lincoln did."

"Fighting the Civil War?"

"No," the First Lady said, chewing on a dry turkey drumstick. "In the traditional, all-American manner."

The President realized at last she was serious, grinned broadly and said in his hoarse Arkansas twang, "I'll make the arrangements right away." He bolted for the door before the bluebird of political correctness could settle on the First Lady's cashmere shoulders.

"While you're at it . . ." the First Lady called tartly.

The President froze. "New Year's?"

"A traditional New Year's. See to it."

"Done," said the President, relaxing all over again. His hand was on the door. He paused to issue a warm sigh of relief and forevermore regretted not flinging open the door and charging through to do his presidential duty.

"But in between, we're doing Kwanzaa," said the Voice of Steel.

The President whirled as if shot in the back. "Kwanzaa? The Black Christmas!"

"It's not Christmas," she corrected gently. "Christmas is the 25th. New Year's is January 1. Kwanzaa is celebrated during the six days in between. And don't say 'Black.' Say 'Afrocentric.' It's more correct."

"Didn't we have this argument once before?" the President said, thick of voice and tongue.

"And I let you win. But the election is over with. We have nothing to lose by celebrating Kwanzaa."

"I won't have to wear a dashiki or anything, will I?"

"No, we light a candle a day and host Afrocentric cultural events."

The President thought that wouldn't be so bad. And the election was behind them. What had they to lose— except a little more of their fading dignity?

"I'll look into it."

"No, you *do* it," the First Lady said, the familiar steel creeping back into her tone. Then she used her perfect white incisors to gouge a hank of dark meat from the bone.

Closing the door behind him, the President was halfway down the red-carpeted hall when he thought he heard the crunching of dry bone. He hoped she didn't choke on a bone fragment. Even for a lawyer, the woman sure had peculiar appetites.

The First Lady didn't choke. Not on the turkey thigh bone. And not on the Kwanzaa deal.

And so on the second day after Christmas, the President of the United States found himself at a Blue Room photo op standing before the African candelabra called a *kinara*, lighting the red candle that the First Lady whispered in his ear stood for the basic principle of *kuji-chagulia*.

"It means 'self-determination,'" she added.

"Maybe *you* should be lighting this one," said the President, holding the long candle lighter, which smelled exactly like the punk cigarettes he used to smoke in his boyhood days in Arkansas.

"Smile and light it," the First Lady urged with her most steely smile. "In that order."

The President applied the flame to the red candle.

"Now pick up the unity cup," she undertoned.

The President blew out the lighter and laid it aside. He took up the small wooden goblet that sat on the table mat on which the *kinara* reposed with quiet dignity.

"I drink to unity," said the President.

Flashbulbs popped in his face. The President looked into the cup. The previous day, after lighting the green unity candle, the fluid had been clear. Water. Now it was red.

"What's this?" he hissed through his own fixed smile.

"Goat blood or something," the First Lady said vaguely.

"I can't drink goat's blood!"

"If you don't, you'll insult our Afro-constituents."

"Let one of *them* drink goat blood."

And overhearing that, the Reverend Juniper Jackman stepped out of the backdrop of Afro-American dignitaries, wearing a gigantic smile and saying, "Allow me to instruct our President on the ways of my people."

The First Lady hissed like a cat. This was mistaken for the hissing of a steam radiator and unnoticed for what it was, while Black national leader and intermittent failed presidential candidate Juniper Jackman brought the cup to his lips and gulped it right down.

When he smiled again, his teeth were as red as melting Chiclets.

"What did I just drink?" he hissed through his own version of the fixed political smile.

"Goat blood," the President and First Lady whispered in chorus.

"We don't use goat blood in our Kwanzaa," Jackman said, still smiling his scarlet-and-ivory smile.

"I improvised," the First Lady said.

And the President clapped his hand on Jackman's back as the flashbulbs popped, stunning their unprotected retinas.

The questions started as the popping subsided.

"Mr. President. How do you feel about celebrating your first Kwanzaa?"

"It's really fun!"

"What is the significance of the red candle?" asked another.

Jackman answered that while the President looked to the First Lady for guidance.

"The red candle stands for the blood of the African people shed by the oppressive white man," he said.

Again the low hissing of the First Lady was mistaken for a leaky radiator valve.

"The green candle stands for our black youth and their future," Jackman continued. "While the middle black candle represents African-Americans as a people."

"I agree with everything Reverend Jackman just said," the President added brightly, happy to be off the hook.

"Mr. President, does it concern you that Kwanzaa has no traditional basis?" a reporter asked.

"What do you mean?"

"It was started in the sixties by a California political-science student who cobbled it together from African harvest feasts he observed during a field trip."

The President looked to the First Lady with an expression that all but said, *Is this true?*

The First Lady, looking blank despite her pearly, professional politician's smile, passed the ball to the Reverend Jackman.

The good reverend looked as blank as anyone in the room as he stared expectantly at the President, who made one of the few snap decisions of his political career. He simply winged an answer.

"Hell, a lot of things started back then that are cultural icons now. Look at Elvis. And the Beatles. Would you ask me the same question if we were celebrating Beatles Day in the White House?"

Since the media never quoted reporters, only their questions, the President hadn't bothered to answer. Another reporter took up the bouncing ball.

"Mr. President, what can you tell us about the event at the BioBubble?"

"Gosh. You got me there," the President said in his best aw-shucks voice. "Are those folks celebrating Kwanzaa, too?"

"No, Mr. President. The BioBubble ecosystem has been destroyed along with all aboard. It just came over the wire."

The President's normally red face went flat dead-fish-belly white. "Oh, my God," he said in a tiny, tight voice.

"Let's get back to Kwanzaa," the Reverend Jackman said quickly, sensing the political spotlight about to shift away from him.

"You do that," the President countered. "I need to look into this."

And he left the First Lady and the Reverend Juniper Jackman to carry the Kwanzaa ball. At the door, he paused to shoot a reassuring wave to the White House press corps—and noticed the First Lady digging two fingernails into Jackman's backside with such pinching force it brought the opportunistic reverend up on his toes in pain. Additional redness came to his welded-on smile—probably from biting his tongue to repress the exquisite agony the First Lady was gleefully inflicting.

All of this was unnoticed by the press.

In the corridor, the President was met by his chief of staff.

"What's this about the BioBubble?" he asked.

"First reports are sketchy," said the chief of staff, following the President into the Oval Office.

"They always are," growled the Chief Executive.

"At an unknown hour this evening, the BioBubble was melted into slag, entombing everyone inside."

"Sabotage?"

"Too early to tell."

"Accident?"

"Think of the BioBubble as a gigantic Habitrail only with people and other animals inside. They don't use gas heat or electricity or anything that isn't natural. Unless the methane inside became combustible, we have to rule an accident out."

"What's NASA saying?"

"Nothing. This isn't their project."

The President looked surprised. "I thought this was a NASA research station."

"A common misconception. The BioBubble is privately funded. They talk up the experimental-Martian-colony angle for the publicity value. So far, NASA has shown no serious interest. Especially with all the gaffes and screwups surrounding the project."

A full-dress Marine guard opened the door to the Oval Office, and the President strode in, his face concerned.

"I gotta call around."

THE DIRECTOR OF THE FBI was at first very helpful. "What can I do for you, Mr. President?"

"The BioBubble just went bust. I want you people to look into it."

"Do you have intelligence pointing to a militia group or interstate or foreign conspiracy?"

"No, I don't," the President admitted.

"Then this is out of our jurisdiction."

"I'm asking you to look into this," the President pressed.

The FBI director's voice became very hushed and anxious. "Mr. President. Sir. Think just a moment. It's a troubled project with communelike factors. It's very controversial. It's in a western state known as an antigovernment hotbed. And something burned it flat. Do you really want federal agents in blue FBI windbreakers traipsing about the smoldering ruins for national media consumption?"

"I take your point," the President said unhappily.

"I knew you would," responded the FBI director, who was polite enough to let the President say goodbye before hanging up in his slack-muscled face.

Next the Chief Executive called the director of the Central Intelligence Agency.

"I have a preliminary report on my desk, Mr. President," the CIA director said crisply.

"That was damn fast. What does it say?"

"BioBubble burned to a crisp. Further details to follow."

"That's no different than what I have!"

"Then we're on the same page, as it were," the director said proudly.

"What's your assessment?"

"I have calls out. We're in touch with our assets in this area."

"What area is that?"

"I like to call it the cosmic area."

"The CIA has a cosmic department?"

"Yes, sir. We do. And as soon as we have something concrete to share, we'll get back to you."

The President allowed his gratitude to shine through his worry. "Let me know soonest."

Hanging up, he turned to his chief of staff. "At least somebody out there is on the ball."

The chief of staff made a face. "I wouldn't believe that bullcrap about a cosmic department. They're so eager over at CIA to justify their post-Cold War existence they'll tell you they have a Kwanzaa department if you wanted it investigated."

"Was that stuff about Kwanzaa being a sixties thing true?"

"Search me. I never heard of Kwanzaa before the First Lady started talking it up two years back."

"Me, neither." The President frowned with all of his puffy face, producing an effect like a cinnamon roll baking. "Get me a federal directory. There must be some agency we can turn to in a situation like this."

"Are you sure we want to? The BioBubble is an orphaned private boondoggle. Nobody even knows the identity of the philanthropist who's backing it now."

"How many people died?"

"Maybe thirty."

"And no one knows how or why?"

"That's so far. But there's talk about a lightning strike."

The President snapped his fingers suddenly. His baggy eyes lit up. "Get me the National Weather

Service. Try for that hurricane expert who's always on TV. He looks like he knows this stuff.''

Twenty minutes later, Dr. Frank Nails of the National Weather Service was patiently explaining to the Chief Executive that a lighting bolt powerful enough to melt fifty tons of glass and steel and everything it housed would be, in his words, ''a thunderbolt you'd have felt in the Oval Office.''

''You're saying it can't be lightning.''

''Not unless the BioBubble was filled with propane and natural gas before the hit.''

''It's all natural. No additives. No artificial colors. Or whatever.''

''And no lightning bolt.''

''People say they heard thunder.''

''They heard an explosion, is my guess. Or an atmospheric pressure wave they mistook for thunder.''

''You've been very helpful,'' said the President, hanging up and looking serious.

Calling the CIA again, the President got the director.

''I was just about to pick up the phone,'' the CIA director said. ''Our intelligence source suggests natural causes.''

''What does that mean?''

''An accident. Propane leak or something.''

''The BioBubble uses no harmful chemicals, any more than the rain forest does.''

''They also claim they don't eat pizza. But there's a lot of loose talk about catering trucks and midnight snacks coming out of Dodona.''

''Who's your source?''

''Confidential. But we've used this person before with acceptable results.''

"What's acceptable?"

"This was the source of our report on the Korean famine, Mr. President."

"I had that warning weeks before CIA gave it to me. Korea was in the middle of a crop failure when the flooding started. Anyone could have predicted famine," the Chief Executive pointed out.

"CIA makes no predictive claims. We confirmed the intelligence."

"Find other sources."

"Yes, sir."

"I don't think these people know what they're doing," the President said after hanging up.

"You're not the first Commander in Chief to come to that conclusion," the chief of staff said ruefully.

The President sat down at his desk, his unhappy head hovering between the brazen busts of Lincoln and Kennedy on the shelf behind him. Outside the imperfect window glass, more than a century old, Andrew Jackson's hickory tree groaned under its burden of pristine snow.

"Let's see what the media says."

Picking up a remote, the chief of staff clicked on the Oval Office TV set, nestled in a mahogany cabinet. "At least this should knock the Kwanzaa story out of the lead," he sighed.

"If not off the newscasts entirely," the President said with ill-disguised relief, forgetting there were four more days to go.

The President frowned as a face and voice familiar to many Americans resolved on the screen that showed the CNN bug on the lower right-hand corner.

"With me is renowned astronomer Dr. Cosmo Pagan of the University of Arizona's Center for Exobiological Research."

The President of the U.S. looked to his chief of staff. "Exo—?"

"I think it means life outside the planet."

"Oh."

The reporter shoved his CNN mike into Dr. Pagan's studious face and asked, "Dr. Pagan, what does the BioBubble disaster mean for the space program?"

"It may mean that someone up there doesn't want us up there," said Dr. Cosmo Pagan in his chipper, singsongy voice.

And the President groaned like a wounded reindeer.

"Are you suggesting an attack from space?"

Dr. Pagan smiled as if the idea of an attack from space would be a wonderful thing and a boon to his career.

"No one can say what kind of life-forms exist in the vast vastness of interstellar spaces. But think of it—billions and billions of stars each, in all probability, orbited by planets—trillions upon trillions of worlds very much like ours. If there is life up there, and they have chosen to make their presence known in this dramatic fashion, it will once and for all answer that age-old question. Is there intelligent life in the cosmos?" Dr. Cosmo Pagan smiled so broadly his onyx eyes twinkled like black holes. "I, for one, find this development very life affirming. And can only hope they'll strike again."

The President sputtered, "Is he nuts?"

"We've got to put a stop to this kind of scare talk," the chief of staff said worriedly. "Remember Orson Welles's 'War of the Worlds' radio broadcast?"

The President looked thoughtfully confused. "You mean H. G. Wells's movie, don't you?"

"It was a book, then a radio program, then a movie. The radio program pretended that the Martians had landed and were frying ass all over New Jersey."

"We've got to find out if any of this is real," decided the President, leaping to his feet.

"Sir?"

"If Martians are out to fry the space program, we've got to take countermeasures."

"What kind of countermeasures could—?"

But the question hung unfinished and unanswered in the empty air. The President of the U.S. had abruptly left the Oval Office, his destination unknown.

UPSTAIRS in the Lincoln Bedroom, the President plopped down on the rosewood bed in the rose red bedroom and removed a cherry red telephone from the cherry-wood nightstand.

It was a standard AT&T desk model, its face as smooth as its red plastic molding. There was no dial or keypad. Just the shiny red receiver attached by a gleaming red coil of insulated wire.

Placing the fiery telephone on his lap, the President picked up the receiver and lifted it to his concerned face. His eyes were grim. He turned on the nightstand radio and tuned it to an oldies station.

The phone began ringing at the opposite end, and instantly a parched, lemony voice said, "Yes, Mr. President?"

"The BioBubble disaster. I want you to look into it."

"Do you have reason to believe its destruction is a national-security issue?"

"All I know is that a major scientific project is dead, and the FBI won't touch it, the CIA is citing unnamed sources and the National Weather Service says it can't be lightning."

"The lightning explanation is preposterous, I admit," said the lemony voice of the man the President knew only as Dr. Smith.

"So you'll take the assignment?"

"No, I will look into it. What is the source of the CIA assessment?"

"I just talked to the director a few minutes ago. He called it natural causes—whatever *that* means."

"One moment."

The silence of the line was perfect. No buzzes, clicks or humming. That was because it was a dedicated line. A buried cable ran from the White House to some unknown point where the director of CURE held forth in secret. The President had no idea where. Sometimes he imagined a basement off in a forgotten Cold War fallout shelter. Other times he envisioned the shadowy thirteenth floor of some massive skyscraper that wasn't supposed to have a thirteenth floor.

The lemony voice came back and it sounded peeved. "The preponderance of telephone-message traffic in and out of Langley is to various commercial hot lines."

"Hot lines?"

"The Prophet's Hot Line. Psychic Buddies Network."

"The CIA is consulting psychics!" the President blurted.

"They have been doing it for years," Smith said dryly, as if nothing the CIA did would ever surprise him again.

"I thought they put that Stargate stuff behind them."

"Evidently not. I would not accept any of their reports at face value."

"Look into this, Smith. Dr. Pagan is talking of death rays from outer space. I don't think people will buy it, but after *Independence Day* and *Mars Attacks* you never know."

"Otherwise intelligent people accepted as fact the 'War of the Worlds' radio broadcast when I was younger. And according to polls, a clear majority of Americans believe in the existence of flying saucers. We have to assume the worst where U.S. public opinion is concerned."

"I already do," the President said ruefully.

And the line went dead.

4

Everything looked good for the return flight to Boston until Remo Williams had to use the terminal rest room and accidentally flushed his fly-padlock key down the john.

No problem, he thought, snapping the tiny padlock shut. *I have a backup.*

For some reason, the airport magnometer went beep when Remo walked through the stainless-steel frame.

"Empty your pockets," said a brown-eyed, auburn-haired airline security woman in a smart blue Wackenhut security uniform.

Remo dutifully placed two quarters and a subway token along with his billfold into the tray receptacle. He wore a white T-shirt and tan chinos, so there was no question of concealed weapons.

The magnometer beeped on his second try. The security agent blocked his path. Her voice became gravelly. A smoker.

"Excuse me, sir. I need to frisk you."

"Like hell," said Remo, picking up his left-hand loafer and shaking the tiny padlock key out into the receptacle. "It's only this thing," he said, going around for a third try.

But the beeper sounded a third time, and the auburn-haired woman said, "Airline rules say I get to frisk you."

"Have to frisk me, you mean."

"Want to frisk you," the auburn-haired woman said. "Frisk you friskily," she added.

"Maybe it's my zipper," suggested Remo.

"Zippers don't register. Otherwise, hunks like you would trip the alarm every time."

"It's got to be this frigging padlock."

"What padlock?"

And Remo lifted his zipper tongue with a fingertip to show her. She bent over, squinting. Remo made the padlock wiggle in the overhead lights.

"Why do you have your fly padlocked?" the security agent wondered aloud, reaching out to help Remo with his wriggling.

"It's a long story," said Remo, stepping back ahead of her exploring fingers.

She pointed to a room marked Security.

"Tell me as I'm frisking you up and down. Now march."

"Look, it's the padlock. Here, it's yours."

And Remo yanked the padlock loose so hard his zipper came tearing out. Both landed in the tray.

"Airline rules require me to peek into your drawers."

"No chance."

"Padlocked zipper. You may be smuggling something in there."

"There's nothing there," Remo protested.

The redhead assumed a disappointed expression, her fists resting on her trim hips.

"That shouldn't be," Remo amended.

The redhead brightened.

That was when Remo remembered he carried in his billfold a useful ID that covered just these situations.

"I'm with the FAA. Let me whip out my ID."

"Whip everything out and let me see it in the light."

Remo started with the ID and announced, "You just passed a random security check with flying colors. Congratulations."

"I still have to frisk you."

"Not in this lifetime."

The redhead shifted gears as smoothly as a high-performance racing car. "How about a date, then?"

"What?"

The redhead drew near, her perfume filling Remo's nostrils like a feathery lavender cloud, her voice growing husky. "A date. You and me. Maybe a hotel room if I get lucky."

Perhaps it was the absurdity of the moment. Or maybe the concept of a date hadn't occurred to Remo in a very long time, because he hesitated a moment before saying, "Can't. Against agency rules."

"I'll quit," the redhead said without skipping a beat.

"I don't date the unemployed," Remo said, collecting his stuff and hurrying to his gate.

The redhead tried to follow. Remo ducked into a men's room, balanced on a stall toilet and slipped out while she was on her hands and knees peeking up into the adjoining stall.

On board, Remo sat with a magazine open in his lap and thought long and hard.

He couldn't remember the last time he had gone out on a certifiable date. He couldn't recall the name or face of his last actual date. Dating was not something

Remo normally did. He had affairs. Sometimes he slept with women as part of a cover personality. But he never dated.

As luck would have it, his flight was staffed with male flight attendants. Although one kept looking at him hungrily, he made no pass. Especially after Remo caught him staring at his lap and made a throat-cutting gesture.

Beyond that, he was not fighting off stewardesses.

It gave him time to think.

Remo did not date because the agency that employed him did not exist. Any more than Remo, once a Newark patrolman, was supposed to exist since that cold day years before when they strapped him into the electric chair at Trenton State Prison and yanked the switch.

Declared dead, Remo Williams became the lone killer arm of that agency, called CURE. Neither the man nor the organization was supposed to exist, because both operated outside the law, breaking the laws of America so that criminals who flouted the Constitution, perverting its letter and spirit to serve their own evil ends, would not escape through the loopholes of the U.S. justice system.

CURE was the brainchild of a President—long ago cut down by an assassin's bullet—who realized something drastic was required to preserve the nation. That drastic something was Remo Williams, trained by his mentor, Chiun, in the ancient martial discipline of Sinanju until he became a one-man strike force, anonymous and unstoppable. And therefore not likely to be captured or killed, which would betray CURE and force America to admit publicly that its constitutional government did not work. Only Smith—who had framed patrolman Remo Williams for a crime he never committed—Remo himself and each successive president were supposed to know about CURE, and none of them was allowed to be linked to the others in public.

But while all that meant Remo couldn't marry or raise children or fall permanently in love, it didn't mean he couldn't have a social life. Assuming he was careful.

Maybe I should start dating, he thought. *Why not? There's nothing in my contract that says I can't. I just can't get involved.*

By the time Remo deplaned at Logan Airport, he had resolved to ask the next attractive woman he saw for a date. Just to see what happened.

But not in the terminal. Too many stewardesses in and out of uniform. The last thing he wanted to date was a stewardess. They were too aggressive. He wanted someone nice. Someone demure. Preferably one with D-cups. C-cups might be acceptable, if she had a really nice walk. If not, D-cups or no cups.

ENTERING the fieldstone church-turned-condominium he called home, Remo found the downstairs kitchen empty and the upstairs rooms likewise. So he followed the sound of the steadily beating heart only his ears could detect to the bell-tower meditation room, and informed the Master of Sinanju of the new leaf he was going to be turning come the New Year.

"I need a date for New Year's Eve."

"I do not recommend this," Chiun said in a low, serious voice entirely unlike his normal excited squeak.

"Why not?"

"They will make you flatulent."

"That's not the kind of date I have in mind," explained Remo patiently.

"Figs also are to be avoided."

"I'm not hungry for dates or figs."

"Then why bring these fruits into the conversation?" asked the deadliest assassin alive.

"We weren't having a conversation until I walked in."

"And I was enjoying peace of mind until that moment. But since you are my adopted son and we are related through circuitous and convoluted ways, I will ignore this and listen to your explanations, although I have already judged them the workings of a possibly demented mind."

"By 'date,' I mean going out with a woman."

This lifted Chiun's wizened face, touching its wrinkles with startled interest. "You have met a woman?"

"Not yet. But I will."

"How do you know this?"

"Because I'm going to keep my eyes open for a woman to take out on New Year's Eve."

The Master of Sinanju stirred on his round reed floor mat. Only a knowledgeable anthropologist would recognize him as a member of the Altaic family, which included Turks, Mongols and Koreans. Chiun was Korean. Born late in the last century, he had youthful hazel eyes that bespoke a vitality that virtually guaranteed he would see the next. There was almost no hair on the smooth egg that was his skull. Two cloudlike puffs tickled the tops of his ears. A wisp of a beard curled from his parchment chin. He was the last Korean Master of Sinanju, head of the House of Sinanju, a lineage of assassins who protected pharaohs and popes, caliphs and czars, rulers of all kinds, in an unbroken chain that stretched back to the thin mists of early human civilization.

"I do not understand this concept, Remo," he said, shifting his golden kimono, whose silken sleeves in his lap formed a tunnel that shielded his hands from view. "Explain it to me."

"New Year's?"

"No. Not that. I fully understand the Western dating errors that insist the year begin in the dead of winter when all sane calendars start with the first blooming promise of spring. What is this other dating?"

"You take a woman out and show her a good time."

"Why?"

Remo growled, "Because you like her and she likes you."

"What then?"

"Depends. Sometimes you date no more. Other times you date forever more."

"You marry?"

"That sometimes happens," Remo admitted.

"You are in need of a wife?" asked Chiun, his voice thinning.

"Not me. I just want to slip into a normal life-style for a change. See how it feels."

"So you will take out a woman you do not know, showering her with undeserved gifts and attention and possibly feeding her?"

"Something like that."

"How do you know this woman will be suitable if you have not yet beheld her conniving face?"

"I won't date anyone who isn't suitable."

"This is a strange concept. If you desire a woman, why not take one?"

"I'm not talking about sex. I'm talking about companionship."

"Leading to what?"

"Sex, I guess."

"Aha!" Chiun crowed. "So why do you not dispense with this dating hysteria and take a woman you like, enjoy her for an evening, possibly two if she possesses sturdy bones, abandon her to the winds of chance and then resume your normal existence?"

"If I want sex, there are willing stewardesses galore."

"Then I leave you to your stewardesses, just as you leave me to my meditations," said Chiun, his gaze going to one of the big square windows that looked out over the seaside town of Quincy, Massachusetts.

"I don't want a stewardess. They just want to climb my tree. I want a woman I can talk to. One who understands me."

"You can talk to me. I understand your unfathomable ways."

"You're not a woman."

"I am wiser than a woman. I have taught you more than any woman could. What disease has attacked your weak mind that you would seek out a woman for companionship and wisdom, women being notorious for their utter lack of those qualities?"

Remo started pacing the square room. "Look, I'm an assassin. I can live with it. But I'd like to do something more with my spare time than parry with you and exercise."

"You sleep?"

"Yes."

"You eat?"

"Yes."

"You have me in your life?"

"Always."

"Therefore, your days are full and rich, and your nights serene. What would a woman bring to them?"

"I'll let you know after I start dating," Remo growled.

"If you seek a wife, I will help you."

"I don't seek a wife."

"If you seek a woman, I will leave the sordid details to you."

"Thanks. Appreciate it," Remo said dryly.

At that point, the telephone on the ironwood taboret rang.

Remo grabbed it.

"Remo." It was Harold Smith. He spoke Remo's name with the same warmth he would put into the phrase "Check, please."

Remo returned the touching sentiment in kind. "Smith."

"I have been asked by the President to look into the BioBubble event."

"Why bother? Everyone knows it's a scam."

"Not that aspect of it. The BioBubble was destroyed earlier this evening."

"By what? Cockroach infestation?"

"No. An unknown power that melted it into sticky glass and slag steel."

Remo blinked. "What would cause that kind of meltdown?"

"That is for you and Chiun to discover. Start with the BioBubble founders."

"Isn't this more the FBI's meat?"

"The FBI is reluctant. And there is some urgency here."

"What kind of urgency?"

"Dr. Cosmo Pagan is telling the media that extra-terrestrials may be behind the BioBubble's collapse."

"Who would believe that crap?" asked Remo.

"As much as fifty percent of the American people."

"Where did you get that figure?"

"That is the number of Americans who believe in UFOs, according to polls. And once Pagan's views are widely disseminated by the media, it could be the start of a nationwide panic."

"Oh," said Remo. "I guess we go to Arizona."

"Be discreet."

"I'll leave my Spock ears behind," said Remo, hanging up. He turned to Chiun.

"You heard?" he asked.

"Yes. But I did not understand."

"There's a place out west where they've duplicated every environment on earth—desert, prairie, rain forest—under sealed glass to study ourselves."

Chiun cocked his head to one side. "Yes?"

"Something melted it flat."

"Good."

"Good?"

"Yes. Why should something so useless take up precious space? Are there not too many people already? Do Americans not dwell too close together and without proper spacing between their houses?"

"There's plenty of room out in Arizona."

"And now there is more," said Chiun.

With that, the Master of Sinanju lifted himself from his lotus position on the floor. He came to his black-sandaled feet like an expanding genie of gold and emerald, the silken folds of his traditional kimono unfolding like tired origami. His hands, emerging from their sleeves, revealed long curved nails, one of which was capped by what might have been a jade thimble.

"Smith said to start at ground zero, so that's where we're going," Remo said.

"Perhaps while we are in Arizona, we will visit your ne'er-do-well relatives," Chiun suggested.

Remo winced. "We're on assignment."

"It may be that our work will take us to the place where your esteemed father dwells."

"Don't count on it. I don't intend to stay in Arizona any longer than I absolutely have to."

"Why not?"

"Because this is a dippy assignment."

"This is new?" asked the Master of Sinanju.

5

No one had ever seen anything like it. No one had ever heard of anything like it.

Project head Amos Bulla walked around the still-warm zone of glazed, brownish glass that surrounded the defunct BioBubble. The striated red sandstone hills of Dodona, Arizona, cooked in the near distance, like Mars without impact craters.

"What could have done this? What the hell could have done this thing?" he was saying over and over again.

"Whatever it was, it produced better than 1600 degrees centigrade of heat," said the planetary geologist from the US Geological Survey in nearby Flagstaff.

"Where do you get that figure, Hulce?" Bulla demanded.

"The name is Pulse. Tom Pulse." He kicked at the red sand with snakeskin boots, pulling the brim of his white Stetson low over his sun-squint eyes. "We know the melting points of glass and steel. Any higher and the thing would have been vaporized."

"Look at it, the glass just ran out like maple syrup."

"No, Mr. Bulla. You are standing on fused molten glass."

"Right. From the dome."

"No. This is new glass. Made by the action of heat on sand."

"Sand turned to glass," Bulla croaked. "My God. What could have done that?"

"A heat source of between 1500 to 1600 degrees centigrade."

"How do you know that?" Bulla demanded.

"No mystery. That's the temperature range at which sand is fused into glass."

"Must have been one hellacious blast."

"Actually all glass is made from superheated sand."

"It is?" Bulla said.

"Yes. Sand, limestone and soda ash. Where did you think glass came from?"

"I don't know, smart-ass. Glass mines, I guess."

"Forget the sand. I think we can rule out a lightning strike."

"It must be a lightning strike."

"The evidence says different. No clouds in the sky to generate an electrical storm. And there are no fulgurites in the sand."

"I can see that." Then catching himself, Bulla added, "No what?"

"Fulgurites. Long tubes of fused glass usually found in sand that has been blasted by a lightning strike. When the electrical charge strikes sand, it naturally follows the metallic pathways in the sand until it expends itself. These pathways fuse into electrically created glass. They're almost works of art in themselves."

Bulla kicked at the red sand. "I still say it's got to be lightning."

Tom Pulse shook his head slowly. He was being paid by the hour. "Lightning might have blown a hole

in the BioBubble," he drawled. "It would have shattered as much as it melted. From what I see, a directed energy source the approximate circumference of
three acres did this."

"Directed energy! You mean this mess is man-
made?"

"If it is, I have never heard of the kind of technology that would focus this much concentrated hell on
a piece of the planet."

"You're sounding like that silly-ass Cosmo Pagan
character."

"You're just saying that because Pagan is against
manned space flight."

"I'm saying this because the man is a sanctimoni-
ous ass. He was the clown who first coined the slur
BioBoondoggle when we refused to hire him as a consultant during our Mars phase. Man threw a hissy fit
to end all hissy fits. You'd think he thought he owned
the copyright on anything to do with Mars. Finally
shut up when we gave up on NASA participation and
went green."

"I hear he's en route."

"Sure. To gloat. Screw him. Don't let him near the
area," Bulla ordered.

"What about federal authorities?"

"Who's coming?"

"Maybe EPA. Could be DoD."

"What would the Department of Defense want with
this sorry slag heap?"

"If they buy Dr. Pagan's extracosmic theory, they'll
be here with bells on and Geiger counters stuttering."

Amos Bulla looked up at the early-morning sky.
Even it looked reddish to the eye. "There's no way a
beam from outer space did this."

"The force was downward. It came from on high. Other than that, it's anybody's guess."

Bulla licked his fleshy lips. "Should we still be standing here like this? Exposed?"

"Why not? Did Uncle Sugar Able nuke Hiroshima twice?"

Bulla blinked. "Uncle who?"

"Military talk for the U.S. of A. Whatever did this got what he, she or it wanted. We're safe."

"I hate you tech types. Never use a simple word when a convoluted one will do."

Tom Pulse smiled a tight smile that said *Sue me.*

Helicopters began to rattle the shimmering red horizon.

"Here they come," Bulla muttered. "I don't know what I'm going to hate worse. The media or the Feds."

"Either way, be sure to smile real friendly-like as they Roto-Rooter your unhappy ass."

Bulla winced. "I liked you better when you talked like a techie, not a Texan," he muttered.

Then he strode off to greet the arriving media.

THEY PILED OUT of their helicopters, unloading video cams, sound systems and enough equipment to record the end of the world. As soon as the equipment was off-loaded, the choppers took off and began circling the site, taping aerial and establishing shots of the glass pancake that had supported Amos Bulla for six fat, happy years.

The media pointedly ignored him as he started wading into their midst, looking to shake hands and make friends before tape rolled and there was no turning back.

No one was having any of it.

In fact, they were so cold Bulla started to wonder whether he had shown up for an exposé with himself scheduled for the hot seat.

"We're ready for you," someone said after the cameras were hefted onto shoulders and the reporters were pointing their microphones at him as if testing his firecracker red necktie for radioactivity.

"I would like to make a brief statement," Bulla began.

The media were having none of that, either.

"What did this?" a reporter asked.

"If I could..." Bulla said, waving the prepared statement.

"Do you believe, as many Americans do, in the existence of extraterrestrial visitants?" another reporter interrupted.

Bulla opened his mouth to reply, and a third question jumped at him.

"Have you ever been abducted by grays?"

"Grays?"

"Highly evolved aliens. Think of little green men—except they're gray. They like to perform medical experiments on humans."

Bulla swallowed his anger. "I have a statement," he said tightly. "It will only take five minutes."

"Too long. We need a soundbite. Thirty seconds or less. Can you boil it down to the pithiest point?"

"Lightning," Amos Bulla said quickly.

"How's that?"

"As far as we can now tell, a gargantuan thunderbolt struck the BioBubble. It was a freak accident. Nobody at fault. Nobody to blame. Let's just keep our heads and the lawyers out of this, shall we?"

"What evidence supports this belief?"

"Fulgurites. They're all over the site. In fact, you could say it's one gigantic fulgurite."

The media failed to ask what a fulgurite was, so Amos Bulla got away with it. Not that he expected otherwise. The media was not one to display its ignorance. At least while the cameras were whirring. Later some would question the lightning-bolt hypothesis. Others would simply report it as fact. By that time, Bulla would know if he were out of a job or not. It sure stank that way from ground zero.

"Will you rebuild?" a new voice asked from in back of the pack.

"That decision has not been made yet," Bulla admitted.

"Who will make it? You?"

"I'm only project director."

"Will the decision be made by the mysterious backer of the project?"

Amos Bulla smiled as he had been instructed to.

"You'll have to ask Mr. Mystery. If you can locate him."

No one laughed or chuckled or even smiled. They were deadly serious. He was hoping for some humor.

"Will BioBubble IV come equipped with a lightning rod?" someone asked.

"This is being looked at," Bulla ad-libbed.

A mistake. He knew it was a mistake the moment the words spilled from his lips. Great communicators did not ad-lib. You tumbled ass over teakettle down the rabbit hole that way.

"Sir, why did the BioBubble, a multimillion-dollar research station, fail to include a common lightning rod—a precaution even the most modest trailer home enjoys?"

"A common lightning rod would not have saved the BioBubble from the gigantic bolt that thundered down from the heavens last night, say our experts," Bulla said, throwing a keep-your-damn-mouth-shut glance over his shoulder to Tom Pulse, who loitered out of camera range.

"Then you anticipated a lightning strike?" a reporter asked quickly.

"No."

"Then you were negligent?" another demanded.

"No one was negligent!" Bulla snapped.

"Then why are nearly thirty scientific volunteers now entombed in glass like so many ants in amber?"

There was no answer for that. No good answer, and Amos Bulla knew that. He swallowed hard and considered giving his reply in cryptic, TV-unfriendly Latin when a scarlet Saturn SLi sedan came down the winding road and out stepped a serious-faced man with short black hair, professorial glasses and the vague air of a professional stage magician. He wore a camel-colored corduroy coat over a brick red turtleneck.

The man stood poised by the scarlet Saturn, saw his arrival was unnoticed and slammed the rear door shut. The sound carried but made no impression. So he opened it again and slammed it harder.

And this time heads turned. Gasps came from those turned heads, and as if the media had been sprinkled with magician's magic dust, they turned their attention from Amos Bulla to the media-friendly presence they all recognized.

"Hey! Isn't that Dr. Pagan?"

"He's always good for a snappy soundbite!"

A concerted rush was made for Dr. Cosmo Pagan, who struck a pose by the scarlet Saturn. He was quickly ringed by a horseshoe of reporters straining their mikes and cameras in his direction.

"Dr. Pagan, what can you tell us about this event?"

"Is this the work of extraterrestrials?"

"The BioBubble people say lightning. Can you refute this?"

"I have not yet examined the site," said Dr. Cosmo Pagan in the singsongy voice that America had first experienced on a famous PBS special many years ago, and revisited on countless science and astronomy specials ever since. He stepped forward.

The converging media abruptly backed up, parting like the Red Sea before a latter-day Moses.

The glass video lenses tracked Dr. Pagan as if he were some kind of glass magnet. The media throng followed like iron filings trailing after a lodestone.

Dr. Pagan walked up to the outer edges of the BioBubble mass, wearing a studious expression. He sucked on an unlit briar pipe. His corduroy coat had felt patches at the elbows, and the Arizona wind played at his hair like a mother's gentle fingers.

"This is not the work of lightning," he announced.

The hovering media crowded close, as if afraid to miss a single crumb of scientific wisdom. No one asked questions. No one questioned him at all. Such was the reverence in which Dr. Cosmo Pagan was held.

"The absence of fulgurites confirms this," he added.

Out of microphone range, Amos Bulla groaned to himself.

Walking farther along, Dr. Pagan purposefully broke the thin-edged glass under his Hush Puppies as if it were a melting ice bank.

"I see blisters and seeds and stones—things that occur when an impure mix is turned to glass."

Geologist Tom Pulse drifted up to Bulla's side, and Bulla asked, "Is he making sense?"

"Not as much as the press thinks. He's throwing glass-manufacturing terminology around. Not applicable here."

"The black color is interesting," Dr. Pagan continued. "It reminds me of obsidian, which is glass produced in the intense natural furnace of erupting volcanoes."

Tom Pulse snorted. "Arizona isn't volcanic."

"But no volcano did this, of course," Dr. Pagan added thoughtfully. "The brownish tinge that glass has at its edge is very suggestive, however." Dr. Pagan turned to face the expectant cameras then. He looked them square in the eye. "Not many laymen know this, but in nuclear power plants, observation windows are forged of special glass because ordinary glass turns brown under exposure to hard radiation."

The press seemed stunned by this pronouncement.

"Hard radiation may be the culprit in this event."

Someone found his voice and lobbed a polite question. "Dr. Pagan, can you speculate as to the source of this hard radiation?"

"There are many possibilities. Billions and billions of them, in truth." Pagan paused. "Billions and billions," he repeated as if tasting the words. "They are endless in their complexity, in their richness, in their sheer wonderment."

Taking the cold briar from his mouth, Pagan pointed to the eastern horizon of red sandstone buttes.

"Not fifty miles in that direction lies Meteor Crater, where an unknown object from space fell, gouging out a rude cup in the hard stone of Earth's mantle that endures to this day.''

"Do you suspect a meteor strike?"

"If this is a meteor-impact site," allowed Dr. Cosmo Pagan, "it is unlike any meteor strike ever recorded by man."

"Then you're saying it's not a meteor strike?" another reporter prompted.

Dr. Pagan shook his head slowly. "Too early to say. For many years, the Tunguska event in Siberia was an unfathomable mystery. Now we think we know that a comet or rocky asteroid exploded before it impacted with our fragile blue planet, flattening a zillion square kilometers of tundra forest. Nothing like it has been documented since."

"Could a comet have done this?"

"No one on Earth knows. We simply don't have the knowledge. This is why our efforts to plumb the depths of space must go on. How can we confront the unknown if we have not ventured beyond our thin atmosphere to challenge it?"

"Are you saying you don't know?" a more astute reporter wondered ahead.

Dr. Pagan shrugged his corduroy shoulders and offered no reply.

At the back of the pack, Amos Bulla nodded. This man knew his stuff. TV, like radio, abhors a vacuum. They would not broadcast his silence. And with it went the reporter's penetrating question.

"Guy's amazing," he said with ill-disguised admiration. "A genius."

Tom Pulse snorted derisively. "Hell, so far all he's done is spout some high-school textbook facts, hardly any of it in his specialty."

"So how come he's famous and you're not?"

"The cameras are pointing his way, not mine," Pulse drawled.

"You got a point there."

"So far, he hasn't offered anything useful you couldn't drag out of an Astronomy 101 student."

Then Dr. Pagan gave the soundbite that led the evening news.

"Visitors from the mighty cosmos can't be ruled out in this inexplicable event. Not with the Hubble telescope discovering new superplanets in distant galaxies every other week. Did you know that igneous meteorites from Mars have been landing on Earth for decades, blown our way by an unknown upheaval? One made planet-fall in Egypt in 1911, killing a dog. We are standing in a perfect approximation of the Martian landscape. Consider the sheer irony, the stupendous odds of a piece of Mars striking the beachhead of man's eventual conquest of the Red Planet. Gives new meaning to the term 'first strike.'"

Pagan took a thoughtful suck on his pipe and added, "It is my fervent hope that the BioBubble, despite its troubled past, will be reconstituted as the forerunner of man's first base on the Red Planet, Mars."

That was it. The media began breaking down their sound equipment and putting away their cameras. The helicopters dropped in response to walkie-talkie summonses and, reloaded once more, they left the site like buzzing electronic locusts.

Dr. Cosmo Pagan hopped into his waiting Saturn and departed, his interest in the BioBubble event seemingly as transient as the media's.

"I don't believe it!" Bulla exploded.

"What?"

"No one cares."

Tom Pulse looked back at the sealed tomb that was the BioBubble and summed it up in two words, "No bodies."

"Say again?"

"No bodies. If you had bodies sticking up from the glass, they'd stay with this story till April Fool's Day."

Bulla shrugged. "I don't want bodies. I want the goddamn media out of my hair."

"Now all you have to deal with are the Feds. And they're not going to accept the lightning-bolt hypothesis."

"Screw them," Bulla snorted.

Pulse lifted his white Stetson, replacing it at a cockier angle than before.

"Whether you're the screwer or the screwee, I don't know. But history tells us the federal government has pretty much the upper hand in screwing folks. I'd be prepared for the worst."

Then Amos Bulla felt a hard tapping on his shoulder, and a cold voice that made him all but jump out of his skin said in his ear, "Remo Kobialka, EPA."

"Where'd you come from?" Bulla sputtered, whirling.

"The taxpayers. They want some answers to some questions."

"You just missed Dr. Cosmo Pagan," Bulla said, deciding to toss the ball into another court entirely. "He said it was aliens."

"You believe that?" asked Remo Kobialka, who looked as much like an EPA investigator in his white T-shirt and tan chinos as Tom Pulse in his white Stetson and snakeskin boots looked like a scientific consultant on earthquakes, volcanos and other Earth hazards.

"I'm only a glorified PR agent. Dr. Pagan is a world-renowned expert," Bulla answered.

"Who once predicted that the firing of the old wells in Kuwait would turn Africa into a winter wonderland," said Remo Kobialka.

"Well, he was off his subject. If it's up in the sky, Pagan knows it inside and out."

"What's your theory?"

"Lightning."

Behind Bulla's back, Pulse shook his head in a slow negative.

"I want to talk to you," said Remo, picking Pulse up bodily and depositing him off to one side like a barbershop pole.

"You can't," Bulla insisted. "He's a hired consultant. Answerable only to BioBubble Inc."

"What are you getting an hour?" Remo asked Pulse.

"One-fifty."

"Not bad. I pay five hundred. Up front."

"Sold."

They left Amos Bulla sputtering.

"What's your take?" asked Remo, drawing the man closer to the BioBubble remnant.

"You got me. It's not lightning. It's not a meteor impact or any of that stuff. Something up there turned a ray or force of something very, very hot on the BioBubble complex."

"How hot?"

"Somewhere between 1400 to 1600 degrees centigrade."

"Where do you get that figure?" Remo wondered aloud.

"Steel melts at between 1400 and 1500 centigrade. To turn raw sand to glass like this, you're talking anywhere in the 1400 to 1600 range. Those are the Bio-Bubble structural components with the highest melting points. Of course, it could be higher."

Remo looked around the site, frowning.

"What's EPA's stake in this?" Pulse wondered aloud.

"The BioThing was full of different environments, right?"

"Yes, but—"

"EPA watchdogs the environment. Something like sixteen pocket environments just went the way of the dodo. This is exactly what the taxpayers pay us to investigate."

"It is?"

"Today it is. Tomorrow we may be giving mouth-to-mouth to the spiny dogfish or doing other important rescues."

The US Geological Survey expert looked Remo up and down, taking in his white-light-deflecting T-shirt and freakishly thick wrists and was about to remark that Remo wasn't exactly dressed for the Arizona heat, when an even more unlikely apparition came fluttering around from the other side of the BioBubble. An ancient Asian with a face like a reanimated mummy's.

"Uh-oh," Pulse muttered. "Looks like the advance man for the harmonic-convergence crowd. I was wondering when the Dodona loonies would start showing up."

"That's Chiun," said Remo.

"You know him?"

"Consultant."

"What's his specialty?"

"Figuring out stuff I can't," said Remo, walking up to the tiny Asian.

If Remo was dressed for one season, Chiun was attired for another. His brocaded kimono was heavy and swayed thickly as he moved. Neither man sweated, which was amazing.

"Find anything?" asked Remo.

"Yes. Melted glass and steel."

"Funny. Besides that, I mean."

Chiun looked around with eyelids slowly compressing until only black pupils showed. "A terrible force did this, Remo."

"No argument there."

"One not of this earth."

Interest flickered across Remo's high-cheekboned face. "Yeah . . ."

"It can be but one thing."

"What's that?" asked Remo.

"A sun dragon."

"Sun dragon?"

"Yes, unquestionably a sun dragon wreaked this terrible havoc."

"I know what a dragon is, but I don't think I've heard of a sun dragon."

"They are rare, but they appear in the heavens in difficult times, presaging calamity. I myself have seen several in my lifetime. One famous sun dragon twice, at the beginning of my life and again more recently."

"You saw a dragon?"

"A sun dragon, which is different from a land-crawling dragon."

Tom Pulse listened to this as if they were making perfect sense.

"Back up," said Remo. "What's a sun dragon?"

"There is a Western word for this. Stolen from the Greek, of course."

"Yeah?"

"The word is 'comet.' "

"A comet did this?"

"Yes. For they breathe fire, as do certain species of land-dwelling dragon. Only sun dragons breathe fire from the tail, not the mouth."

Remo gave Chiun a skeptical look. "A fire-farting dragon?"

Chiun made an offended face. "Is there not one lurking in the heavens even now?"

Remo shrugged. "Search me."

"He means Hale-Bopp," said Pulse, joining the conversation.

"He does?"

"Comet Hale-Bopp has been visible most of the year. It's on the other side of the sun right now, but it's still up there. When it reemerges, they say its tail will be a sight to see. Brighter and better than Comet Hayakute II was."

"It is not lurking behind the sun," Chiun snapped. "It has pounced upon this place, melting it with its withering breath as a warning to Westerners to mend their ways."

"What are Westerners doing that would upset a comet?" asked Remo.

Chiun composed his face thoughtfully. His hazel eyes narrowed in interesting ways. "They are mistreating Koreans, that is what."

Remo threw up his hands. "I should have seen that one coming."

"Do not become upset, Remo. Doubtless the comet has not taken notice of your existence. You are safe. Especially if you remain dutifully at my side."

"Comets are millions upon millions of miles out in space."

"If this is true, why can they be seen from Earth?" countered Chiun. "If they were so far away, they would be unfindable to all but the keenest of eyes."

"They're very big and they glow. No mystery there."

"So is the den of inequity called Las Vegas. It is not so very distant from here. Yet I cannot see it. Can you?"

"No," Remo admitted.

"Nor can I see many-towered Boston, a mere three thousand miles east."

"That's because of the curvature of the earth."

"A myth. I look in all directions and I see flatness. I look into the sky and I see no so-called comet, though many beheld its fiery tail in the sky not very many weeks ago. Therefore, it has descended to earth."

"Comets when they get too close to the sun are hard to see," Remo argued.

"They are dragons which live in the sun and venture out to punish the wicked. One swooped down upon this very spot, wreaking justice and righteousness."

"It killed thirty people."

"Deserving people," countered Chiun. "Were they not imprisoned for an allotted period of time?"

"Look, let's just save this for another time," said Remo in an exasperated voice. "For right now, all you have to offer is a comet sideswiped this place?"

"Yes. There can be no question."

"Fine. Put that in your report. I'm going to look around some more."

But before Remo could act on his decision, a wrenching scream pierced the dry desert air from the other side of the flat silicon pancake that had been the BioBubble.

"Sounds like Bulla!" Tom Pulse said tightly.

6

When the butter-colored official telephone jangled discordantly, Major-General Iyona Stankevitch picked it up without thinking.

The butter-colored direct line to the Kremlin was forever ringing these days, what with rumors of plots and putsches and coups in the offing. Most were spurious. After all, who would want Russia in its present state?

"Da?" said Major-General Stankevitch.

"General, there is a report out of the United States that a space-research dome was reduced to molten metal in the dead of night."

"Yes?"

"There is talk of lightning. But according to our best scientists, no lightning could produce this catastrophe."

"Yes?" repeated the general, vaguely bored. Who cared what happened in the faraway U.S. when Mother Russia was crumbling like old black bread?

"There are two schools of thinking here. That the Americans are testing a new superweapon of destructive power, or that some unidentified power is testing it on U.S. targets, and Washington will naturally blame this event upon us."

"Why would they do that?"

"It is the historic reality of the relationship between the two superpowers."

The general started to point out that Russia—he refused to say Commonwealth of Independent States—was no longer a superpower. But if the leadership insisted upon clinging to dashed illusions, who was the director of the former KGB—now known as the FSK, or the Federal Security Service—to tell him otherwise?

"I see your point," said the general politely.

"That idiot Zhirinovsky is on NTV, warning that the Americans now have the dreaded Elipticon."

"There is no Elipticon. Zhirinovsky made up this conceit to frighten the credulous West."

"And now he is trying to frighten the East by ascribing its awesome power to Pentagon warmongers."

Stankevitch sighed. He hated the old, stale phrases. They suggested an inability to face geopolitical realities. "What would you have me do?"

"Search your files. Try to discover what this weapon might be and who controls it."

"Search my files?"

"It is a first step. Once I have your report, we will issue a directive for action."

Shrugging, the general hung up the butter-colored handset and buzzed his secretary.

"Have all available clerks search all available records for a weapon of destructive power."

"We have no weapons on file," the dull-witted secretary said stonily.

"I meant for intelligence on such a device," Major-General Stankevitch returned tightly.

"Then why did you not say this in the first place?" The secretary harrumphed, disconnecting.

Settling back in his seat, Major-General Stankevitch closed his Slavic green eyes to the lowly state to which he had sunk. If the clock could only be turned back, he could have the dull, impertinent secretary stood before a firing squad and the answers to his inquiry would be on his desk before the body thudded to the bloodstained brick.

But this was late-twentieth-century Russia, harried and abused by former satellites, NATO forces encroaching on her near abroad, her Black Sea fleet operating out of what now amounted to a foreign port, her major cities overrun by gangsters and capitalists, her aging babushkas supplementing meager pensions by selling their own medicines on street corners, while indolent teenagers guzzled Coca-Cola instead of homemade *KVASS*, which could hardly be found anymore, and grew fat on greasy fast food, and male life expectancy fell to third-world levels.

He leaned back in his creaky chair and napped to relieve the tedium of his position. Outside in the former Dzerzhinsky Square, now Lubyanka Ploschad, traffic hummed and blared in a monotonous cacophony. One thing at least had not changed. The soothing sounds of Moscow.

The answer came by midafternoon in the form of a manila folder stamped Cosmic Secret. To be Stored Forever.

Accepting the folder, Major General Stankevitch frowned. "Cosmic Secret" was the old classification for the utmost secret possible.

Untying the fading red ribbon that sealed the folder from all but the most elevated eyes, he pulled out the sheaf of papers.

At the name Zemyatin, Stankevitch's eyes lost their bored look.

Field Marshal Alexi Zemyatin was the grand old man of the Soviet Republic. He had been with Lenin. He was loved by Stalin. Khrushchev trusted him. As did Brezhnev. Andropov. And on down to the last-gasp Chernenko regime.

He was a tactical and strategic genius who had disappeared off the face of the earth some eleven years ago under circumstances that suggested CIA involvement—except that the CIA would never have dared to liquidate him. Personally Stankevitch had suspected the historical criminal Gorbachev of the foul deed.

The report detailed an incident that had taken place when Major-General Stankevitch was but a lowly KGB captain. He remembered hearing vague rumors. A Russian missile battery had been neutralized by an unknown agency. This was suppressed at the time, only coming out later. It was the later rumors that Stankevitch had overheard.

This report in his hands explained the incident.

An American superweapon had concentrated terrible energies, incapacitating the electronics of the missile battery. Many died horribly from hard radiation of unknown origin.

World War III had nearly resulted. Only a cooperative effort by the USA and USSR—seeing these four initials made a lump of nostalgia rise in Stankevitch's throat—had averted global conflagration.

The file ended with a disclaimer:

Should such a weapon ever be unleashed upon
Soviet soil again, an immediate retaliatory strike
must be implemented without consultation or
delay.

The words stared at Major-General Stankevitch like
a cold horror.

Under current FSK rules, he was duty bound to report this to the Kremlin.

On the other hand, if he did, some dunderheaded
bureaucrat might actually implement it, trigger-
ing a U.S. counterstrike—or was it a counter-
counterstrike?—with the greatly shrunken and de-
fanged Russia doubtless coming out a poor, smoking
second.

Swallowing hard, Major-General Stankevitch
weighed his duty to the Motherland against his desire
to live out his normal life span.

In the end, self-preservation won out. The direcfive
clearly specified action if such a weapon were directed against the USSR. It was not. It was directed
against the U.S. Those two missing initials, Stankevitch grimly reflected, spelled the difference between the world going on happily or becoming a
charred ball of charcoal.

The thought then crossed his mind. *What if the
Americans train this weapon upon us next?*

Within five minutes, he formulated his response.

The directive clearly said the USSR. There was no
more USSR. Only a CIS, and Major-General Stankevitch decided he now loved those inelegant and
weak-sounding initials.

"I am a citizen of the CIS," he said. "I love being
a citizen of the CIS. The Americans will never attack

the CIS. What is there to gain? We have nothing any-more.''

When he had recited these reassuring words over and over like a mantra until they lowered his blood pressure, Major-General Stankevitch picked up the butter-hued official phone and pressed the Cyrillic letter *K*.

''Report,'' an officious voice said.

''We have found nothing.''

''This is unfortunate.''

''Perhaps,'' Stankevitch said guardedly.

''It may be that the KGB files in question were sold to the highest bidder during the chaos of the breakup.''

''I do not think so,'' said Major-General Stan-kevitch sincerely, cold sweat breaking out on his brow. For he himself had sold some of those very files, as had many of his underlings. But photocopies only. He had no wish to be shot as a traitor to the motherland, now very much in her elderly phase of life.

''Say nothing of this to anyone,'' said the voice from the Kremlin.

''Da,'' said Major General Stankevitch, hanging up.

With relief, he gathered together the manila folder and its contents and was in the act of retying the red ribbon before sending it back to its file cabinet, when he noticed the faded line at one end of the ribbon. An age mark. The ribbon was discolored where it had been tied once before. Tied and untied.

Someone had consulted this Cosmic Secret file in the eleven years it had been under lock and key.

There may have been good reason for this. Perhaps not. But it suggested the file had been duplicated—and not by Major-General Stankevitch, who made a point of consulting every file before selling its copy—for who knew whom some of the shady bidders represented?

As he buzzed for the dull secretary to come to restore the file to its proper place in the old KGB archives, a chilling thought ghosted through Major-General Iyona Stankevitch's bureaucratic brain.

Who had the copy, and could that copy cause difficulties for Stankevitch and FSK in the near future?

The worry haunted him all the rest of the working day, until he went home to his apartment directly behind Lubyanka Prison, which was well stocked with the imported, German-made Gorbatschew Vodka—so much better than the thin swill available in the kiosks and markets here in the capital of a dead and dying empire—and drowned his vague fears.

7

They found Amos Bulla squatting in the red sand-stone dust clutching his eyes and screaming inarticulately.

Reaching down, Remo got his wrists and pulled him to his feet.

Bulla kept screaming, so Chiun brought a sandaled toe down on his instep with excruciating pressure. Bulla took his tongue between his teeth and nearly bit it in half. The Master of Sinanju eased back on the pressure, and Bulla stopped howling.

"What is wrong with you, loud one?" Chiun demanded.

"Blind! I'm blind!" he burbled.

"What happened?" asked Remo.

"I can't see, you idjit!"

"Before that."

"The damn alien did it," Bulla wailed. "He burned out my eyes."

"I'm looking at your eyes. They're still in your head."

"But I can't see."

"Settle down," said Remo, pressing on Bulla's other instep until the bones crackled. "What did you see?"

"It looked like a Martian," Bulla gasped. "Had its back to me. I walked up to it, and it spun around real sudden-like. It had a rod in its hand. Damn thing flashed at me. Felt like hot needles jabbing my eye-balls." Bulla's voice cracked. "Now I can't see my fingers before my poor face."

Remo and planetary geologist Tom Pulse ex-changed glances while Bulla waved his hands in front of his blinking bloodshot eyes. There was so much red in the whites, the blue of his eyes looked purple by contrast.

Pulse shrugged helplessly. "I can't vouch for him. We only met today."

Remo looked into Bulla's sightless eyes and said, "Try closing them."

"They *are* closed!" Bulla insisted, all evidence to the contrary.

"Then open and close them."

Bulla did. They got wider and, if possible, redder.

"Any difference?"

"No. I can't see, open *or* closed."

"Keep them closed. Just relax. We'll figure this out."

Bulla began walking around in aimless circles, moaning and blubbering.

Remo sat him down and knelt beside him. "You said Martian?" he asked calmly.

"Yeah. It was a Martian."

"How do you know it was a Martian?"

"It *looked* like a Martian," Bulla said.

"You know what a Martian looks like?"

"No. 'Course not. But he was man shaped. Wore a quilted space suit with a square black glass porthole in front of his face. Had gloves and boots on and was looking around the way the old Apollo astronauts used to poke around the moon. You know, careful and clumsy-like at the same time.''

"That doesn't make him a Martian," Remo declared.

"He sure wasn't press!" Bulla said bitterly.

Remo stood up and faced the Master of Sinanju. "Little Father, let's look around some more."

"We will discover who committed this foul deed," Chiun squeaked.

Remo called back to Tom Pulse, "Keep an eye on him."

"Sure thing."

Starting off, Remo undertoned to the old Korean, "He could be making this story up."

"Why?"

"To get the heat off the project."

The Master of Sinanju looked back at the rim of the BioBubble shimmering up heat waves under the broiling Arizona sun.

"If so, he is far too late."

"Not that kind of heat. You saw the way the press was acting when we pulled up."

"Yes. It was good that we remained away from their noise and insanity. Otherwise, they would have committed some barbaric indiscretion, such as interviewing you instead of a more worthy person."

"I don't believe in men from Mars," said Remo, walking with such care that his Italian loafers left no impression on the rust-colored Arizona sands. Chiun likewise disturbed nothing with his sandaled tread.

"Is Mars not a world like this one?"

"Yeah. But there's no air up there. It can't support life. It's a big red desert, kinda like this one."

"If no man of Earth has ever been there, how can you know this?" asked Chiun.

"We sent probes. They sent back video."

"Television probes?"

"Yeah."

Chiun scrunched up his chin. His wispy beard stuck out from under his lower lip like a fluttering tendril of smoke.

"And if there were men dwelling on the Fire Planet as there are Earth men, would they not have have seen these probes coming and showed them deceitful pictures of arid deserts and desolation to confound suspecting Earth men into thinking no one lived there?"

"I don't think so," said Remo, frowning.

They came to a set of footprints that trampled the sandstone ground with no discernible purpose or direction. The prints were humanlike, but heelless and corrugated for extra traction like a pair of running shoes.

Chiun indicated this confusion of prints with the curved jade nail protector that protected his right index finger.

"Behold, Remo. Proof!"

"Of what?"

"That a man of Mars stood on this very spot."

"All I see are boot prints."

"Examine the markings more closely. Do the heels not consist of the Greek letter *Mu?*"

Remo looked closer.

"Yeah, now that you point it out, the tread is a stack of *M's*. So what?"

"*Mu's*. Men from Mars. Clearly the Martians are wearing Martian-made boots."

"Come off it. If there were Martians, they wouldn't advertise their existence with brand-name boots. Besides that, the Martians don't use the English alphabet."

"So you admit Martians do exist?" said Chiun loftily.

"No, I don't."

"Even with the proof etched in the red dust at your feet?"

"Look, let's collar this guy and find out if he's a Martian or not."

"I will agree to this. Let the Martian decide this argument."

"Fine. Let's go."

The footprints led through eroded red rock and sand until, without warning, they just stopped.

"Where'd they go?" Remo said, looking around.

Chiun frowned. "They stop."

"I can see that. How is that possible?"

"It is simple. The Martian entered his space chariot at this spot and was whisked back to his home desert."

"No sale. It don't see landing-gear marks."

"Further proof!" Chiun crowed.

"Of what?"

"That Martians truly exist."

"How?"

"You would not look for the marks of their space chariots if you did not secretly accept their existence," Chiun sniffed.

Remo started to throw up his hands, decided against it and knelt instead. "Something's wrong here," he muttered.

"That is obvious," Chiun sniffed.

"No. This patch of ground. Feel it with your sandals."

Chiun scratched at the red sand experimentally.

"It does not shift like loose sand," he said, papery lips thinning.

"Yeah. It's fixed. Like the sand grains are cemented down."

Exploring with his hands, Remo found that the sand in a sizable rectangle had the feel and texture of coarse-grained sandpaper, and beyond a well-defined area, it became loose and granular again.

"This isn't natural," said Remo.

Then his questing fingers found the ring under a flat rock. It was literally a brass ring, except it was hand, not finger, sized.

Stepping back, Remo lifted the ring up—and up came a long, rectangular trapdoor. The trap fell back, exposing a cavity that was lined with concrete. Remo looked down.

"Looks like a secret tunnel. So much for Martians."

"I accept nothing until it is proved or disproved," Chiun said aridly.

"Let's go," Remo said, dropping into the hole.

It was a tunnel. The beaming sunlight illuminated it for a dozen yards, and then it became as dark as the jungle tunnels Remo used to infiltrate during his Vietnam days.

They advanced through the zone of light into shadow, the visual purple in their eyes compensating until they could see shadows and shapes. Ultimately the details of the tunnel resolved as clearly as if they were in gray twilight.

Odors began drifting to their sensitive nostrils.

"I smell stuff," said Remo.

"Food," said Chiun.

"Yeah. That, too. But a chemical smell, too."

"Skulking Martians," suggested Chiun.

"Not having the faintest clue what a Martian smells like, I take a pass on the argument."

"Therefore, I win," said Chiun.

The tunnel right-angled once and then again. It was taking them unerringly in the direction of the collapsed BioBubble.

After the second turn, the space opened up, and the smell of potatoes and lettuce and other familiar foodstuffs filled their noses. The familiar humming of ordinary refrigerators made the still air vibrate.

The vast, shadowy area was crammed with familiar appliances.

Remo stopped, blurting, "Looks like a restaurant kitchen."

They moved among the stoves and refrigerators and meat lockers, opening them. They found prime rib in plastic, frozen TV dinners and assorted bottled beverages, including thirty gallons of whole milk under refrigeration.

"Still in code," said Remo, replacing a gallon and slamming the refrigerator shut. He went to a big black range and turned on a burner. Blue gas flames *whuffed* up. A stainless-steel range hood collected the heat and waste gas.

"It is a Martian secret base," said Chiun.

"A food dump?" Remo said incredulously. "Come off it. It's the secret kitchen of the BioBubble. This is where they make their forbidden pizza. This probably explains why the air levels have been screwed up. They cook with gas, and it eats up their oxygen."

"I see no Martian. Nor do I smell one."

"Looks like they get some of their heat from the stoves," said Remo, studying the acoustical-tile ceiling. "There's gotta be a way up into the BioBubble from here. Come on."

Leading the way, Remo found a simple folding aluminum step-ladder. It stood under a submarine-style airlock hatch. It was up in the closed position.

"BioBubble's directly above," he said.

"So, too, is the Martian foe," Chiun said sternly.

Remo climbed the ladder, undogging the hatch with a twirl of his index finger. The hatch squealed in protest, then dropped like a hungry steel mouth. Remo made it look effortless, but three bodybuilders with a monkey wrench couldn't have budged it.

Remo poked his head up into the open space. It smelled of sulphur.

"What do you see, Remo?"

"Looks like the inside of a melted marble. Stinks, too."

"You cannot smell the Martian?"

"Unless his body-odor smell leans toward glass and plastic, no," Remo called down.

Twisting around on the ladder, Remo tried looking in different directions, then said, "I'm going in."

"I am following," said the Master of Sinanju.

Chiun floated up the ladder and joined Remo in what appeared to be a distorted air pocket that had formed when the BioBubble settled and cooled. There were weird flowing tunnels going in three directions from the central pocket.

"Pick a tunnel, any tunnel," said Remo.

Chiun sniffed the air delicately. "I smell nothing that smells like a man of Mars, therefore I pick this tunnel."

"Why that one?" Remo pressed.

"Why not?" And the Master of Sinanju padded into it.

Remo took the adjacent tunnel and ducked in. It was only five feet high at its highest point, and he moved along it carefully.

The walls were mostly glass. Dimly Remo could make out streaks of color and at one point a skeletal human hand, scorched to black bone, evidence of a BioBubble inhabitatant having been cooked in a cauldron of molten glass. He saw an aluminum chair, bright as the day it was forged, suspended in a glass matrix.

It was like walking through a weird aquarium of rippled glass and bizarre objects. There were an awful lot of bugs. Mostly roaches, their feelers wilted.

The ceiling dropped lower and lower. Remo was about to turn back when he detected a muffled heartbeat. It was pounding.

He froze.

And before Remo could zero in on the source of the sound, something flared white-hot, and the tunnel turned the whitest white Remo had ever beheld. He knew before his eyes could completely shut he had been blinded. The searing pain stabbing deep into his optic nerve told him that. The pain went straight to his toenails, and deep in the pit of his stomach he experienced a growing and alien fear....

THE MASTER OF SINANJU was moving through a tunnel of glass whose sides felt slick to his touch. It was like nothing he had ever before encountered, and he therefore resolved to write of this in the scrolls that were passed down from Master to Master for the edification of future Masters of the House of Sinanju.

Chiun had come to a place where the tunnel swelled, forming a dome where the air was especially foul. Standing there, hands in the sleeves of his kimono, he stepped around, his hazel eyes taking in the strange sight of ordinary objects and cockroaches floating unmoving in cooled glass.

A moment's scrutiny assured him that no skulker lurked in this chamber of glass, so Chiun turned to retrace his steps.

At that moment, the glass to one side flared brightly, and through the tunnel came the wordless scream of his adopted son.

"Remo! My son!"

Throwing back his kimono sleeves, the Master of Sinanju flew back through the surreal tunnel of rehardened glass toward the sound of his pupil's scream of soul-searing pain.

8

The Master of Sinanju emerged from his tunnel just as a strange figure backed out of the glass tube into which Remo had gone.

The figure was not Remo Williams.

From the back, the Master of Sinanju discerned a bulky gray quilted suit of armor that made him think of Chinese warriors of the old Qing Dynasty. But the style was not Chinese. The head was encased in a featureless bullet of some dull silver material.

"Turn and face your doom, Man of Mars," Chiun thundered.

The creature turned, sweeping a long rod of some white metal that glowed red at the tip before him. It sought him with its evil glimmerings. But no warrior of this or any world was equal to a Master of Sinanju.

Closing his eyes protectively, Chiun twisted his pipestem body, lifting one foot high while pivoting on the opposite toe.

Turning in midair, he spun a complete circle. It looked like a slow-motion windup to some ferocious stroke, but as the turning toe reached a point horizontal with the Master of Sinanju's chin, it accelerated to an unreadable blur.

The toe struck the side of the bullet head just as the square black panel of glass that hid the fearsome foe's face finished turning in Chiun's direction.

The black top of Chiun's sandal connected just as the red rod emitted a burst of pristine white light so pure it shocked Chiun's eyes, even though they were tightly sealed by his papery eyelids.

Chiun felt the impact, recoiled from it and recovered as the body of his foe went *whump* on the floor of the air pocket at the heart of the BioBubble.

Only when the rattle of death reached his ears did the Master of Sinanju open his eyes and face the defeated one.

Carefully Chiun padded up to the bulky shape on the floor.

The body lay like a bloated starfish, limbs splayed to the four quarters. Where the head should be was an empty space.

That sight satisfied Chiun, who then flew down the tunnel, seeking his pupil.

He found Remo leaning against a glassy wall with one hand. The other was groping at his face. His eyes were open, but they were sightless, the pupils contracted to shocked pinpoints, the whites shot with angry scarlet threads.

For a moment, the Master of Sinanju paused, stricken by the paralyzed expression on his pupil's formerly proud countenance.

Then, steeling himself, he stepped forward. "Remo! What is it?"

Remo's reply came in a squeezed voice. "Chiun, I— I can't see."

Chiun's wrinkled visage flinched like a web touched by a stick. "What do you see in this condition?"

"Everything is white."

"Not black?"

"No. White."

"This is strange. If you are blind, you should see blackness."

"That guy was in here. Be careful."

"I encountered him. He is no more, Remo. You have been avenged."

Remo hesitated before replying in a thick voice. "Thanks, Little Father."

"I would do the same for any other adopted son, if I had one."

Remo waved a helpless hand in Chiun's direction. "Give me a hand."

Chiun took three quick steps, then halted. No, this was not the time or place to coddle Remo.

"No," he said.

"No? What do you mean, no?"

"If you are blind, you must learn to use your other senses."

"Look, just give me a hand out of here," Remo said angrily.

"No. You know the path that you took to the place of your downfall. You have only to retrace your fool-hardy steps."

Remo made a stiff face. He looked to be on the verge of losing his temper. Then, straightening his spine and composing his face, he oriented himself using only his senses of hearing and touch.

At first he employed the tips of his fingers to guide him along the glassy walls. As confidence returned, his hand dropped free and he used his supersharp ears. No doubt the beating of the Master of Sinanju's heart guided him.

Chiun willed his heart to be momentarily still. It did not stop. It merely beat with exceeding slowness, a technique that, if prolonged, would result in a catalepsy that simulated death.

"No fair," Remo complained. "I can't hear your heartbeat."

Chiun said nothing. He was holding his breath. He stepped backward with exceeding caution, his sandaled feet making no sound on the glassy floor. He moved aside to allow Remo to pass him unsuspecting.

Without tripping or stumbling, Remo made it down the glass tube and into the central air pocket, where he immediately fell over the body of the defeated one.

"Is this him?" Remo asked, feeling the padded body.

"Yes," said Chiun, allowing his heart and lungs to function normally once more.

"I don't feel any head."

"Proof of its undeniable Martianness. For it has none."

"I saw him. For just a second. It had a head."

"A helmet. I removed it. But no head lay beneath it."

Remo felt the shoulders, then brought his hands together.

"Feels like there's a stump."

Frowning, Chiun went to the bullet helmet and lifted it up.

Shaking it vigorously, he got a head to fall out with an audible *bonk*.

"Was that what I think it was?" asked Remo, getting to his feet.

"Yes," returned Chiun thinly. "The head."

"What's it look like?"

"Ugly."

"How ugly?" asked Remo, drawing near, his face curious.

"Exceedingly ugly."

"What color skin?"

"Yellow."

"The Martian is yellow skinned?"

"Yes. With hideous eyes and a flat nose."

"Better save it for Smith, then."

"Of course," said Chiun, dropping the head into its helmet and carrying it like a baseball in a catcher's mitt. "Now it is time that we leave this place of shame."

Remo fell in behind the Master of Sinanju, his face and voice dazed and dull. "I only caught a glimpse of him—it," he said thickly. "I was moving on him, and everything went white."

"You see whiteness still?"

"Yeah. What does that mean? Anything?"

Chiun frowned. "I do not know. Perhaps because you are white, this is normal."

Remo shook his head and felt for the stepladder top rung with his feet. "Blind people see darkness. Everybody knows that."

Chiun said nothing in response. His eyes were clouded and troubled.

Remo descended with careful movements. Chiun followed. They worked their way back through the underground kitchen to the camouflage trapdoor and emerged into the hot Arizona air once more.

"Follow me," said Chiun.

Remo did. He said nothing. His face was loose with a kind of dull shock. Several times he licked his lips as if he wanted to say something, but instead compressed them. The color of his face was very, very pale. His breathing was out of rhythm.

Chiun let these things pass. There was no danger here, so it was not important. No danger. No future, either. Not for Remo. Not for the House.

They came upon Amos Bulla and Tom Pulse near the collapsed BioBubble.

"Something happened inside the BioBubble," Pulse said when he saw them.

"It is not important," Chiun said thinly.

"The whole thing shone white for a moment. It was like a big light bulb. Or a flying saucer about to take off."

"Yeah," said Amos Bulla. "I saw it with my own eyes."

Chiun's voice climbed to the sky. "What! You saw?"

"Yeah."

"You were blind."

"My eyes cleared up."

Turning, Chiun cried, "Remo, did you hear that?"

"Of course. I'm not deaf. Just blind."

"And you are only blind for now. For the affliction is not permanent."

"Whew!" said Remo in relief.

"He got you, too?" Bulla asked.

"Yeah, but we got him," said Remo, sitting down to wait for his sight to clear.

Bulla and Pulse gathered around the Master of Sinanju.

"Is that what I think it is?" Bulla asked, indicating the silver helmet in Chiun's long-nailed grasp.

"Yes. It is his head."

"How'd it come off?"

"It was loose. A mere tap unbalanced it."

"Martians must be made of flimsy stuff," Bulla said, avoiding the sight of the head in the helmet.

"I don't believe in men from Mars," said Remo, not wanting to be left out of the conversation even if he couldn't see what was under discussion.

"It has a yellow visage and horrible, catlike eyes," said Chiun.

"Yeah?"

"Truly."

"Hey!" said Remo suddenly, "I think I'm starting to see again." He stood up. Blinking his eyelids, he waved his fingers before his face. After a while, his features brightened and the pinpoint pupils slowly relaxed to normal size.

"I can see again. I can see again!"

"Clearly?" asked Chiun, concealing his joy with a stern tone.

"No, just my fingers. They're a blur. But it's coming back."

"Try closing your eyes. That'll help some," said Bulla.

Remo did.

"When the whiteness becomes red, you'll know you're okay," Bulla offered.

"It's starting to happen," said Remo.

"Open your eyes, Remo," Chiun instructed.

Remo obliged. The whites of his eyes had already lost much of their thready redness. His Sinanju-enhanced system accelerated the healing process.

He found himself looking at the Martian's dead face. "*That's* the Martian?" he blurted.

"Yes. Is his countenance not terrible to behold?" said Chiun.

Frowning, Remo took the head in both hands. "This Martian looks suspiciously Chinese."

"I have always wondered about the Chinese. They seem unsuited for this planet," Chiun sniffed.

"This guy *is* Chinese," Remo exploded.

"There's something written inside this helmet," Pulse said.

"What's it say?" asked Remo, striding up.

"'Property of FORTEC.'"

"What the hell is FORTEC?" asked Amos Bulla.

"It's the Foreign Technology Department of the U.S. Air Force," Tom Pulse supplied.

"Never heard of it," Bulla scoffed.

"It's ultrasecret. People say it investigates alien technology."

"Space aliens?" said Remo.

"That's the rumor. The truth is they're interested in exotic technology. Foreign to the U.S. Unusual propulsion systems. New laser applications. That sort of thing."

"So they could investigate flying saucers if they took a mind to?" Bulla asked.

"It's in their mission. Technically."

"This Chinese guy is one of *ours*?" Remo asked.

"He is not one of mine," spat Chiun, dropping the head back into its helmet and kicking the gleaming shell away.

From the cell phone in their rented car, Remo put in a call to Harold Smith at Folcroft Sanitarium, the cover for CURE.

"Ever hear of FORTEC?" Remo asked Smith after the call was rerouted through sixteen states and scrambled to avoid eavesdropping by National Security Agency monitors.

"Yes. You have FORTEC credentials yourself, and have used them in the past."

"I can't keep track of all my covers," Remo growled.

"Why do you ask?"

"They sent one of their guys out here. He blinded me with something that looks like a flashlight."

"Laser blinding technology is under development by the Army."

"He was wearing some kind of quilted spacesuit," added Remo.

"A high-tech battle suit also under Army development."

"Why wear combat gear on an investigation?"

"Perhaps because he is not certain what he will encounter," suggested Smith. "You could ask him."

"I could, but Chiun knocked his block off. So to speak."

Smith groaned. "Are there witnesses?"

"Not to the act, but a crowd is gathering around the head."

Smith groaned again. "Pull out," he ordered.

"We haven't got anything. Unless you like Chiun's theory."

"Which is?"

"A sun dragon. It's Korean for 'comet.'"

"The Korean word for 'comet' is *hyesong*," returned Harold Smith.

"I stand corrected," Remo said dryly.

"If you have nothing better," said Smith, "pull out."

"The BioBubble PR head is here."

"Find out who is backing the project."

"That should be easy. Hold the line."

Remo walked up to Amos Bulla and said, "We found the big kitchen under the BioBubble."

"I'm only director of public relations. I don't handle logistics or supply."

"But you're not supposed to have any kitchen," Remo persisted.

"You'll have to take that up with the the project's angel."

"Angel?" said Chiun.

"Another word for financial backer."

"Who is he?"

"No clue. I was hired by telephone. His name is Mavors. Ruber Mavors. That's all I know. I don't know who he is or how to reach him."

Chiun narrowed his eyes suspiciously. "You have never met this Ruber Mavors?"

"No. He's just a voice on the telephone who gives me my instructions."

"He tell you to install a full kitchen?" asked Remo.

Bulla wiped sweat off his face. "If there's a kitchen, it was built before my tenure. I came in after the Mars-colony scam—I mean phase—went belly-up. The whole Mars colony project was supposed to be a joint U.S.-USSR space mission. Neither country could do it alone. Folks thought it would be a great way to encourage superpower cooperation. Then the Soviets up and died, and the project went bankrupt. That's when Mr. Mavors came in, hired me and bailed the project out. It's been an ecological-research station ever since."

"This man called Mavors," said Chiun, fingering his beard, "does his voice fall strangely upon your ears?"

"Yeah. He kinda sounds like Rod Serling, if you really want to know the honest truth." Bulla squinted at the Master of Sinanju. "How'd you know that?"

"Yeah, Little Father," said Remo. "How did you know that?"

"Because," intoned Chiun, "in the Latin of old Rome, Ruber Mavors means 'Red Mars.'"

"That's as phony a name as I've ever heard," said Remo.

"It's the name he gave me," Bulla insisted.

"He is telling the truth," Chiun confirmed.

"Yeah, I can hear," said Remo disappointedly.

"Hear what?" asked Bulla.

"Your heartbeat. If it accelerated, that would tip us off. It didn't, so you're telling the truth."

Bulla touched his heart as if to make sure it was still beating.

Remo went back to the telephone and filled in Harold Smith.

"A dead end," said Smith when Remo was through. "I will search through Bulla's telephone records. Something may turn up. You and Chiun leave immediately."

Hanging up, Remo rejoined the others.

Amos Bulla was kicking at the red sands of Arizona disconsolately. "Well, if that's the end of EPA's investigation, I guess I'm out of here—and out of a job, too. Unless Mavors wants to start from scratch." Bulla shot a sick parting glance at the flattened dome of rehardened glass. "Sure would like to know what caused this flop, though."

Everyone took a final look at the BioBubble, baking in the Arizona sun like a candy-glass flapjack.

"A sun dragon," intoned the Master of Sinanju. "Mark my words. A sun dragon is loose in the heavens and will strike again."

No one disputed him this time. The sheer size of the destroyed research station beggared any better explanation.

The bad news came by e-mail:

> To: RM@qnm.com
> From: R&D@qnm.com
> Subject: Possible product failure
> Staff here in R&D feel that the situation in Arizona may be a by-product of current testing, which at first appeared to suggest product failure, but which now appears to be the result of a bug in the software.

Long pale fingers hesitated at the keyboard and, after a moment, typed a furious reply while rain beat a steady tattoo on an office window.

> To: R&D@qnm.com
> From: RM@qnm.com
> Subject: Your mail
> Explain software glitch.

The reply was not long in coming:

> To: RM@qnm.com
> From: R&D@qnm.com
> Subject: Your mail

Probable cause is defective Platinum chip unknowingly installed in guidance system.

Pale fingers typed swiftly.

To: R&D@qnm.com
From: RM@qnm.com
Subject: Your mail.
Defective chip installed where?

To: RM@qnm.com
From: R&D@qnm.com
Subject: Your mail
In working prototype.

And the pale hands went paler.
They shook as they pecked out a response.

To: R&D@qnm.com
From: RM@qnm.com
Subject: Ozone layer
Does product failure have any impact on ozone layer?

The reply: "Why do you always ask that?"
To which, the pale fingers shot back: "None of your damn business. Answer the question."
"None." The reply made the pale fingers relax.
Color slowly returned to the poised fingers. The owner cracked his knuckles and attacked the keyboard with renewed energy.

To: R&D@qnm.com
From: RM@qnm.com

Subject: Your mail

I am on vacation. I have been on vacation for two weeks. Erase this e-mail and all previous electronic communications. I will do same. Project ParaSol is defunded this date. Furlough all nonessential personnel. Remember—loose lips sink careers.

10

The BioBubble event was the best thing to happen to astronomer Cosmo Pagan since he'd married his third wife. Or the *Galileo* flyby. Or maybe Shoemaker-Levy colliding with Jupiter. It was hard to say, on a cosmic scale. All were pretty spectacular events in the Big Bang that was his terrestrial sojourn.

Every time the heavens burst forth with a new wonder, or Cosmo Pagan fell in love, his career went up like a happy rocket. It was amazing. It was life affirming. It was exhilarating.

And it all started around the time the *Viking 1* probe landed on the red sands of Mars and began transmitting pictures of the dead planet's arid surface.

Cosmo Pagan was an untenured astronomy professor in those days back at the University of Arizona. There, he met Stella, tawny, tenured and on the fast track, career-wise.

"So how does a guy get tenure in a place like this?" Cosmo asked on their first date at the Lowell Observatory on Mars Hill outside Flagstaff, where they took turns looking up at red Mars through the same refractor Percival Lowell had used to study the canals of the Red Planet a century ago.

"You earn it. Usually by publishing."

Cosmo swallowed. "That sounds like work. I'm a people person. I do better in front of a class than on the printed page."

"There isn't a back door to enter, you know," Stella reminded him.

But Cosmo Pagan found one. First he married Stella Redstone, then after two years of marital stargazing, he popped the real question. "Why don't we collaborate on your next book?"

"Why?"

"Because you have tenure and I need it."

Stella thought about it. She thought about it hard. She had a growing academic reputation to protect.

"We'll give it a shot," she said guardedly. "But you have to pull your own weight."

"Deal," said Cosmo, shaking hands with his wife of two years—three tops, if things worked out. He was already *shtupping* the occasional undergrad.

They started with a strict division of labor, just as they did with the household dishes. Stella did the research, Cosmo the first draft and she the polish.

But typing was not Cosmo Pagan's strong suit, and no one could read the smeary Sanskrit that passed for his penmanship.

So they tried alternating chapters. Cosmo kept getting sick when his turn rolled around. Or he made Stella redo her chapter before he tackled his. The project fell further and further behind schedule.

Then in exasperation, Stella pulled out of the project. "You write your damn book. I'll write mine."

That's when Cosmo Pagan filed suit for divorce and his half of the book, as yet untitled.

It took three months of protracted litigation, arguments over commas, theories and metaphors until Stella threw in the towel.

"Look, just give me my freedom from that lazy leech," she told her lawyer. "He can have the book, the house, everything."

When *Universe* was published, it sold better than anyone ever dreamed, earning Cosmo Pagan full tenure and a cool quarter-million dollars, an unheard-of sum for a popular-science textbook at that time.

While the book was climbing the bestseller lists, Pagan received a telegram from his ex wife: "You turned my elegantly written prose into popular junk."

Cosmo fired back an equally succinct reply. On a postcard. "Popular junk is the future of this country."

When PBS approached Cosmo to adapt *Universe* for a twelve-part science special, Cosmo Pagan saw an opportunity undreamed of by tenured professors of astronomy.

"I have to write it. And host it," he insisted to his agent.

The PBS executive producer turned him down cold.

"How can he do this?" Pagan asked his agent.

"She. Her name's Venus. And she calls the shots over there."

"Did you say Venus?"

"Yeah. Venus Brown."

"I never slept—I mean met a woman named after a planet," Cosmo said wonderingly. "Especially one as interesting as Venus. It's my second-favorite planet after Mars."

So Cosmo Pagan asked her out. On the third date, he asked Venus Brown to marry him. She turned him down flat. It took two more tries until she succumbed to his boyish charm, but finally they were married in a brisk outdoor ceremony with the planets Mars and Venus hurtling through the evening sky overhead.

On the honeymoon, after visiting multiple cataclysmic orgasms on his new bride, Cosmo Pagan popped the question again: "Let me write and host the show."

"Why should I do that?" the newly named Venus Pagan asked.

"Because I'm your husband and you want me to succeed in life," Cosmo answered with his usual boyish directness.

She wrapped him up in a warm hug and said, "You already succeeded. Wildly. And repeatedly."

"I need to succeed bigger. And better."

"Let me sleep on it. Okay?"

"I haven't given you the galactic orgasm yet."

"Galactic orgasm?"

"It's the one after you scream you can't handle another one," Cosmo explained. "The perturbations are marvelous."

"Oh, really?"

Three orgasms later, she said "Yes! Yes! Yes!" to the heavens, and Cosmo Pagan took that as his green light. And no morning-after protestations of temporary nuptial insanity were accepted.

It was a wonderful marriage. It led to fame, wealth, a Tucson, Arizona, suburban home with its own private astronomical observatory where the seeing was best and more groupies than even a studiously handsome astronomy professor in the space age could ever wish for.

It might have gone on forever and ever if Cosmo Pagan hadn't gotten caught *in flagrante delicto*.

"We're done," Venus Pagan snapped after slapping Cosmo's face in both directions while the future unnamed third party in the divorce suit yanked on her panties.

"You can't divorce me," Cosmo blurted.

"Why not?"

"Think of how our careers are intertwined."

"What careers? You're famous. I'm a behind-the-scenes producer. You get all the glory. Hell, you hog it. I'm Mrs. Cosmo Pagan who gets thanked on the dedication page in small print."

"Look," Pagan said, getting down on bended knee, "we have a lifetime of split royalties ahead of us. Don't tear that apart over one eager-beaver blonde."

"You must be thinking of a prior beaver," Venus said tartly. "That was a brunette who just scampered away."

Cosmo made his voice as serious as nature would allow. "I won't give up the house."

"The Mars observatory, you mean. I'm sick of it. Don't think I don't know you point that kaleidoscope of yours at the neighbors' windows."

"It's called a telescope. And what about the children?"

"What children?"

"The two asteroids orbiting the sun named after us. They're our celestial offspring. They'll be together long after we're gone."

"Maybe they'll break up, too," Venus said thinly.

And the door slammed.

It might have been a career wrecker, except neat cosmic stuff kept happening. Comet Kohoutek.

Comet Halley's return. The *Challenger* disaster. Shoemaker-Levy. Every time the cosmos hiccuped, Dr. Pagan was invited on news programs and talk shows to interpret the burp.

When comet fragments struck Jupiter, Pagan was on the phone trying to convince the planetary society to strike the name Asteroid Venus until further notice.

"We've never had a precedent for renaming an asteroid," he was told.

"I can't orbit the solar system with my ex-wife for all eternity," Pagan lamented. "Think of how bad it looks. Besides, I'll probably remarry. Just leave the name blank until then. I guarantee my next new wife will be worthy of celestial immortality."

The response was disappointing: "No. Sorry. Not even for you."

Hanging up, Dr. Pagan silently vowed to get around the galactic red tape somehow.

He found it while flipping through interview requests from news organizations interested in interviewing him on the Jupiter-impact event.

A name both familiar and unfamiliar leaped out at him.

"Who's this Venus Mango?" he asked his secretary.

"CNN reporter."

"Is she cute?"

"Depends on your taste."

"Is she up and coming?"

"Yes."

"Tell her we're on."

Venus Mango was in fact what Pagan liked to call a heavenly body. And she was science editor for CNN.

She knew the Crab Nebula from the Trifid, and recognized over fifty other Messier objects. That made them compatible in Cosmo Pagan's eyes.

Dr. Pagan invited her to dinner after the interview. Of course, she accepted. Who wouldn't say yes to the famous boyish face, the erudite manner and easily tousled hair?

"Marry me," Cosmo asked in the middle of dessert, a red Jell-O dome with black-licorice decorations that Cosmo called Martian Moon Jelly.

"What!"

"I love you, Venus."

"You say 'Venus' as if you've been saying it all your life."

"Marry me and I promise to have an asteroid named after you," Cosmo promised.

The future Venus Pagan said yes in the second hour of their first date. They were married by the weekend, and Cosmo Pagan proudly showed her the documentation on their honeymoon at China's Purple Mountain Observatory by the light of a nifty lunar eclipse.

"Why is this dated ten years ago?" Venus asked.

"I had a premonition."

Venus Pagan wept openly. "This is the most amazing thing any man has ever done for me."

"Wait'll you experience the galactic orgasm."

Venus Pagan in truth didn't so much advance Cosmo Pagan's career as she maintained it. Cosmo decided to settle for that. He wasn't a spring chicken anymore. There was an actual worry line seaming his high forehead now. Fortunately on-camera makeup shielded his adoring public from the unnerving sight.

Besides, how high could an astronomer go?

For the first time in his life, Cosmo Pagan was content to settle down for the easy ride.

This year was turning out to be a comet year. Hayakute II. Then Hale-Bopp. The public lapped it up, and Dr. Pagan was only too happy to feed their curiosity.

So when the BioBubble burst, it was just another cosmic event engineered to further that career, and a break from explaining the Oort Cloud for the gazillionth time.

The phone began ringing off the hook immediately. Of course, the first call he returned was Venus's. Cosmo was no fool. Where was he going to find another earthbound Venus who could do anything for his career?

By the next morning, he was quoted in virtually every newspaper and TV news program in the nation and beyond.

This time he discovered they played it for laughs.

"'Someone up there doesn't like us'?" he sputtered, reading back his own quote. "Everyone used that comment! It was a throwaway. I gave a detailed, reasoned, poetic analysis, and they print a side-of-the-mouth attempt at levity?"

"You gave a windy speech to a TV camera," Venus returned. "You know better. All TV wants is soundbites."

"I'm used to having a forum," Cosmo lamented. "And editorial control."

"Not this time, honey. Get over it."

But Dr. Cosmo Pagan wasn't about to get over it. Twenty-five years of popularizing astronomy and the heavens had made him famous from Anchorage to Asia, but one last honor still eluded him.

Respect from his fellow astronomers. They hated him to a man.

"I have to do something about this," he fumed.

"Why bother? The story has a half life of maybe three days."

"I'm going to the BioBubble."

"I won't recommend being tied to this one. The BioBubble is a joke. You said so yourself."

"That was when it first started. I've since changed my mind," he growled.

"Suit yourself."

And Dr. Pagan did. He drove his Mars red Saturn with the license plate that read BARSOOM-1 to the Martian-like landscape of Dodona, Arizona, and stole the spotlight out from under the BioBubble people.

By the time he had returned home, the ink was drying on the print-media story.

"'Dr. Pagan says Martians crushed BioBubble!'" he screamed. "I never said that!"

"I saw it on CNN," Venus said. "You came darn close."

"I said visitors from outer space. I was being poetic. By 'visitor,' I meant an asteroid or meteor. Not little green men!"

"Nobody says 'little green men' anymore. They say 'grays' now."

"I don't believe in that UFO conspiracy crap."

"You don't believe in the current shuttle program, either."

"Listen, there's an entire cosmos out there I'll never get to explore at the current technological rate. We went to the moon. It was a dusty rock. Big deal. The next logical step is Mars. But do we take it? No. We just send these stupid space trucks into low Earth orbit and bring them back. I'd rather see deep-space probes, sending back images that I can see in this lifetime. Screw the shuttle. They won't get to Mars until after they sprinkle my ashes in Tunguska.''

''You said visitors. They took you literally. Relax. By the time Hale-Bopp comes back, this will all be forgotten.''

Dr. Cosmo Pagan screamed like a cow in distress. ''I'm going to be pilloried by every astronomy society on the planet. And beyond.''

''Poor baby,'' Venus II said, hugging him tightly. ''Look at it this way—at least you still have me. And we'll orbit the sun until the end of time.''

''I need some face time.''

''I need some suck-face time,'' his wife returned, pinching his boyish cheek.

Cosmo considered this. ''Trade?''

''Throw in a galactic orgasm. I haven't had one in moons.''

''That's going to take all night, knowing you.''

''What will a few hours' delay cost you?'' Venus said, giving his hair a muss and starting to pop his shirt buttons with her strong white teeth.

11

On a beach in Cancún, a pale man in a Speedo bathing suit lounged on a candy-cane folding beach chair as turquoise waves creamed against the pristine sands.

Unfolding his laptop, he booted up his system and began typing.

To: R&D@qnm.com
From: RM@qnm.com
Subject: Current project status. Update, please.

The reply took twenty minutes, even by e-mail. In that time, his skin began to burn. And remembering how fragile the ozone shield had gotten in the past eleven years, he applied supersunblock to every exposed area. He smeared his forearms as he read.

To: RM@qnm.com
From: R&D@qnm.com
Subject: Update
No feedback from corporate. Media currently ascribing event to space aliens. Specifically Martians determined to nip planned NASA Mars colony in the bud.

The fingers, greasy with sunblock, pecked out a response.

To: R&D@qnm.com
From: RM@qnm.com
Subject: Update
Sounds good. Go with it.

The reply came back almost instantly through the miracle of orbiting communications satellites: "What do you mean, go with it?"

Greasy fingers went to work: "Encourage media's thinking."

The reply: "How?"

To which, the greasy fingers typed: "That's your job. If you can't do it, I'll find someone who can."

A long time—by information-age standards—passed before the next e-mail appeared on the laptop screen. Actually it was only twelve minutes.

To: RM@qnm.com
From: R&D@qnm.com
Subject: Directive
What about legal ramifications?

The man on the beach snapped out an impatient response:

To: R&D@qnm.com
From: RM@qnm.com
Subject: Re: Directive
You're protected by the corporate shield. Do what's best for the corporation.

There was no response to that, and the pale hands powered down the laptop, folded it up and went back to enjoying vacation.

After a while, the pale man on the beach threw on a gaudy Hawaiian shirt. With all that UV radiation pouring down from the sky, there was no sense in taking chances. Basal-cell skin-cancer rates over the last decade had skyrocketed higher than the stock market.

12

Somewhere over the Ozarks, Remo Williams leafed through a newspaper.

"It says here that Hale-Bopp was last seen three thousand years ago."

"How do they know this?" demanded Chiun.

"Search me. It orbits the sun, and once every three thousand years or so, it comes within sight of the earth." Remo frowned. "Who was Master three thousand years ago?"

"If you were a true Master of Sinanju, you would not need to ask such a question."

"I know the lineage of the Masters. I can recite almost every Master's name, but I can't reconcile them with Western dating."

Chiun puckered up his facial wrinkles. "Yes. Of course."

"What do you mean, of course?"

"You were raised to worship the crucified carpenter. To those of your doubtful creed, the universe began only two thousand years ago."

"That's not true—" Remo started to protest.

"Before the carpenter, there was nothing. All was darkness, without form, without light, without substance," Chiun said bitterly.

"That's not how it works. There was a time before Jesus. We just count the years backward from that point. Three B.C. is three years Before Christ."

"We count forward from Tangun, who created the first Korean. That was five thousand years ago. Before then, no one was."

"According to modern science, man has been around for about three million years or so."

"Your hairy-ape ancestors, perhaps. But not Koreans. We came along to rectify the wrongs done to this world by your simian forebears."

Remo started to protest, but decided it wasn't worth it. They had had this argument before. Instead, he changed the subject. "How's the nail?" he asked.

Chiun winced painfully.

For several months, he had been wearing the horn-like jade nail protector to guard his maimed right index fingernail, which had been sliced off by a foe wielding a supersword. It was unheard-of for a modern Master of Sinanju to be bested in close combat. Chiun was still sensitive about it.

"It grows apace," he said aridly.

"Good."

"But it lacks its full length yet. Thus, I am forced to wear this."

"It goes with the kimono."

"That is the problem. I am forced to wear only kimonos whose colors harmonize with jade. I have not worn my royal purple kimono in months. The black lies folded in darkness, wondering if it has been abandoned forever. The cinnabar wilts from disuse. The pink—"

"You'll be back in pink before you know it."

"It was Master Salbyol."

"Who?"

"Master Salbyol. He was Master when the sun dragon of three thousand years ago was seen."

Remo lifted an interested eyebrow. "Any interesting legends go with him?"

Chiun considered. "He was an indolent Master. Egypt was too far for him to travel, so he relied on Japan and China, who were not as rich as Egypt in those days."

Remo shrugged. "The House got by, I guess."

"There is no excuse for sloth," Chiun sniffed. "He blamed it on the arrow star, not himself."

"Arrow star?"

"The thing you call a comet was unknown in the Korean sky of the days of Salbyol the Indolent. It was called the arrow star because it flew like a feathered shaft through the slower stars, and was considered an evil omen. Much later other such stars appeared, and a wiser Master determined that the arrow star was no star at all, but a sun dragon."

"How'd he come to that brilliant conclusion?"

"Very simply, Remo. Every time a sun dragon rampaged among the Korean stars, a calamity would result. No arrow brought such bad luck. Therefore, it could only be a dragon."

"You know, there probably isn't a time when there isn't a calamity somewhere."

"What are you saying?" asked Chiun, eyes thinning.

"Comets don't cause calamities. That's all. It's just superstition."

"I agree with you. They do not."

"Good."

"They merely presage misfortune."

Remo suddenly noticed the full-figured woman with the cloudy black hair and jade green eyes and said, "Excuse me."

"Where are you going?" Chiun queried.

"I promised myself I'd ask the next gorgeous woman I saw for a date and I just saw her."

"She is fat."

"Voluptuous."

"Fat."

"Catch you later," said Remo, unlocking his seat belt and moving back to the rear of the cabin.

The woman sauntered as far as midcabin, where she began stretching in a way that made Remo look forward to their first date. That she would say yes was guaranteed. No woman ever turned down a Master of Sinanju. Remo sometimes thought the attraction was pheromones. The perfect grace of a body in harmony with itself might also explain the phenomenon. He'd once read that the human brain was programmed by nature to respond positively to a certain symmetry of form. Sinanju training had symmetrically harmonized Remo's body. Where most people had one eye or hand or side of their body larger than the other because the muscles were used more, Remo's form had achieved total symmetry.

Women sensed this symmetry, even if they didn't perceive it on a conscious level. This was part of Remo's innate sexual attraction.

Any way it was sliced, the green-eyed woman wasn't going to say no.

"Hi," said Remo, putting on his best disarming smile.

"Hello," she said, her voice smoky, like dry sherry. "My name is Coral."

"Remo. Going to Boston?"

"I live there."

"Me, too."

"That's great," she said, inching closer.

"I have some free time tonight."

"Me, too."

"Why don't we get together, have dinner?"

Coral was beaming now. "I'd love to." Her breath was a moist, inviting musk.

"Great," said Remo, thinking this was the way to go.

"Let me clear it with Fred first."

"Sure. Who's Fred?"

"I'll be right back."

The cloudy-haired brunette brushed past him, leaving the scent of White Diamonds on Remo's lean body, and he tried to enjoy the fragrance while she went back to her seat. He ended up having to close off his olfactory receptors. The scent, though subtle, was too powerful for his highly sensitive sense of smell. He made a mental note to ask her to go scentless on their first date.

The woman came back and said, "Fred's a little out of sorts, but it's okay."

"He'll get over it," Remo said agreeably. "Who's Fred?"

"My husband."

"Husband?"

The woman lifted her left hand and let the overhead lights play on a plain gold wedding band.

"Why didn't you tell me you were married?" Remo said angrily.

"Why didn't you look at my ring finger?" She was smiling as if it were no big deal.

"Out of practice," Remo said dispiritedly.

"I'll help you with that," she said brushing up against him with her bullet-shaped bosom.

"Look, I don't do married women."

She ran long gold nails down the front of Remo's T-shirt and purred like a lion. "Fred will get over it. He always does."

"Not the point. I don't poach on another man's preserve."

"Hey, don't I get a say in this?"

"Sure. You get to say goodbye. Goodbye," said Remo, retreating to his seat.

"You have your date?" asked the Master of Sinanju blandly.

Remo folded his arms. "Don't give me that. You overheard every word, you old reprobate."

"I would prefer to hear the story from your own lips."

"She's married."

"I knew that."

"Goody for you."

"In this land, Remo, it is customary for a married woman to wear a gold circlet about the ring finger of the hand that is closest to the heart. This signifies a woman who is taken."

"I know that!" Remo flared.

"It is good that you did not take her."

"There are other women."

"You are going about this the improper way," Chiun warned.

"Go grow your nail," growled Remo unhappily.

"And you may jump over the moon as you chase your white cows," the Master of Sinanju said huffily.

13

The director of operations for NASA's shuttle program was only too happy to answer reporters' questions.

Shuttle flights were so routine the press didn't bother to cover them live anymore. There was always a token media presence, of course. The *Challenger* disaster guaranteed that. Everyone wanted tape if another in-flight catastrophe shook the world. So the national media duly sent a sprinkling of bored reporters each and every time an orbiter was launched.

This time it was the newest of the shuttle fleet, the *Reliant.* It was to be her maiden voyage. Task—deploy a National Reconnaissance Office spy satellite, name and mission classified.

Usually the reporters showed up the day before launch and waited. Sometimes the wait stretched out over three or four days, and they grumbled. They always grumbled. They especially grumbled when the launch went off without a hitch. Sometimes they cursed and complained bitterly that the pictures were "always the same."

"What do you want?" the director once asked a CBS reporter. "Another *Challenger?*"

Without hesitation, the reporter said, "Hell, yes."

The director of operations walked away rather than clean the man's blue-bearded clock.

Today the *Reliant* stood on the gigantic crawler-transporter that moved her toward the launch pad, and the reporters were already here. In droves. The weather had been cold for Florida in late December. Maybe they had hopes of a catastrophic failure, the director thought angrily.

The media assembled in the director's office, which looked down over the most reinforced road in the world, with Launch Complex 39-A in the background. The crawler-transporter was rumbling along. It was a 2500-ton battleship gray converted surface coal-mining machine as big as a baseball diamond moving at a sedate three and a half miles per hour on four double-tracked tractor units. Each of the shoes that made up one of the massive treads was capable of exerting thirty-three tons of crushing force. Strapped to the gigantic external tank and flanked by the dual rocketlike boosters, the shuttle sat upright as if poised for launch, as it was borne to the launch pad.

It was an impressive sight, but since it wasn't spewing smoke and flame, the press showed no interest in it.

"Are you afraid for this mission?" asked one reporter.

"Why should I be?" the director shot back.

"If Martians did fry the BioBubble, wouldn't NASA be high on their target list?"

"There are no Martians, and there is no target list. Get off it."

"How do you know that?"

"Because I saw the *Viking* and *Mariner* probe pictures. It's a dead world."

"Then why is NASA talking about going there in thirty years?"

"It's not completely dead. There are probably lichen. Maybe some microbes or one-celled organisms."

"How do we know one-celled microbes aren't advanced enough to point death rays at Earth?" a seasoned science reporter asked.

"Because," the director of operations patiently explained, "a one-cell organism doesn't have a brain. It's a primitive life-form." He swallowed his biting *Like reporters, only smarter.*

"We don't know what a one-celled Martian might be like. Maybe the cell is all brain."

"Yes, a giant brain," a reporter piped up from in back.

"If he was all brain," the director of operations said with ill-concealed impatience, "then he wouldn't have hands to point his death ray with, now would he?"

"Maybe some of his Martian comrades are just hands. Or feet. They gang up and make a whole person. Nassau'd be a sitting duck."

"It's NASA, not Nassau," he returned, correcting a sacrilegious mispronunciation reporters had been committing since the halcyon days of the Mercury Program. "And the program is not at risk. Take my word for it."

"You don't mind if we film the crawl?" one said.

"Be my guest."

Cameras were set up all around the giant transporter. They recorded every laborious inch and foot as the gigantic treads crept along. It typically took a full day to move a shuttle from the launch-assembly hangar to the pad. The media dutifully committed to tape every millisecond of the transfer.

Somewhere past midnight, after the launch director had gone home for the evening, the tireless cameras recorded the biggest disaster to strike NASA since the *Challenger* dropped into the Atlantic Ocean.

Floodlights bathed the gleaming white shuttle. The crawler crawled along the crawlerway with painful ponderousness, making a low mutter.

Without warning, night turned to day.

There came a white-hot flash, a thunderous *baroom,* and the space shuttle *Reliant* was instantly consumed, along with her wilting twin solid booster rockets. The big, empty external tank fed the blaze, its thin orange skin turned black in the instant before it collapsed utterly.

Shuttle, tank, boosters and transporter were fused into a single hot blob. Most of it melted down into molten metals and sublimed rubber and other toxic fumes. Heat-resistant ceramic tiles rained down—literally rained. They came down as white-hot liquid precipitation that made smoking black teardrops on the ground.

The remote cameras were also consumed, so there was no footage.

Except for one still camera.

A *National Enquirer* photographer, denied admission to the facility on general principles, happened to be shooting from a vantage point in the marshes outside of NASA property.

He was taking shots of the *Reliant* silhouetted against the moonlit sky, clicking the shutter rapidly, not paying much attention, knowing that at least one good shot would emerge from the roll.

The image in the viewfinder was so small he missed seeing the important phenomenon in person. It was only after he developed the roll, looking for the "before" shot to go with the "after" image of the cataclysmic disaster he had captured, that the faintly glowing letters in the sky were discovered.

Because of what they spelled, all hell would break loose on both hemispheres.

14

The President of the U.S. was awakened from a sound sleep by the urgent voice of his chief of staff.

"The new shuttle blew up, sir."

The President roused from the rosy haze of his dream life.

"Shuttle?"

"The *Reliant*. It went the same way as the Bio-Bubble."

"Damn. Don't tell my wife. She'll find a way to blame me."

A stern kick to his ankle reminded the President of the U.S. that he happened to be in bed with his wife—contrary to his interrupted dream.

"Sorry. Didn't recognize the new hairdo," he muttered, throwing off the bed covers.

His chief of staff followed as the Chief Executive hurried from the room, tying a blue terry-cloth robe with the Presidential seal about his waist.

"You have to give a speech to reassure the nation," the chief of staff said anxiously.

"Have it written," the President snapped.

"We have to come up with a plausible explanation that won't trigger nationwide panic."

"I'll leave that up to you," the President said, stepping into the tiny White House elevator.

The chief of staff started to step aboard but a pudgy Presidential hand pushed him back.

"Meet me in the Oval Office. Ten minutes."

"Where are you going?"

"Upstairs."

"Oh."

The elevator took the President to the Lincoln Bedroom, where he got the tireless Smith on the line. Smith sounded sleepy for almost five seconds, then the lemonade started coming out in his voice.

"Smith, the space shuttle *Reliant* was just destroyed. It looks like whatever melted the BioBubble got it."

"I will look into it."

"I thought you *were* looking into it."

"I did. My people came up with nothing tangible. Although I am pursuing leads."

"How do I explain this to the American people? It looks like Martians are attacking the space program."

"The BioBubble was not part of the space program," Smith clarified.

"Try convincing the American public of that. With Dr. Pagan telling everyone space aliens are angry at us, they're sure not going to believe *me*. I don't have his credibility."

"Do your best. I will put my people on it."

The President lowered his voice, knowing the First Lady's office was just down the hall.

"Do you think someone *is* out to crush our space program?"

Smith cleared his throat. "The possibility cannot be excluded."

"The Russians, maybe. They're getting shirty again."

"Except for the Mir space station, their space program is in the doldrums."

"And they're on short rations up there ever since their shuttle failed to dock with Mir last month."

"Exactly. Russian involvement makes no sense. Should they have an emergency on Mir, their best rescue option rests with our shuttle fleet."

"Guess you're right. We can scratch the Russians off our short list."

"The French, the Chinese and the Japanese all have active commercial space programs and are trying to compete with NASA," Smith continued, "but I cannot conceive any of those nations targeting our space agency. The technology is beyond them."

"The Japanese have been pretty mad at us lately. I'm not even sure why."

Smith said nothing to that. He knew why. He had ordered Remo and Chiun to punish a certain Japanese conglomerate for acts of commercial sabotage the President knew nothing about. The Japanese understood America had been behind the dropping of a steam locomotive on Nishitsu headquarters in Osaka, but couldn't complain without exposing their own complicity in an attempt to destroy the U.S. rail system.

"I will be back to you, Mr. President," Smith said, terminating the conversation.

The President hung up, knotted his bathrobe and shuffled in his fuzzy slippers to the White House elevator. Just once he'd like a major crisis to come in the afternoon. He hated being pulled out of bed at these ungodly hours. If he didn't get his ten hours' sleep, he was out of sorts all day.

HAROLD W. SMITH HAD excused himself from his marital bed, and was rewarded by a brief interruption in his wife's steady snoring before taking the briefcase containing his satellite uplink to the CURE telephone line. It was the only weak link in his direct line to the White House. When he wasn't at Folcroft, the call was forwarded through his computer system to the briefcase, which also contained his laptop connection with Folcroft.

Of course, the line was scrambled. But a conversation that was relayed from a ground station to an ordinary communications satellite and down again could be intercepted. Theoretically it could be unscrambled—if one had the correct technology and perhaps five years in which to untwist the conversation. By that time, the conversation would be moot, Smith assumed. Thus, he felt reasonably safe with this emergency-only link.

After he terminated the White House call, Smith hit the autodial button to Remo Williams's Massachusetts home. He was a gray man with gray eyes and hair, the complexion of weathered, unpainted wood and a matching personality. Even in his CIA days, more than thirty years ago, he was known as the Gray Ghost.

Smith waited patiently, knowing that the Master of Sinanju would ignore the ringing and Remo would, depending on his mood, also ignore it because Chiun was ignoring it, or possibly break the telephone and keep on sleeping.

It was an unlisted number. Neither man had anything remotely like a social life, but these days telephone salesmen were unafraid to call at the most ridiculous hours, and Remo had no patience for such interruptions.

Fifty rings later, Remo answered, clear as a bell but slightly peeved. "If you're selling something, I'm going to spoon-feed you the contents of your scrotum."

Smith cleared his voice. "It's me."

"Me who?"

"You know my voice," Smith said carefully, knowing this was an uplinked call.

"I know a lot of voices."

Smith decided to skip the game-playing. "The space shuttle *Reliant* was destroyed on its transporter midway between the launch-assembly building and the launch pad."

Remo's voice sobered instantly. "Anybody killed?"

"Unknown at this time. But no astronauts were aboard." Smith paused. "Remo, it was hit by a bolt from the night sky, turning it to slag."

"Damn. Somebody's trying to wreck the space program."

"The BioBubble wasn't part of the space program," Smith said testily.

"Maybe whoever's doing this doesn't know that."

"It is possible."

"Speaking of which," said Remo, "any luck on tracking down the mystery guy who funded the BioBubble?"

"No," Smith admitted. "I have combed Amos Bulla's personal and business telephone records, and accounted for all persons and calls. None trace back to a man named Ruber Mavors."

"There's no such person. Not going by that name."

"I looked into the backgrounds of everyone in those records. None had the financial wherewithal to rescue the BioBubble project."

"Unless you believe in Latin-speaking Martians with a sense of humor, you're overlooking something," Remo said dryly.

"Remo, see what you can learn at the Kennedy Space Center."

"Won't the place be crawling with investigators?"

"Yes. But you saw the BioBubble aftermath. I want positive confirmation that these two events were the work of the same agency."

"That's all?"

"Perhaps you will stumble upon something."

"Should I leave Chiun behind?"

"Why would you do that?"

"Because he doesn't exactly blend in with a high-security investigation," Remo said dryly.

"Will he agree to remain behind?" Smith asked doubtfully.

"Sure. Why wouldn't he?"

"You know him better than I. Go in as a National Transportation Safety Board investigator."

"NTSB! Aren't they just airplane and train crashes?"

"Yes, but every other logical agency will be represented. Any other cover would put you in contact and conflict with legitimate representatives of other agencies."

"Gotcha. I'll call you from Florida."

The line went dead.

When Remo padded to Chiun's room at the other end of the L-shaped building, the Master of Sinanju was already rolling up his sleeping mat, attired in an avocado-trimmed ivory kimono.

"I am going with you," he squeaked.

Remo decided on the nonconfrontational approach. "It's not a good idea, Little Father."

"I will be the judge of that."

"It's going to be a zoo."

"Perhaps I will encounter some apes I have never before beheld," Chiun said aridly.

"Just give me one reason why you should go when you don't need or have to."

Chiun's hazel eyes flared in a brief twinkle that quickly died. "I have read that the Americans are taking Japanese into space now."

"Yeah, some Japanese astronaut went up on the shuttle to help salvage a Japanese satellite earlier this year. What's that got to do with anything?"

"If a Japanese can go into space, why can not a Korean?"

"It's not that simple. You have to be selected. Then you have to train for years."

"I have trained all my life."

"Not for outer space."

"Are there deadly assassins and killers in outer space?" Chiun demanded.

"Not that we've found so far," Remo admitted.

"I have slain the most-ferocious killers on this world. Why can I not visit the celestial realm, where death does not walk in human form?"

Remo thought fast. Chiun was looking up at him hopefully, and his bald head only came up to Remo's breastbone.

"Because you're too short," he said quickly.

"What!"

"It's true, Little Father. Cross my heart and hope to die in old age. Astronauts have to meet a height requirement."

"There is nothing wrong with my stature!" Chiun flared.

"You gotta wear a protective space suit, and they don't come in your size. I think you're at least two inches shy of regulation astronaut height."

Remo held his breath as Chiun studied his face for signs of insincerity.

"And I suppose you will be allowed to ascend the heavens, stilt-legged one?" Chiun asked at length.

"I'm not planning to go into orbit, Chiun. Honest."

"The Chinese promised that I would be the first Korean into space when I was last in China."

"They were trying to launch you into the Void, Chiun. You know that. They wanted you dead. They figured a fast ride on an ICBM would be the quickest way to get rid of you."

"The Chinese know I work for America now. As do the Russians. As do many of this nation's mortal enemies."

"Yeah. So what? They don't know about CURE or Smith or even me."

"If the nations of this world know this, it cannot be the nations of this world who are attacking the New Rome. Fear of Sinanju wrath would stay their treacherous hand. Therefore, it can only be the work of a nation from some other world."

"Let's leave the Martians out of this. Come on. Let's just go, if you're going."

"I am going," Chiun said firmly.

"No steamer trunks this time."

"I will not pack for the voyage into space until I have been formally invited," Chiun sniffed. "I have my pride."

"Good. I don't suppose you still have that three-piece suit from a few years back when you were on your last Western kick?"

"Will wearing such a garment increase my opportunities for travel beyond this world?"

"Can't hurt," said Remo.

"Then prepare the scarlet chariot. I will join you."

Grinning, Remo went downstairs to wake up the chariot.

It was Harold Smith's latest attempt to fulfill a contractual obligation Remo had insisted upon. He needed a vehicle that was equal to Boston traffic and capable of being sideswiped, rear-ended and otherwise abused by insane Boston drivers. And it had to be red.

The last chariot, an armored personnel carrier, had been APC-jacked. The replacement was a little more down-market, but Remo had decided it would do. After all, if the Humvee was good enough for Arnold Schwarzenegger, it was good enough for Remo Williams.

The engine turned over without any trouble despite the subzero temperature.

The Master of Sinanju floated out of the condo-castle a moment later, wearing a severe black three-piece suit that was ordinary in every way except the tailor had widened the sleeves so that they flapped like bell-bottom pant legs.

This sartorial compromise enabled the Master of Sinanju to conceal his hands in his sleeves, hiding the shame of his maimed fingernail from an uncaring world.

Chiun took the passenger seat, and Remo backed out, the Humvee engine surging powerfully.

It was night and the Southeast Expressway was all but deserted. They took the new Ted Williams Tunnel to Logan International Airport, parked and grabbed the first flight to Orlando, Florida. Which turned out to be the last flight of the night.

It wasn't empty, but the stewardesses outnumbered the passengers by half. Remo, realizing they would probably fill the idle flying hours by trying to sit on his lap all at once, told the Master of Sinanju, "Tell them I'm in a coma."

"You are not."

"I didn't say I was. Just fib for me."

"I will tell my own lies, not yours," Chiun snapped.

"Just so long as I get to sleep the flight away, undisturbed," said Remo, slapping a pillow behind his head and nodding off without further ado.

The first stewardess to check on their aisle after the 747 vaulted into the night sky was told, "Do not bother. He is gay."

"He does look kinda gay."

"He is very gay."

"Damn."

The second stewardess came up and said, "When he wakes up, will you let me know?"

"Why?" asked Chiun.

"Because I have a thing for gay guys."

"He is also VIP positive."

"He's famous?"

"He is diseased."

"Double rubbers. They work for me. Tell him, okay?"

"Of course."

The third stewardess came up, took one look at Remo and lamented, "Why are all the good ones married or gay?"

"Because they cannot be both," replied the Master of Sinanju.

The braking of the wheels touching tarmac triggered Remo's waking reflexes, and he looked out the window at the blue runway lights speeding by.

"We're there?" he asked Chiun.

"Yes."

"Any problem with the stewardesses?"

"I told the first that you were very happy, the second that you were a VIP and not to be disturbed under any circumstances, and the third expressed regret that you were married."

"You told her that I was married?"

"No, it was her idea," said Chiun blandly. "I merely did not contradict her mistaken impression."

"Nice going, Little Father. I owe you one."

"And I will collect in a time and place of my own choosing."

As they left the plane, the flight attendants said their goodbyes, insisting on shaking Remo's hands warmly, and Remo accepted because they had been good enough to leave him alone.

Once in the terminal, he opened his fist to check the folded papers they had surreptitiously slipped him, thinking they were the usual hastily scribbled phone numbers.

"Why did all three give me AIDS-prevention pamphlets?" Remo wondered aloud, tossing them into the nearest trash can.

"Perhaps they recognize you for the promiscuous rake that you are."

"I'm the reverse of promiscuous."

"If you fall into the foul habit of dating women, promiscuity will be your epitaph."

"You sure you didn't put them up to this?"

"Lust kills," sniffed Chiun. "Remember this as you sow your wild goats."

"It's 'wild oats.' And stop trying to get my goat."

"Do not complain to me if your voracious goat consumes all of your wild oats and you have none left when you are my age."

15

Sometimes Radomir Eduardovitch Rushenko forgot himself. It was very easy to forget. Just as it was very difficult to fully lose the old Red ways.

Rushenko parked his dull black Volga automobile within sight of Iz Tsvetoka's modest tailor shop on Tverskaya Street, not far from the hideous yellow double arches of the most popular McDonald's restaurant in the heart of gray Moscow. It was very gray now, with the heavily overcast skies like lead and the freshening smell of snow coming out of Siberia.

The bell over the door tinkled as Rushenko stepped down from the sidewalk to the sunken establishment.

The balding, fuzzy-haired tailor did not look up from pressing a pair of trousers until Rushenko said, "Good morning, *tovaritch.*"

"I am not your comrade," the tailor said harshly.

"Excuse me. I meant, good morning, *sudar.*"

The tailor nodded, satisfied.

Rushenko laid his suit on the counter and said, "It requires special attention."

The tailor gestured to the fitting room. Rushenko stepped inside, drew closed the red curtain and, just as the surly tailor made his pants presser spurt steam, Rushenko gave a coat hook a certain twist.

The rear panel of the fitting room pivoted on a middle hinge, and Rushenko quickly stepped back. The panel finished its revolution, and it was as if he had stepped off the face of the earth instead of entering the bowels of the most secret security organization in Russian history.

There had been at one time the Czarist secret police. Then the Cheka. Then VCheka. After that OGPU, NKVD, NKGB, MVD and KGB. Now there was the FSK, a toothless organization good for nothing more than wardening the old KGB files and taking horrific casualties in Chechnya.

The best and brightest of the old KGB, having no stomach for détente, *perestroika, glasnost* and the cold consequences of these failed policies, had banded together to form a clandestine ministry that was responsible to no one in the sickeningly democratized Kremlin. Until the red-letter day Soviet rule would be restored, they would operate in secret, overseeing, manipulating and protecting Mother Russia from its deadliest enemies—which in these days was itself, and its drunken, incompetent leaders.

His footsteps echoing down the corridor, Rushenko came to a blank nickel-steel door. There was no name on the door. To place a name there would be to give a name to the ministry that had no official existence.

In the beginning, it had been called Shchit— Shield—a name suggested by the sword-and-shield emblem of the old KGB. It was completely paperless, having no files or public phone number. But after a while, it became clear even a name was a security risk. So a formal name was dispensed with. A ministry that enjoyed no official sanction should not enjoy a name, reasoned the architect of Shield, Colonel Rushenko.

The headquarters of the ministry changed from time to time. At first it was a Moscow prison. Later it masqueraded as a publishing company specializing in Russian-language sequels to *Gone with the Wind*.

The current incarnation had been the brainchild of Rushenko, because it enabled his people to keep an eye on the American FBI, which in this most insane of eras had itself established a branch office in the very same part of Moscow.

Rushenko stood before an ivory panel, his firm mouth addressing a copper microphone grille. A laser lens emitted a steady crimson glow at eye level.

A voice crackled, ''Identify.''

''Radomir Eduardovitch. Colonel.''

''Place your fingertips to the five lighted spots.''

Touching a fan of five points of light that appeared beneath the laser eye, Rushenko allowed the optical reader to scan his fingerprints. He was then asked to peer into the red laser lens.

The laser—harmless unless his fingerprints were not found on file—scanned the unique vein pattern in his retina, and only then did the door hum open. The alternative was a smoking hole bored from brow to the back of his skull.

Inside was a reception area done in old-style socialist heroic decor, with a honey blond woman in a simple maroon skirt and red turtleneck jersey seated at a massive desk. It was a different blond woman each month. A different heroine of the Motherland who would willingly drink poison in the event of unauthorized penetration so that the secrets of Shield would go to the grave with her.

"You are expected, *tovaritch.*"

And Rushenko smiled to hear the old form of address again.

"Thank you, comrade."

Nowadays people were *sudar*—"sir"—or *gospodin*—"Mr." It sounded too elitist for Rushenko and his socialist ears for he had been educated under the old system. Only here in the labyrinth of Shield was it acceptable to address others as "comrade."

In a red-walled conference room without windows but illuminated by high-intensity floor lamps to defeat the depressive psychological effects lack of sunlight caused, Rushenko met with the other section chiefs of Shield. They only convened in case of crisis or intelligence and policy discussion. It was safer that way. All wore the insignialess black uniforms of the defunct Red Army, as did Colonel Rushenko, revealed when he removed his greatcoat and astrakhan hat.

"There has been an event in the United States," he was told by a man whose name he didn't know, a former KGB operative like himself.

"Interesting," said Colonel Rushenko.

"An installation called the BioBubble was destroyed utterly by a power of unknown destructiveness."

"A bomb?"

"We think not. We think a ray."

"A laser?"

"No laser is this powerful. To do this, the laser beam would have to possess a circumference of three acres."

Glances of unease passed among stone-faced men. For security reasons, no one knew the identity of his comrades. The people's hero who had recruited them had taken his life once his task was accomplished to ensure their anonymity.

"Star Wars?"

Rushenko shook his head. "Such a laser in orbit would be so large as to reveal itself. It is not a new weapon of the supposedly cancelled U.S. Strategic Defense Initiative."

"Could it be ours?" a shaggy-haired man with suspicious Georgian eyes asked.

"Zhirinovsky talks of the Elipticon," an Estonian remarked.

Colonel Rushenko shook his heavy Kazakh face. "Zhirinovsky talks of foolishness. But he is useful to us."

"Colonel Rushenko, I have in my possession a file copied from the old KGB archives. It speaks of a weapon such as this."

"I am listening."

"It is a very dangerous weapon. If deployed, it could render our nuclear deterrent obsolete."

Colonel Rushenko frowned darkly. "Our nuclear deterrent is all but obsolete. Half the missiles are inoperative or under repair. We no longer test, so there is no way to know if they will launch or detonate on impact. For all we know, the current leadership has its collective finger on the trigger of a water pistol."

"You mistake my meaning, comrade. This weapon could make the surviving good missiles useless hulks resting in their silos and launchers like so many loaves of bread in so many paper sacks."

"How?"

"We have only a flimsy grasp of the event, but if the Americans are experimenting with this device, we will stand naked beneath it."

"We have assets in the Evil Empire?"

"Yes. Kinga the Bitch."

Rushenko shuddered. "A true nutcracker, that one."

"Let us send her into the field. Perhaps she will learn something useful."

"And if she is caught?"

"She has been hypnotized to give up under interrogation the name of an FSK control she once dallied with and who left her. Let the FSK take the blame."

Colonel Rushenko nodded. "Then I will see that it's done."

With that, the meeting was adjourned, and Rushenko was left with a computer linked to a Chinese-red telephone that, thanks to a friendly telephone lineman, ran through the FSK switchboard and thus accessed the superior government Vertushka phone system.

It took three hours to obtain a modem connection with the international Internet. It was another embarrassing proof of how much Russian technology had deteriorated since the old regime was overthrown.

In the glory days of the USSR, it would never have taken more than two.

16

When Dr. Cosmo Pagan heard that the U.S. space shuttle had been melted down en route to the launch pad, he was trying to find Mars through the twenty-four-inch antique refractor at Lowell Observatory outside Flagstaff.

As observatories went, it wasn't much—a white, wood-frame Victorian structure perched on a promontory. In the cloudless dry Arizona air, it was a perfect spot to observe the Red Planet.

Here, Percival Lowell had mapped out the canals that later astronomers sought in vain. But Lowell had seen them, and before he died, Cosmo Pagan wanted to see them, too.

Mars wasn't being cooperative. Unable to sight it by fiddling with the right ascension and declination, Pagan swung the blue telescope tube by hand and peered through the brass-bound sighter.

Finally he got a fix.

There it was, the Red Planet, just as Lowell had described it in his notebooks over a century ago. Lowell saw a dying planet kept alive by a planetwide network of irrigation canals. His findings had fired the imaginations of H. G. Wells, Edgar Rice Burroughs and other great chroniclers of the Mars that had in turn ignited Pagan's youthful dreams.

Regrettably the Mars of canals and princesses and four-armed, green-skinned giants had evaporated with the *Viking* and *Mariner* probes and subsequent discoveries.

It was too bad. Even at his mature age, Dr. Pagan would rather green Martians than red deserts. After all, there were red deserts on earth, too. Here in Arizona. And in Mongolia, where the Red Gobi had an uncannily distinct Martian feel to it—not that Dr. Pagan had ever been to the Red Gobi. There were no news cameras in the Red Gobi. He never went anywhere where there wasn't the possibility of face time—or at least good black ink.

Though discredited, Lowell hadn't toiled in vain, Cosmo thought. If not for him, there would have been no "War of the Worlds" or *Warlord of Mars* to set Cosmo Pagan on the road to his red destiny. By that reasoning, Percival Lowell had not lived in vain.

And it was Cosmo Pagan's deepest wish to one night see the phenomenon that had caused a great astronomer to believe he saw Martian canals.

His cellular phone shrilled as he was drinking in the sight of Mars, and without taking his eyes from the eyepiece, he flipped it open and began speaking.

"Dr. Cosmo Pagan, world-renowned authority on the universe and everything under the heavens."

"Dr. Pagan, this is the Associated Press."

"Would you like a quote?"

"Exactly."

"The universe is transcendent in its awesome greatness. An ocean of stars in a whirling cosmic whirlpool whirling about, oblivious to the paltry human concerns of us mere molecular bio-machines."

"That's great, but I was looking for a specific quote."

"Right now I am looking at the Red Planet, Mars—seat of war, according to the ancient Romans. But to me it is a place of peace and scarlet tranquillity. Some day man will set foot on Mars, but for all its grandeur it is but the stepping-stone to the greater, grander cosmos."

The AP man cleared his throat and tried again. "Dr. Pagan, do you think Martians are behind the shuttle meltdown tonight?"

"I wish..." he breathed. Then, catching himself, he blurted, "Meltdown? What shuttle?"

"The *Reliant* was turned to molten metal not twenty minutes ago."

"Wonderful," Pagan breathed.

"What?"

"Mars. It seems to be looking back at me. The north polar icecap looks like the cool wink of a painted concubine. No canals, though. Lowell saw canals. I'd love to see the canals he saw, even if that turned out to be just lichen patterns."

"So you think the Martians theory has credence?"

"I think," said Dr. Cosmo Pagan, "the universe loves me."

"Say again?"

"Every time I have a lull in my lecture itinerary or I'm between specials, the universe conjures up an event to perpetuate my name."

The AP man grew tense of voice. "Dr. Pagan, I'd like a comment on the shuttle disaster."

"I regret the loss of our brave astronauts' lives."

"No astronauts died. It was a prelaunch accident."

"Then perhaps it was for the best."

"Sir?"

"Do you know how much vile carcinogens one of those thundering monsters puts out? The noise pollution alone is enough to deafen the manatees in the Straits of Florida. Migratory birds are driven away from their natural flight paths. And that doesn't even take into account the damage to the ozone layer. Do you know that at the rate we're depleting the biomass, our polar icecaps are going to start melting, raising the ocean level everywhere? Spaceship Earth could go the way of dead Mars. For all we know, we earthlings are repeating history. Martian history."

"I thought you were pro-space flight, Dr. Pagan."

"I am pro-peaceful exploration of space. One missile. One probe. The shuttles require a main external fuel tank and two boosters. That's three times the noise, three times the pollution and for what? We're only filling the near heavens with junk that falls to earth and might hit somebody. They go 125 miles up. Hell, Chris Columbus went farther than that in a wooden sailing ship. The human tribe needs to look beyond our Earth-moon ghetto to Mars, then the better neighborhood of the Jovian planets, and ultimately Alpha Centauri and beyond. That's using space to our advantage."

"One last question."

"Go ahead."

"Do you think the shuttle was destroyed by the same power that melted the BioBubble, and if so, why?"

"Perhaps," Dr. Pagan said thoughtfully, "it has something to do with our thinning ozone layer. The way those shuttles tear through the ozone shield, it's a miracle we all don't have basal-cell scalp sarcoma."

"Thanks, Dr. Pagan. That's just what I needed."

"I'll send you a bill," Dr. Cosmo Pagan said smoothly. Hanging up, he exulted, "The universe loves me. It truly, truly does." Taking a last, wistful peek into the eyepiece, he sighed. "But I have eyes for only you, my scarlet hussy."

IN CELEBRATION, FLORIDA, an always-running Compaq computer beeped twice, signaling an incoming e-mail message.

Kinga Zongar heard it even in the early sleep of the sultry Florida night with the cold moonlight coming through her bedroom screens like cool fingers of silver and steel.

Throwing off a scarlet satin cover, she strode nude to the system, whose color monitor splashed varicolored light against the sitting-room walls. Her long russet hair, brushed back from her high brow, fell back in a ponytail that swished with her every step.

Accessing her e-mail file, she read the message in the Cyrillic language:

To: AuntTamara@aol.com
From: UncleVanya@shield.su.min
Subject: Assignment
Greetings from the Motherland. Consider yourself activated this date. Go now to Cape Canaveral, where an unknown force has reduced an American space shuttle to worthless, bubbling materials. This appears to be the same phenomenon which, as you may have read, similarly destroyed the BioBubble. Learn what you can. Report everything.

Kinga erased the message from her system. She didn't know who Uncle Vanya was, other than the commissar of Shield—or whatever they were calling it this year. Neither mattered. Only her sacred duty to the Motherland.

She dressed with brisk care, a demure maroon dress that bespoke casual professionalism. A notebook and press card completed her cover ensemble.

It was amazing, Kinga thought as she claimed her bloodred Maxima GTE and sent it spinning out into the evening, how America allowed just anyone to obtain journalist credentials. Were journalists not de facto spies without portfolio? Yet this was how it was done in America.

And since this was how it was done, this was how Kinga Zongar would do it.

If it became necessary to resort to "wet measures," well, there were other slots in other newspapers for an expatriate Hungarian reporter, if Kinga the Bitch was forced to revert to type.

Secretly she hoped it would come to that. It had been a long time since she had killed a man in the line of duty.

Far too long, she thought, licking her very scarlet lips.

17

Getting past the gate to the Kennedy Space Center at Cape Canaveral was the easy part.

The area was a crush of reporters doing stand-ups, supported by white satellite trucks and floodlights.

Behind the gate, an eerie whitish exhalation arose from the spot where the shuttle *Reliant* had melted down like an ice-cream cone under withering sunlight.

Remo and Chiun moved through the media throng as if they were two molecules slipping through a placer miner's pan.

At the gate, there were two white-faced Air Force guards at a guard box.

Remo presented himself and his ID. "Remo Cupper, NTSB. This is my assistant, Chiun."

Chiun started to bow, then remembering his Western garments, nodded instead.

"NTSB? What are you guys doing here?"

"It was a transportation accident, right?" said Remo.

"Technically."

"Nobody can say NTSB isn't on the job, no matter where the trouble is," explained Remo.

The two airmen exchanged dubious glances.

"Let me kick this upstairs," said one. "Our orders are firm—keep all non-NASA personnel out."

"Can't let you do that," said Remo, taking the telephone from his hand.

The man stared at his empty hand as if doubting the evidence of his own eyes. His hand was still in clutch mode. It held only air and the vague memory of plastic contours. Yet he had gripped the handset tightly. He was sure it would be impossible to remove the handset without disturbing his grip. But there it was.

The second airman sputtered, "What do you mean by this?"

"It's not an investigation if the brass has a chance to cover this up," explained Remo.

"Nobody's covering up anything. It's all over the TV."

"Just open the gate," said Remo, handing the phone to Chiun, who broke it in two and returned the pieces to the airman who was still trying to figure out the physics of Remo's telephone trick.

"Very well, sir," the man said, handing over a pair of clip-on passes. "But you didn't have to break the phone."

"Next time, don't try to cover for your bosses," retorted Remo.

"Nor impede the wrathful agents of the NAACP," added Chiun as the gate rolled aside electronically.

The press, seeing an opening, decided to take a run at the gate, figuring that once they were in, there would be too many of them to throw out.

Remo and Chiun slipped in, and the guard threw the gate into fast reverse. A female reporter got her boobs caught in the closing gate and shrieked a protest that could be heard on the moon—if anyone up there had ears.

This gave the others their opportunity. All the guards converged on the moving wall of press, and no one paid any attention to the pair of NTSB investigators who had been passed through.

REMO AND CHIUN WALKED unnoticed to the accident site. If the BioBubble resembled a glass pancake, this was more like a metallic waffle. Chunks and lumps of unmelted matter protruded from the rehardened crawler that was now spread out like a stepped-on aircraft carrier.

Amazingly they were unchallenged by the emergency crews and frantic blue-coated managers scurrying around. Some wore gas-and-particle-filter masks against the chemical fumes of the destroyed shuttle.

The 165,000-pound space plane was no longer recognizable as the most ambitious feat of engineering ever accomplished by man. Remo recalled that shuttles were so complicated that it was a miracle every time one went up without a hitch. When they landed intact, it was considered another miracle.

Personally, Remo thought, he would rather drive a Yugo against traffic in the Indy 500 than go up in one of those things, but he was risk averse, being only a professional assassin.

"What do you think, Little Father? And don't say dragon."

"I will not say dragon. But I am thinking dragon."

"Don't even think it."

"Too late. I am thinking it."

A beefy-faced manager whose sweat had nothing to do with the humidity of the night noticed them and demanded to know who they were.

Remo did the honors.

The manager read the ID card and exploded, "NTSB? What the hell are you guys doing here?"

"We came for the black box," Remo said in a measured voice.

The manager looked perplexed for all of a minute.

Remo could tell by the dull gleam in his eyes that he was middle management and had no idea if there was a black box, or whether the NTSB could legally lay claim to it if there was.

This conclusion was confirmed by the man's next words.

"I gotta take your request up with my immediate superior."

"You do that," said Remo politely, knowing that his superior would take it to his superior and so on up the line to who knew how many redundant management layers.

By the time a possible no thundered back down the chain of command, Remo figured it would be Christmas again.

Moving among the packed NASA personnel, Remo flashed his NTSB ID card and asked repeatedly, "Anybody see the incident?"

A fresh-faced technician in what Remo at first thought was an Izod smock but quickly realized that impression was merely the result of sneezing without benefit of a handkerchief said, "I did."

"I want to hear all about it," Remo said sharply.

"The transporter was—"

"What transporter?"

The man looked at the gargantuan pile of hardening metal and ceramic, and a dazed expression spread over his face.

"It was incredible. The shuttle transporter is the largest piece of machinery of its type ever built. The shuttle was riding atop her. The most complicated machine ever built riding the biggest one ever constructed. And just like that, it was turned into solder."

"What did it?" asked Remo.

"Lord alone knows. I saw a cone of white light. It bathed the machine, then went away. The heat must have been fierce. Glass melted in the observation room. Glass doesn't melt easily, you know."

"Lately it does," said Remo.

The man went on. "The light evaporated, then came the pressure wave."

"Yeah?"

"It sounded like thunder. But it couldn't have been thunder. What I saw wasn't lightning. Not forked lightning, bolt lightning and certainly not ball lightning. I know lightning. It's one of our biggest concerns when we're taking the spacecraft out of the launch-assembly building."

"Look like a ray to you?" asked Remo.

"If it was a ray, it was the biggest ray ever generated."

"Makes sense. The biggest ray to knock out the two biggest machines ever built, right?"

Chiun nodded as if this made perfect sense to him.

The technician's voice became hollow. "It was also as hot as the surface of the sun. We're finding black droplets we think are the shuttle's heat-resistant tiles. They're supposed to protect the orbiter from reentry heat and are designed to withstand temperatures up to 1,200 degrees Fahrenheit. They came close to being sublimed. That means turned to gas.''

"Sounds hot," said Remo.

"We're looking for any carbon-carbon from the nose and leading-edge wing insulation. Carbon-carbon will withstand 1,600 degrees. But so far, there's no trace.''

"Sounds superhot," said Remo.

"You know," the technician said, looking up at the red dot that was Mars high in the Florida sky, "I got into the space business because I used to read a lot of science fiction when I was a kid. You grow up, you shake off a lot of wild notions. Space men. UFOs. All that foolishness. But after what I saw tonight, it all came back at me like that past fifteen years never happened. I look up at the stars now and I'm reminded how small we are and how insignificant. Makes a man shiver deep into his soul.''

"You shiver for both of us," returned Remo, "I have work to do.''

They left the technician staring up at Mars with his mouth hung half-open.

"You will see that I am correct," intoned Chiun, examining the pile of mixed molten metals that had been the *Reliant*.

"I will admit you're right when there's no other way to go.''

"Why stumble through the maze of doubt when the true way has been shown to you?''

"I like doing things *my* way.''

"I give you my permission to stumble about blindly and confused. Meanwhile, I will stand here and guard against malevolent Martians.''

"Try to capture the next one alive, okay?"

"If he does not force my hand," Chiun said, thin of voice.

MOVING AWAY from the Master of Sinanju, Remo retreated to get a longer view of the situation. The air was sticky, and interior floodlights made the tall launch-assembly building down the marsh-bordered road look as if it were about to launch itself into orbit.

From farther back, the shuttle was even more impressive somehow. What remained of it.

Remo was thinking that something very, very powerful had done this when he almost bumped into one of the most beautiful women he had ever seen.

She was tall yet shapely. Her long hair reminded Remo of a chestnut mare the way it hung down to the small of her back in a long ponytail, twitching skittishly. The color of her intelligent eyes was mahogany. She filled out her dress exactly the way Remo thought a woman should.

Remembering a promise he'd made to himself, Remo put on his most disarming smile and said, "What's a gorgeous girl like you doing in a place like this?"

"I am not a girl," she said in a severe accent.

"Woman. Sorry. The question stands."

"I am journalist."

"Remo Cupper, NTSB." He flashed his card.

Cool interest made her intelligent eyebrows bunch together. "You are investigating this tragedy?"

"Yeah."

"Then I will consent to interview you. Even though you are impertinent."

Remo frowned. He tried again. "Trade you an interview for a late dinner?"

"I am here to work, not eat."

"I meant dinner as in let's get to know each other."

"I am here to work, not make new friends," the woman retorted.

Remo blinked. Normally women didn't act this coolly toward him. He decided to take the direct approach. "Did I say friends? I really want to jump your bones."

"I do not know this, please."

"I want to kiss you all over."

The woman made a disapproving face. "This does not appeal to me, thank you."

"Suit yourself. But your interview is walking away." And Remo turned to go.

"Wait. I am hasty. I will consent to have Beeg Mek with you."

"What's that?"

"Delicious American fast food."

"You mean a Big Mac?"

"Yes, we will share Beeg Mek and much information. It will be of mutual benefit to us."

Remo shrugged. "It's a start."

"It is the best I will do to accommodate you. What is your name, please?"

"Remo."

"I am Kinga Zongar."

"Nice name for a—"

"I am sometimes known as Kinga the Butch."

"That explains it," said Remo.

"Although I do not consider myself a butch," Kinga added.

Remo blinked. "You mean bitch?"

"Perhaps that is correct term. In my language it is *szuka*."

Remo frowned. "I don't know a lot of languages."

"Mine is a very fine language. 'Merry Christmas' is said this way—*Boldog Karácsony*."

"I like plain old 'Merry Christmas' better. Let's find a place we can talk."

"You may talk. I will listen attentively and absorb your words."

"It's a start," said Remo.

There was a NASA commissary and it was in full swing dispensing coffee and hot food to carry NASA employees through the long night. In all the controlled excitement, they were not noticed, never mind challenged.

Over black coffee and mineral water—Remo had the water because caffeine affected his system the way speed affects an ordinary person's system—Remo let Kinga pepper him with questions.

"What is your frank opinion concerning this catastrophe?" Kinga asked.

"It wasn't Martians."

"Who has said Martians?"

"The press. You should know that."

"There are no Martians, according to science."

"That's my theory," said Remo, grinning.

Kinga blinked. "What is your theory?"

"That there are no Martians here or on Mars."

"Yes. Of course. But what is your theory as to the shuttle disaster?"

"Something unknown. Maybe an enemy nation."

"Which is most likely?"

Remo shrugged. "Search me. The Russians are pretty quiet these days. But it's somebody out to get our space program."

"This is not logical," Kinga said flatly.

"You got a better theory?" Remo asked.

"The correct English is, 'Do you have a better theory?'"

"Thank you for the elocution lesson," said Remo, wondering why the woman wasn't trying to flirt with him. He decided to start first, just to hone his flirting skills.

"You are stepping on my toe," Kinga said firmly.

"It's called playing footsies."

"The correct term is 'foot.' Where were you educated, please?"

"In an orphanage," Remo replied truthfully.

"That is no excuse for not speaking your native tongue correctly. I myself speak three languages, including Russian."

Withdrawing his foot, Remo said, "You're different than other women I usually meet."

"I am Hungarian by birth."

"Hungarian women all like you?"

"How do you mean by this question?"

"Never mind," said Remo, who decided that as dates went, Kinga Zongar was a wet firecracker. Finishing his water, he said, "Well, gotta get back to my investigation."

Kinga stood up, flinging back her long tail of chestnut hair. "I will observe, if you do not mind."

"If you can keep up, feel free," Remo said, thinking that, on the other hand, it was refreshing to meet a woman who wasn't scratching at his fly like a cat trying to come in on a cold night.

"I can keep up," she said confidently.

WHEN REMO FOUND the Master of Sinanju again, Chiun was moving through the press of technicians and middle managers in a posture that clearly told Remo that he was stalking someone.

Remo fell in behind him, forgetting all about Kinga Zongar.

In his dark suit, Chiun was a shadow with an instinct for other shadows. And with all the floodlights and flashlights, there were plenty of stark shadows between the patches of incandescent light.

Remo moved more openly. Behind him, Kinga asked, "Who are you following?"

"Do you see me following anyone?"

"I see you following a person, but I do not see the person it is you are following."

"If you could, I'd be worried."

On the other side of the giant tower that was the launch-assembly building, Chiun paused.

Remo came up behind him, and Chiun waved him to hold back. Of course, Chiun was aware of Remo, even if he had given no sign until now. He could sense a flea leaping at a hundred yards by the tiny *sproing* of its legs.

Obediently Remo hung back. "What's up?" he called in a low, carrying tone that would register in Chiun's ears but no one else's.

A thin squeak floated back. "I am following a Martian."

"Where?"

"If I knew the where, I would hie ahead of him and await him at his destination, unsuspected," Chiun hissed back.

Remo frowned. He sniffed the air. The only scent that came through the harsh tang of burned metals was human sweat and a faint whiff of what seemed to be chocolate.

"To whom are you speaking?" asked Kinga, peering into the dark blots between shards of light.

"And tell your Russian friend to hold her tongue," added Chiun.

"She's—" Remo started to say.

"Hungarian," Kinga said for him.

Chiun turned, looked at Kinga squarely and sniffed the air delicately. "Russian. But one who has dwelt in this land many years."

"Who said that?" asked Kinga, peering deeper into the shadows.

"That patch of black up ahead," said Remo.

"I see nothing in the patch."

"You heard the voice?"

"Yes. Of course. It sounded like Mickey the Mouse and Donald the Duck speaking in unison."

"Let's hope he takes that as a compliment," said Remo.

"I do not," the squeaking voice from the shadows returned.

And suddenly Chiun was moving on.

Remo slipped up behind him. It was then that he saw the object of the Master of Sinanju's interest.

He looked like a NASA technician. He was stepping back, his head canted, his eyes fixed on the giant ruined transporter-crawler down the long road that stretched between the launch-assembly building and the forlorn tower that was the launch gantry. Clutched in his hand was a candy bar, still in its cream-colored wrapper. He nibbled at the exposed bar of chocolate as he surveyed the damage.

"Nothing suspicious about this guy," Remo said quietly, joining the Master of Sinanju in the lee of a blob that still had a few half-smelted tractor treads sticking from it. It had been dragged here for examination.

"He is a secret Martian agent," Chiun hissed.

"What makes you say—?" Then Remo caught a glimpse of the candy wrapper. Too late to stop the Master of Sinanju, who flitted forward and seized the technician by one unsuspecting wrist.

Chiun's hand clamped down as the technician sank to one knee, his face looking the way Remo imagined his own did when they threw the juice to him in the electric chair.

He jumped, twisted and kept jittering as Chiun's voice lifted in an accusatory tone. "You have been captured, agent of Mars. Confess the name of your warlord, or perish on this spot."

"What—"

Remo stepped in at that moment, saying, "Chiun! Let him go."

"He was sent here by the insidious Mars Incorporated—therefore, he knows what transpired here. Speak, alien one."

The technician squealed like a speeded-up voice recording. "My name is Otis Kline. I'm from Boca Raton. And I don't know what you're talking about."

Remo flashed his NTSB ID and said, "I think there's a little misunderstanding here."

Chiun squeezed harder, and the man's eyes began to bug out. His face became purple and rubbery, his nostrils flaring.

"Behold, his true countenance is revealing itself. See how the eyes protrude unhumanly?" Chiun said triumphantly.

"You're doing that to him," Remo countered.

"I am merely encouraging him to resume his normal appearance," Chiun returned.

"He's going to need plastic surgery if you keep that up."

Stooping, Remo picked up the dropped candy bar. He held it to the moonlight so the bold red letters were visible.

"Is this your clue?" he asked Chiun.

"Yes. This spy is on a world that is to him alien, and he must consume food from his home planet to survive."

"Chiun, this is a Mars bar."

"Yes. From Mars."

"No, it's not."

"Read the small print," Chiun sniffed.

Remo did. "Says 'Copyright Mars Inc.'"

"Proof!" said Chiun, giving his captured Martian another squeeze. He got even purpler.

"Hackettstown, New Jersey," Remo finished. "I'm from New Jersey. And I'm not even remotely Martian."

"Obviously, that refers to the Martian New Jersey."

"There is no Martian New Jersey."

"There is a Jupiter, Florida, is there not?" Chiun demanded.

"But there's no Hackettstown, New Jersey, Planet Mars. Trust me, I used to eat these things when I was a kid."

"That exact same?"

"Well, the wrapper's different from what I remember."

"Hah! Therefore, this is a shoddy counterfeit."

"They're selling these over at the commissary. Okay?"

Chiun narrowed his hazel eyes until they were unreadable slits.

Gently Remo extracted the hapless technician from the Master of Sinanju's fierce clutch.

"Misunderstanding. You can go now."

"But we will be watching you," Chiun called after him in a cold voice.

The NASA technician stumbled away.

His hands retreating into the belled sleeves of his coat, Chiun regarded Remo with thin disapproval. His eyes flicked to Kinga. "Who is this?"

"Kinga. She's a reporter."

"Why is she following you?"

"It's okay. She's the first woman in a zillion years who doesn't want to jump my bones."

"I do not know this phrase," Kinga said. "What does it mean, please?"

"*Ya tebya lyublu*," said Chiun.

"*Prastee'te?*" Kinga replied.

Chiun leveled accusing eyes at Kinga. "She is Russian, not Hungarian."

"I am Hungarian, but I speak fluent Russian."

"*Bocsánat,*" said Chiun.

"*Köszönöm,*" replied Kinga. Then in English, "You speak Magyar?"

"Obviously," said Chiun.

"What's Magyar?" asked Remo.

"The Hungarian national language," said Kinga.

"I thought the Hungarian national language was Hungarian."

"Only an American could be so ignorant not to know of Magyar," Kinga scoffed.

"Well, Polish people speak Polish," Remo said.

"That is a different matter entirely. Poles are Slavs."

"How many fingers do I hold up?" asked Chiun, displaying four fingers.

"*Négy*," said Kinga.

"Not *chety're?*"

"That is the Russian word. I will reply to your question in Russian if you wish."

"You smell Russian. You smell of borscht and black bread."

"I have eaten these foods, but not recently. I much prefer American foods exclusively since I come to this country. Especially Beeg Meks and chizburgers."

"You will die young and in pain, then," spat Chiun.

"Who is this fulminating little man?" Kinga asked Remo.

"That's Chiun. My partner."

"He is very unusual. Such frankness of speech to a stranger."

Chiun made a nasal sound like a polite snort. He had the Mars bar and was examining it critically.

"This is unfit for human consumption."

"It's chocolate, caramel and nougat," Remo said.

"Fit only for Martian stomachs."

Remo sighed. "Look, we're getting nowhere at this rate. Let's get serious or get out of here. We've seen that whatever did this was the same thing that zapped the BioBubble."

"What do you know of the BioBubble disaster?" asked Kinga suddenly.

"That it was a mercy killing," said Chiun, bustling up. "What do you know of this, Russian?"

"I am Hungarian," Kinga insisted.

"Perhaps. Answer the question."

"I am reporter. I am interested in your theory as to what force or agency is responsible for what has transpired here."

"Martians," said Chiun, turning on his heel.

Remo started after him, calling over his shoulder, "You coming or not?"

"I am coming. I find you both very interesting."

"That's a start," said Remo.

"I do not understand you very well," Kinga said, a plaintive note coming into her cultured voice.

"The feeling's mutual," returned Remo.

"Men are from Mars, women are from Venus," sniffed Chiun. "And if you both are wise, you will remain in your own spheres."

"I hear Mars needs women," countered Remo, grinning.

Kinga fixed them with a look that could only be called askance.

18

In a darkened Orlando hotel room, a roll of film was coming out of the portable developer. Once exposed, the film would have far-reaching geopolitical consequences, though no one would recognize this until it was too late to turn back the doomsday clock on humanity.

Travis "Red" Rust took a jeweler's magnifying eyepiece to the contact sheet and was going through each shot looking for the best one.

He got to shot thirteen, moved on, then jumped back so fast and hard he bruised his eye.

When the tearing stopped, he looked at the image with his right eye, then the left, then the right again to make triply sure what he was looking at wasn't an emulsion glitch.

Rust started to reach for the telephone, then thought better of it.

"This is worth more to the networks than to that rag," he muttered. "It's red-hot."

He got to work developing print thirteen.

At the local CBS affiliate, the news director was having none of it. "It's a still picture. We're TV. We need tape. Still pictures make viewers reach for their clickers."

"It shows the exact instant before the ray hit the *Reliant*," Red said urgently.

"You got the moment of the explosion?"

"No. But I got some great after shots. Shows the thing actually hissing and spitting like a volcano."

"We might be able to use them. Leave them, and we'll get back to you."

"It's the before shot that's important. Everyone knows the *Reliant* was torched. But no one know what did it. This picture may be the only clue."

The news director got interested. Grabbing the picture, he looked at it and made assorted faces. "What am I looking for?"

"Letters in the sky."

He looked closer and saw the white configurations against the background star constellations just behind the *Reliant*.

"Those?"

"Yeah. See? They spell out a word, probably in an alien language."

"Looks like plain English to me."

"Look closer. The *N* is backward."

"Okay, it's backward. And it's a little *p* not a big *P.* So what?"

"But the *M* and the *P* face frontward," Rust said excitedly.

"I repeat my *so?*"

"That means it's not an *M* and a *P.* Not *our M* or *P.*"

"What are you saying, Rust?"

"I think this is a signal from Mars."

"Oh, get off it."

"Okay, maybe not Mars, but some language from beyond our earth. Maybe this was a warning. Stop launching shuttles or you're all toast."

The CBS news director cast a skeptical eye in Travis Rust's specific direction. "*M*, backward *N* and *P* say all that?"

"They could," Rust said hopefully.

"They could be the call letters for Martian TV, too.... Who did you say you work for, Rust?"

"I'm free-lance," Rust said quickly.

"Who's your best client?"

Rust swallowed. "The *Enquirer*," he admitted.

Print thirteen went sailing toward the exit.

"Follow it out. No sale."

At the ABC and NBC affiliates, the doors were slammed in his face before Rust could barge past the lobby guards.

"We were warned about you," he was told at both locations.

That left Fox.

At Fox, they were very interested. Very.

"Our ratings on the alien-autopsy special were so high we had to show it all over again the next week," the Fox news broadcaster said gleefully as he shuffled through Rust's stack of photographs.

"Then you'll take it?"

"We've got a news organization now. Of course we'll take it. But it's gotta be a world Fox exclusive. And you come along as part of the package."

"Package?"

"These are stills. I need a talking-head expert to tell the story, and you're the only game in town."

"Twenty thousand bucks," Rust said quickly.

"Deal."

Fox had a news special on the air within the hour. Travis Rust found himself happily sweating on national television, explaining what he was doing in the marshlands outside the Kennedy Space Center, what he saw, what he didn't see and his theory on the alien letters that appeared in the sky before an unknown power had puddled the orbiter *Reliant*.

The program went out live, and Rust had visions of fame and fortune. Not to mention a career change. The media was always hungry for telegenic experts. Travis Rust would be only too happy to pontificate on the extraterrestrial threat to Earth—a subject on which he was an unqualified expert, having read the *National Enquirer* every week since 1984.

That was before the three men in the charcoal black suits and impenetrable sunglasses burst in on midtelecast and confiscated every photo in sight. Travis Rust, too.

"Who are you people?" the hapless interviewer was saying as Rust was picked up by his elbows and escorted off camera with his shoe heels barely dragging the floor.

"Government agents," one of the trio barked, failing to display ID.

"They're the men in black!" Travis Rust screamed. "They cover up stuff like this!"

The newscaster followed with a microphone. "What?"

"My *Enquirer* editor will know! Tell him what happened here!"

And that was the last the public saw of Travis Rust until the world had been dragged to the brink and beyond.

19

Dr. Harold W. Smith was toiling under the shaky fluorescent lights of Folcroft Sanitarium in Rye, New York. His computer beeped at him, alerting him of a mission-pertinent story moving on the wire.

It was out of AP. They were carrying a report that Fox TV was broadcasting a live interview with a news photographer who had snapped critical shots of the *Reliant* disaster.

The touch of a hot-key transformed Smith's amber monochrome screen into a color TV set. He got the local Fox affiliate by entering another code.

The picture resolved just as Travis Rust was being escorted from the studio by three faceless men in dark sunglasses and dull black business suits, calling out something about men in black.

"What are men in black?" Smith wondered aloud.

Putting the question aside, he watched as the stammering Fox broadcaster tried to fill the dead air now that he was alone in the studio facing an empty guest's chair that still spun from the velocity with which Travis Rust had been taken away.

"That was Travis 'Red' Rust, being carried off by three men purporting to be from the government. To recap, Mr. Rust snapped what may be the single most important photograph in the chain of events that began with the BioBubble disaster and progressed to the *Reliant* catastrophe. Just moments before the *Reliant* collapsed into a bubbling metallic mass, an ominous word appeared in the night sky. Consisting of three letters, two seemingly in our Roman alphabet, but the middle one looking like a reversed *N*."

The camera came in for a tight shot of the broadcaster's serious, sweat-dappled face.

"Are these acts of sabotage warnings from a hostile intelligence from beyond our own atmosphere?"

"Rubbish," said Smith, starting to reach for the hot-key that would restore normal computer functions.

Then tape was played of the photo under discussion.

Harold Smith froze. His gray eyes took in the three letters. They blinked. His firm mouth, normally compressed in concentration, made a round, bloodless hole just before his jaw dropped on slack muscles.

"My God!" he croaked.

Blindly Smith reached for the red telephone that connected him with the White House.

THE PRESIDENT of the United States was conferring with his national-security advisers when the call came in.

When he had first taken over the Oval Office and the previous Chief Executive had explained about CURE and the hotline, he said that he had set up a baby monitor in the Lincoln Bedroom two flights above so that when the red telephone rang, he would know it if he were anywhere in the White House.

And the outgoing President had surrendered the portable baby monitor, saying, "It's your worry now."

The thing was ringing now, and the President said, "Excuse me. Been sitting here so long, I gotta pee up a storm."

His advisers were working the phones, trying to discover which—if any—agency was kidnapping journalists on live TV, and hardly noticed. They were pale and haggard of face and baggy of eye. The office TV was flickering in its cabinet niche.

The tiny elevator took the Commander in Chief to the red telephone, which was still ringing. He snapped up the handset.

"Go ahead, Smith."

"Mr. President. There is a strange report on Fox TV."

"Yeah. I heard. Some goofball *Enquirer* photographer."

"I do not think so."

"They're talking up Martians."

"The letters are not Martian, Mr. President. They are Cyrillic."

"What's that?"

"The letters of the Russian alphabet devised by Saint Cyril in the ninth century. They are based on the Greek alphabet, so there are many letters in common."

Smith's voice was low and urgent and more than a little hoarse. The President decided to let him explain.

"They show three letters," Smith continued. "*M,* a backward *N,* and a *P.*"

"Yes?"

"In Cyrillic Russian, these letters are pronounced *meer.*"

"How do you get *meer* out of 'MNP'?"

"The backward *N* is pronounced double *E*. The *M* is equivalent to our *M*. But the *P* is actually an *R*."

"I'm with you so far."

"Transliterated from the Russian, 'MNP' becomes 'MIR.'"

"Mir, Mir..."

"The word means 'Peace,'" supplied Smith.

The President's voice brightened. "That's good, isn't it?"

"Mir is the name of the Russian space station orbiting the earth even as we speak."

"Uh-oh," muttered the President. "Are you saying the Russians are attacking our space program?"

"I am saying that in the instant before the *Reliant* was obliterated, the Russian word for 'peace,' the name of their space station, appeared very high in the sky over the target area," said Harold Smith in a patient but tight voice. "No more, no less."

"Oh, man," the President groaned. "I think I'd rather it be the Martians."

"There are no Martians," Harold Smith said testily.

"I wouldn't be so sure of that," the President confided.

"What do you mean?"

"I was watching the Fox telecast when those three goons claiming to be from Washington came and hauled that photographer off. We've checked with CIA, NSA, DoD, everyone I could think of. They all disavow sending any agents."

"I fail to follow."

The President lowered his voice to a hoarse hush. "Before Rust was dragged off, he was taking about men in black."

"That term is not one I am familiar with," Smith admitted.

"Men in black are these mysterious guys who go around confiscating UFO evidence. Some say they're CIA. Others that they're Air Force." The Chief Executive's voice dropped lower. "A lot of people think they're really space aliens."

"I trust you do not believe the latter theory," Smith said thinly.

"A smart President doesn't rule anything in or out when dealing with national-security issues. Especially one who watches 'The X-Files' faithfully."

"I will look into the Russian aspects of this," Smith said unhappily.

"How?"

"If necessary, I will send my people to Russia."

"I can't believe the Russians would attack us like this. And why advertise themselves?"

"I do not know, but I take some of their recent space activity as very suggestive."

"You mean that shuttle launch last month?"

"Yes. It was strange that they reactivated their shuttle program. *Buran 1* was retired after one unmanned orbital flight in 1988. *Buran 2* orbiter was placed in storage years ago and never flown until now."

"It was a colossal joke. The thing's so unsafe they don't dare send up cosmonauts in it."

"To the contrary, Mr. President. The fact that the *Buran* could be launched and returned to Earth safely by robot is an advantage over U.S. shuttle technology."

"None of this computes, Smith. Russians or Martians. Why would Martians attack us? We never attacked them."

"I will get back to you," said Harold Smith, disconnecting.

AT FOLCROFT, Smith searched the net for some link or data base that would enable him to fix space station Mir's orbital position at the time of the *Reliant* disaster. He had a feeling it wasn't going to be an easy task, so he called up his best brute-force search engine, set it to autosearch U.S. military data banks and moved on to other tasks.

The phone rang not an hour into this process.

It was Remo.

"Smith. We're at a Holiday Inn near Kennedy. Looks like the same thing zapped the *Reliant* that popped the BioBubble. But there's no telling what it is except very, very hot. It turned the shuttle's tiles to tar."

"It may be a Russian operation," Smith said.

"Where do you get that?"

"A photographer captured the Cyrillic word for 'peace' in the sky the instant before the explosion. That is the name of the Russian space station circling up there."

"Isn't it a peaceful research station?" said Remo.

"That is the story. But remember that Mir was launched under the old Soviet system. And it recently attempted to dock with the Russian version of the shuttle."

"Last time that thing went up, they deployed a doomsday device."

"Yes. The Sword of Damocles. You and Chiun dealt with that. There is reason to believe the *Buran* carried a new doomsday device to Mir."

"They'd have to be crazy to attack us."

"Facts do not fit the circumstances completely. I want you and Chiun to stand by."

"Okay. But I have a hot date."

"Excuse me?"

"A date. You know, dinner and—"

"With whom?"

"Her name's Kinga Zongar. She's a reporter with the *Orlando Sentinel*."

"I disapprove," said Smith.

"Disapprove afterward. I don't think I'm going to get anywhere with her."

"Allow me to run a background check."

"On my date?"

"It is a wise precaution."

"Save it. I like surprises," said Remo, who then hung up.

Smith returned to his multitasking. It was going to be a long night, and he expected nothing to make sense until dawn at the earliest.

20

"It's the Russians," said Remo, hanging up.

"I told you she was a Russian," spat Chiun.

"I am Hungarian," Kinga said, an edge creeping into her cultured voice.

"Not her. I just finished talking to Smith. Someone snapped a photo of the shuttle just before it blew. The Russian letters for Mir were up in the sky."

"What is this!" Kinga flared.

"It's on TV, according to our boss," Remo told her.

Kinga turned on the Holiday Inn TV without asking and flipped the channels until she got a report that held her attention.

"All America is asking one question—are these letters in the Martian alphabet?" a newscaster was saying. "If so, did actual Martians barge into this studio and haul off the only eyewitness to their handiwork on earth?"

"If that was true," said Remo, "they'd have hauled your butt out of the room, too."

"Hush," said Kinga, raising the volume until both Remo and Chiun winced from the sensory overload.

Remo confiscated the clicker and lowered the volume.

The broadcaster was saying, "Here again is the world-exclusive photograph that is sending chills up and down the spines of Fox viewers everywhere."

Everyone watched. The screen showed a star-sprinkled sky and the distinct white configuration of bizarre letters.

"It is Russian," said Chiun.

"Of course it is Russian," said Kinga. "It means 'Peace.'"

"That's the space-station name," said Remo.

"Space station Mir is not responsible for these events," Kinga said heatedly.

"How would you know?" Remo asked.

Kinga said, "It is inconceivable otherwise."

"You are very positive for a Hungarian," said Chiun, drawing near.

"Easy, Chiun," Remo warned.

Chiun inclined his shiny head in Kinga's direction. "I will grant you the privilege of interrogating this Russian."

Remo stepped between Kinga and the TV and folded his lean bare arms. He was facing Kinga, his dark eyes intent. "What makes you so sure the Russians aren't behind this?" he asked.

"It is illogical. If Mir is sending down death rays, why would they advertise their complicity by painting the sky with their own name?"

"Maybe it's a computer glitch."

"Pish! Mir is not designed to flash its name from orbit."

"Only a Russian would possess such knowledge, Remo," Chiun said pointedly.

"Stay out of this, Little Father," Remo said evenly.

"These facts are commonly available. I am only stating the obvious." Kinga stood up. "I must go now."

"What about our date?"

"I will take rain check. I must file story with my newspaper."

"We're not done yet," said Remo.

"We are done with you," said Chiun, handing Kinga her purse.

She took it quickly. "Thank you. I must go now."

"Goodbye," said Chiun.

Remo started to reach out for Kinga, but the Master of Sinanju deflected his hand with a hard blocking wrist.

After she had gone, Remo confronted the Master of Sinanju. "Why'd you let her just go like that?"

"For two reasons. She is not interested in you the way you are in her."

"I don't know how interested I am in her. She's different from most other women."

"And I have her wallet," added Chiun, producing a kid wallet from up his sleeve.

Remo took it.

Inside there was a driver's license, giving an address in Celebration, Florida.

"You figure we should follow her?" Remo asked Chiun.

"It is devious, but we are dealing with a devious person."

"I didn't see any deviousness in her at all. She was perfectly direct. Too direct, maybe."

"She did not throw herself at your feet."

"So?"

"Perhaps because she is not attracted to you."

"I never met a woman who wasn't attracted to me."

"Perhaps because she is not a woman of this world," suggested Chiun.

"Oh, come off it. A moment ago, you were saying she was a Russian, when she's only Hungarian."

"I said she smelled like a Russian. But her features are Magyar."

"Meaning?"

Chiun's eyes grew hooded of lid. "Perhaps she is a Martian who wears an imperfect mask."

Remo rolled his eyes. "Look, let's see what we find at her place."

"Be prepared to weep if you love this woman."

"I don't love anyone," Remo growled.

"That is regrettably true."

"I didn't mean you, Little Father."

"It is too late to call back the canard," said the Master of Sinanju, breezing out the door one step ahead of his pupil.

21

In Cancún's Diamond Resort Playacar Hotel, the occupant of room 33-D sat nervously on the edge of the rumpled king-size bed, his laptop balanced on his hairy-legged lap, his eyes staring at the room TV, which was tuned to CNN. Moonlight streamed in through the half-closed curtains.

On the screen, a steely-eyed anchor sat with a graphic floating beside his silvery pompadour. The graphic showed a starry sky against which floated three letters: "МИр."

The newscaster was saying, "... obviously a hoax inasmuch as the purported alien letters are of earthly origin."

"I don't believe it," the man on the bed said.

"A hoax so shoddily constructed that the middle consonant was flopped," the newscaster added.

"Thank God thank God thank God for flopping."

The graphic was replaced by a shot of the shapeless blob of space-age metals and ceramics that was once a U.S. space shuttle.

"At the Kennedy Space Center, NASA officials remain tight-lipped about the loss of the *Reliant*, which jeopardizes the International Space Station, whose first components were scheduled to fly on the *Reliant* next year and will not be completed until the year 2001.''

"Tough. Build another shuttle."

"With us now, by satellite from his private observatory, is renowned astronomer and exobiologist, Dr. Cosmo Pagan of the University of Arizona's Center for Exobiological Studies. Dr. Pagan, what motive would anyone have for destroying a U.S. space shuttle?''

Dr. Pagan appeared on one side of the split screen, his face sober, his voice sonorous, his speaking cadence strange, the accents falling on improbable syllables and words.

"Brad, we cannot rule out an asteroid strike. A small impactor, not a Tunguska-size bludgeon. Otherwise, we would have lost Florida, and not an unimportant shuttle. You see, striking asteroids pack the punch of a nuclear device. Recently we sky watchers have begun to classify them, threat-wise. They include the aforementioned ten-megaton Tunguskas, hundred-megaton regional bludgeons capable of obliterating a continent, hundred-gigaton, hemisphere-demolishing small extinctors, and the Tyrannosaurus rex of asteroids, the great extinctors.''

"How serious *is* this threat?"

"Quite small. We can expect a ten-megaton impact once every century. So this event, coming ninety years after Tunguska, is about on schedule.''

"Earlier in the day, you were quoted by AP as pointing to the ozone layer.''

"An ozone-layer rupture is also a possibility," said Dr. Pagan.

"You say this, but the phenomenon appeared in two highly localized spots thousands of miles apart. How would an ozone hole account for both events?"

"Perhaps we are looking at a floating hole in Earth's ozone shield," Dr. Pagan said without skipping a beat.

"In other words, you really don't know?"

"I know the possibilities. The universe is ruled by mathematical possibilities. Billions upon trillions upon zillions of possibilities. I am merely enumerating them. I am a scientist, not a seer."

"Pick a damn theory and stick with it!" the occupant of room 33-D railed at the unheeding screen.

"I see," said the CNN anchor. "Dr. Pagan, let's address the question of sabotage. Who would profit from the shuttle's destruction?"

"Besides my career, you mean?"

The laptop beeped, and the occupant of room 33-D looked down at his liquid-crystal screen.

"You have mail!" the system was flashing.

Calling it up, the man read quickly as the singsong voice of Dr. Cosmo Pagan evaded the question artfully.

To: RM@qnm.com
From: R&D@qnm.com
Subject: New problem
Last-quarter report is out, and firm lost big. Heads are rolling. Upper management is on our backs for a progress update on ParaSol. And they're looking for you for stockholder-impact report.

"Damn," said the man in 33-D.

He pecked out a reply.

To: R&D@qnm.com
From: RM@qnm.com
Subject: Re: New problem
Do they know where I am?

He hit Send and went back to watching Dr. Pagan, who had somehow gotten on the subject of comets.

"A comet is nothing more than a dirty snowball locked in a perpetual orbit around our mundane sun. Comets rarely strike Earth. But asteroid strikes are very common. A great extinctor created the Chicxulub crater in Yucatán, which threw up so much obscuring dust it blocked out the sun and set off the eco-chain reaction that killed the late, lamented dinosaurs. I would be more concerned with a nameless asteroid landing on Washington than Hale-Bopp or some future comet that's merely booming by our planet."

"Shut the eff up," the occupant of room 33-D snarled. "Do you want the board to hear you?"

The reply from research and development was succinct: "Unknown."

Then the system flashed the new-mail signal, and it popped up automatically.

To: RM@qnm.com
From: Evelyn@qnm.com
Subject: Mr. Gaunt
Mr. Gaunt asked me to request that you make yourself available for early-morning meeting at your hotel. He is en route.

"Shit! That pencil-necked beancounter is coming here. What do I do? What do I do?"

On CNN, Dr. Cosmo Pagan was into his biography.

"I owe it all to Edgar Rice Burroughs, H. G. Wells and Ray Bradbury. They all wrote about Mars. Not the Mars that's up there now but the Mars of imagination. The Mars of the human spirit. Someday soon, lowly man will walk on the Red Planet, and that day will be a glorious one. Let me urge NASA to launch a crash Mars-colonization program before mankind succumbs to the next great extinctor."

The occupant of room 33-D grasped the remote control and hit Mute. Dr. Pagan kept talking anyway. He just didn't make any sound.

"I didn't get this e-mail. That's it! I was out. My system is down. I can't be held accountable for mail I don't receive."

Hastily he reaccessed the last R&D message and hit the Reply key.

"Cease all communications until further notice," he typed. "Erase all e-mail from me. We have not been in contact. Don't even answer this. I never sent this message."

Then he folded up his laptop and called down to the main desk.

"I'm checking out. Immediately. Urgent business. Gotta get back to the States."

Packing furiously, he muttered, "Let Gaunt come here. I'll go back to Seattle. It's the last place he'll think of looking. If he complains, that'll teach him to get on an international flight without waiting for confirmation of my whereabouts."

The occupant of room 33-D left without shutting off the TV. Oblivious, Dr. Cosmo Pagan continued lecturing a dark, empty room.

"It might interest my loyal viewers to know that geologic evidence recently came to light suggesting that the Chesapeake Bay was created as a direct result of a meteorite impact approximately thirty-five million—that's million not billion—years ago. And just last May, Asteroid 1996 JA-1 missed our earth by a mere 279,000 miles—a near miss on the grand scale of the cosmos...."

22

On the way back to her apartment, Kinga Zongar broke the speed limit in her bloodred Maxima GTE all the length of the Central Florida Greenway.

Somewhere past Kissimmee, a black-and-gold Florida State Highway Patrol car came wailing after her.

Kinga considered her options. She must not be deterred in getting word to Moscow.

On the other hand, if she managed to evade this state person, others would pursue her, arousing great suspicions where none existed.

In the end, it was her long period of relative inactivity that decided Kinga. She pulled over onto the shoulder of the road and sat quietly as the highway-patrol car pulled behind her, its roof lights making a discordant multihued web of color in the humid air.

When the highway patrolman came striding up in his gray-and-black whipcord uniform, his straw Stetson cocked at a rakish angle, Kinga smiled with quiet pleasure. He was very big for an American. His life would require at least three bullets.

From the drink receptacle between the front seats, Kinga extracted her choice of weapon. A matte-finish Ruger. It was a very satisfying firearm with which to kill enemies.

A touch of the dash button brought the window humming down, and Kinga turned her head so the patrolman could see her flawless womanly face.

"I am sorry to bother you, Officer. Was I exceeding the speed limit?"

Whether the patrolman was disarmed by her polite manner or her refined if unplaceable accent did not matter. He thumbed his Stetson back off his head and drawled, "I'm afraid so, ma'am."

He was very solicitous and polite. So Kinga did him the courtesy of shooting him directly in the face so that he would experience no pain or discomfort in the brief, helpless interval before he struck the macadam in death.

She left him jittering in his insensate death throes, pulling away reluctantly because these wet affairs were always so stimulating. Especially after going so long without them.

Reaching her apartment without further incident, Kinga locked up her vehicle and entered her apartment quietly, so as not to disturb the neighbors who never showed her reciprocal courtesy. But this was America, after all.

The Compaq was running as always. She took the red leather chair and logged on to the net, typing in Cyrillic with professional precision.

To: UncleVanya@shield.su.min
From: AuntTamara@aol.com
Subject: Findings
Preliminary investigation fails to disclose cause of accident in question. National media reporting sighting of three glowing letters in sky prior to event. Media speculating letters of cosmic ori-

gin. Clearly they are not, unless extraordinary coincidence at work. Letters are "МИр."

Further, have made contact with investigators from NTSB, who are not what they pretend to be. One is elderly Asian gentleman with North Korean accent. The other is American companion. Does this suggest anything to you?

Kinga pressed the Send key and waited. Knowing the Russian telephone system, it could be a minute or three days before a response came back. She decided to wait until drowsiness overcame her alertness. It was an exceedingly sultry night, and sleeping would be difficult at best.

Twenty minutes passed before she decided to call it a night. If a reply came, the machine would emit an electronic call that invariably pulled Kinga out of the deepest sleep.

Deep in the night, the chime sounded and Kinga flung off her red satin bedcover before her eyes quite opened. She dropped into the chair, squinting to read the green letters in the humid darkness. As a gesture to modesty, she left the room light off.

The Cyrillic message popped up at the touch of a key.

To: AuntTamara@aol.com
From: UncleVanya@shield.su.min
Subject: Report
Mir story incredible. We have queried Glavkosmos contacts.

Your North Korean possible Master of Sinanju, now known to be in employ of Washington through unknown agency. Request courtesy liquidation. Good luck.

Kinga Zongar smiled in the greenish phosphor glow. It would be the greatest of pleasures to undertake a sanctioned wet affair of such magnitude here in the United States.

Reaching out to erase the message, Kinga hesitated only briefly. The brief interval proved to be unfortunate.

A hand, cool as steel and equally hard, arrested her wrist.

Trained for dangerous contingencies, she stifled a sharp intake of breath and said in a moderate voice, "I am unarmed, as well as nude."

"I noticed," said a friendly, familiar male voice. "Move your head so we can read."

"You! My goodness, Remo. I did not hear you enter."

"But we heard you enter," said the squeaky voice of the elderly Korean, Chiun.

"You have been in my apartment all this time?"

"We almost waved when the highway patrolman pulled you over. But we were in a rush," said Remo in an insolent voice.

"You are staring at my bosom," Kinga said thinly.

"Can't help it. It's in the light."

"I must protest this intrusion on my privacy."

Remo pointed at the screen. "Check this out, Chiun."

"It is in Russian."

"I figured that much out. What's it say?"

"She has been instructed to liquidate me," the Master of Sinanju said thinly. He did not sound so very angry as annoyed in a minor way. This fell strangely on Kinga's ears.

"What about me?" asked Remo in a tone also not angry, but casual in its interest.

"You are not mentioned, lesser one."

Kinga said nothing. Her eyes were on the screen, and her heart was beginning to pound. Another moment, and she would have erased the incriminating message for all time. Now the Cyrillic letters glared greenly at her like burning crystals.

"I would not have harmed you, Remo," she said quietly.

"Why not?"

"I admire you."

"You have a pretty cool way of showing it."

"I am very shy with men."

"Is this why your walls are covered with salacious portraits of women?" Chiun asked, gesturing broadly in the eerie green glow. His face resembled a shriveled lime with thin eyes.

Kinga said, "I fail to grasp your meaning."

The light went on, illuminating the walls. Here and there were hung lithographs and reproductions of studies and paintings. The subjects were all of a single theme. The female form.

"Looks like you have a one-track mind," said Remo, looking around admiringly.

"You are speaking nonsense. These are reproductions of works of fine art. Have you no culture?"

"I don't see any equal opportunity for men."

"A nude man is a vulgar sight. A woman's unclothed form is pleasing to both sexes," Kinga said.

"I kinda like what I see," Remo admitted.

"You are very uncouth, barging into my flat and—"

"Tough. You're pretty rude yourself, coming to this country to spy."

"I am not spy."

"You are not Hungarian, either."

"I will speak the truth. I am half-Hungarian. My paternal parent was Russian. I am ashamed of this because there was a rape involved in my conception. It is very painful to admit this, but it is nonetheless true."

"Let's skip the personal history," said Remo, cutting in. "Who do you work for?"

"I am free-lance. The highest bidders command my allegiance. No other."

"Liar," said Chiun.

"I speak the truth. And now that you have read my instructions, I would like to erase them, please. They are no longer of consequence now that you have seen them."

This time it was the elderly Korean who arrested her reaching hands. But his touch was not steel, but acid. Needles dipped in acid. Injecting Kinga with a deadly venom that burned along the nerves until her lush body lay on the floor quivering.

"Who do you work for, Russian?" the Korean voice demanded through the mounting pain.

"I cannot tell," Kinga gasped through clenching teeth. She tongued a cyanide pill out of a hollow wisdom tooth. The maneuver was surreptitious in the extreme. But it didn't go unnoticed.

The pain redoubled, and her tongue shot out. The pill fell to the rug, and a sandal crushed it utterly, then returned to exerting pressure on her head.

Kinga could hold it back no longer. "FSK! FSK! I am FSK! My control is Stankevitch, FSK!"

Remo turned to the Master of Sinanju. "What's the FSK?"

"I do not know," said Chiun. "But I do know that I am done with this would-be slayer of me."

"She couldn't kill you if she had a neutron bomb tucked in her bra."

"That is not the point," said Chiun, bringing a black sandal down on Kinga Zongar's disheveled head. The heel touched the side of her head, paused, then dipped a quarter inch.

Kinga Zongar's head burst like an erupting melon.

"Chiun! For crying out loud, that was my date."

"You have terrible taste in women," sniffed Chiun, scuffing his sole clean against the carpet.

"She was going to be the first date I've had in I don't know how many years. I didn't even get to first base."

"Nor would you have. She does not love men, only women."

Looking around the room again, Remo said, "I guess you're right. But I gotta admit it was nice having a conversation with a woman who didn't lust after me."

"There are other lesbians, if that is your desire," said Chiun.

"Not funny," said Remo, picking up the telephone and calling Harold Smith by the simple expedient of depressing the 1 button until an automatic relay embedded in the telephone system routed the call to Folcroft Sanitarium via Dixville Notch, New Hampshire.

"Remo?" Smith asked.

"Who else?"

"I have run up against a blank wall."

"On the Russian angle?"

"No, on Kinga Zongar. According to my research, she does not exist prior to 1988."

"Well, she's not going to get past 1996 either."

Smith's voice grew sharp. "What do you mean?"

"Chiun just wasted her."

"With cause?"

"We tracked her back to her apartment, where she got a computer message from someone writing what Chiun says is Russian."

"It *is* Russian, as was the woman," Chiun piped up.

"Whoever gives Kinga her orders, they ordered her to hit Chiun. They figured out who he was."

"It is obvious who I am, even to Russians," said Chiun.

Turning the phone away from the Master of Sinanju, Remo told Smith, "I'd read you the message on the screen, but it's full of backward *N*'s and *R*'s and upside-down letters I don't recognize."

"Where are you?"

"Kinga's apartment. I think it's going to be available by the first of the year if you're interested," Remo added dryly.

"One moment. I am tracing your call."

Remo hesitated. While he did, he said to Chiun, "Why don't you throw a blanket over her? She's naked."

"She is your date. You cover her nakedness," Chiun sniffed as he read the screen.

Smith came back and said, "I have accessed the computer."

"How'd you do that?"

"The supporting telephone line is listed in Kinga Zongar's name, as is the line you are calling from."

"Oh," said Remo. "Pretty slick."

The line hummed for a moment. Then Smith said, "I am attempting to retrace the e-mail to its sender."

"How can you do that?"

"The e-mail address at the top."

Remo looked. "Which one is that?"

"Top line."

"I see a *W,* a backward *N* and a *T.*"

"It is pronounced like a certain foul English word."

"Which one?" asked Remo.

Smith said, "The *W* is the Cyrillic *Sh.* The backward *N* is pronounced like a double *e* but transliterates as *I,* while the *T* equals our *T.*"

"I'm a little slow today, Smitty. Care to spell it out for me?"

"Never mind," put in Smith. "The word means 'shield,' and I am coming up with an e-mail account in Moscow."

"She said she was with the FSK, whatever that is."

"The Russian Federal Security Service. It used to be the KGB. But the e-mail account is not coming from the former KGB headquarters in the former Dzerzhinsky Square."

"Probably a blind."

"Unfortunately I cannot get a definite address."

"So we're at a dead end?"

"No. I have it narrowed down to four blocks on Gorky Street. I think it would be useful for you and Chiun to go there and discover what you can."

"Not much of a lead," said Remo.

"According to the e-mail from Moscow, her superiors are attempting to learn what they can about this from Glavkosmos, the Russian space agency. If you find nothing in Moscow, that will be your second stop."

"Sounds pretty thin."

"Nevertheless, it is a direction, and we desperately need a direction right now. Especially with Dr. Pagan giving hourly public theories."

"What's he saying now?"

"Currently he is vacillating between an asteroid strike and a floating hole in the ozone layer."

"No asteroid could have done what Chiun and I saw."

"The American public will have to be educated to understand that. In the meantime, panic is growing and we are making no progress."

"Okay. Next stop Moscow," said Remo, looking to Chiun for his reaction.

That was when he noticed the red smudge on Kinga's index fingernail.

"Hold the phone, Smith."

Remo called out. "Check this out. She was wearing some kind of fake nails."

"Do not remind me of my shame," sniffed Chiun.

"This isn't about you." Kneeling, Remo lifted the cooling hand. It was the color of porcelain. Under the exposed natural fingernail were three letters seemingly tattooed to the cuticle: "ЩИТ."

"Looks like the Russian word for 'shield,'" said Remo.

"Yes, it is the Russian word for 'shield,'" said Chiun.

Returning to the phone, Remo said, "She's got 'shield' tattooed under her fingernail. Smitty, what do you make of that?"

"A recognition sign."

"Her code name maybe?"

"That, or the name of the organization for which she works. Let me consult my data base."

The speed with which Smith came back on the line surprised Remo.

"I have something." Smith's voice was troubled. "Do you recall the event at the Rumpp Tower a few years ago where you and Chiun encountered Russian agents?"

"Yeah. It was the last time we fought that crazy Russian klepto who could walk through walls."

"During that assignment, a Russian thug you captured blurted out the Russian word for 'shield' when asked his affiliation."

"I execute my assignments, I don't commit them to memory," Remo growled.

"Remo, it might be useful to throw the word 'shield' around in Moscow."

"Gotta have the Russian pronunciation."

"Sheet."

"What's the matter?" asked Remo. "Got a paper cut?"

The momentary pause on the line made Remo think Harold Smith was fuming in silence. When he spoke again his tone was distasteful.

"Report as needed."

The line went dead.

On the way out, Remo tossed the red satin bed cover over Kinga's lush lines, telling her, "That's the biz, sweetheart."

23

It was a long flight to Moscow from Orlando, Florida.

The reservation clerk said, "It's a ten-hour trip. You'll have to fly to Berlin, then catch Aeroflot's Budapest flight to Bucharest and Moscow."

"Sounds like it involves a lot of stewardesses," Remo said unhappily.

"I'm sure they'll treat you right," the clerk said with a wink.

"Let me think about it."

"The next available flight leaves in fifty minutes."

"I'll get back to you on that."

Remo found the Master of Sinanju guarding the luggage carousel from thieves. He was doing a good job of it. Nobody was stealing any luggage. Nobody was getting their luggage back, either. The carousel kept going around and around as an angry mob pressed closer and closer like Transylvanian villagers confronting Frankenstein's dying monster.

"What are you doing?" Remo asked Chiun.

"I am protecting valuable property from thieves," said Chiun, swiping the air before him like an angry cougar. The ring of people flinched as one.

"They look like passengers to me."

"Let them prove it. I have seen on television how luggage is stolen daily by thieves pretending to be tourists."

"We don't have any luggage with us," Remo reminded.

"If we strike terror into would-be thieves now, the next time we bring luggage, my trunks will be safe."

"That's a nice theory, but we have to get to Moscow this year," Remo sighed.

"I cannot go to Moscow trunkless."

"Well, we can't go to Moscow until I figure out a way to get there without inciting stewardesses of five or six nationalities to commit crimes of passion against my body."

Chiun stepped in front of a woman who came slithering closer on her belly. She slithered back like a blue-jeaned serpent, hissing in defeated frustration.

"You must control yourself, Remo."

"It's not me who needs control."

"If you knew the secret of harnessing your natural allures, you would not have this problem."

Remo's dark eyes brightened. "Teach them to me?"

Chiun shook his aged head. "You are too young. You have not yet given me a suitable heir."

"There's gotta be another way to do this."

"There is. My way."

Having no other recourse, Remo decided to address the crowd. "Anyone here know a good way to fly without attracting a lot of attention?" he asked.

"Are you a terrorist?" a bright-eyed fat man asked.

"No. I'm just allergic to amorous flight attendants."

"That Tourister is mine. Hand it over, and I'll make special arrangements for you."

"It's a deal."

Remo handed over the Tourister, and the bright-eyed fat man beckoned Remo to follow him out of the terminal. A reluctant Chiun trailed.

After that, there was a mad rush for the carousel, followed by another mad rush for connecting flights and taxicabs.

In back of a moving cab, Remo asked the bright-eyed fat man, "You a travel agent?"

"In a way," he said happily.

"In what way?" asked Chiun.

"I ship people all over the world without a problem. But you'll have to rough it."

"I can rough it," said Remo.

"I will fly first class if you are roughing it," Chiun insisted.

"You can accompany him. I'll arrange that, too," the fat man said in a pleasant voice. Too pleasant for someone who had had his luggage held hostage, Remo thought. But he wasn't about to look a gift horse in the mouth.

"Sounds like half a plan," said Remo.

He was more than a little surprised when the taxi let them off at a funeral home. The gilt sign said Pope-joy Funeral Home. "You work here?" Remo asked the fat man.

"I own this establishment," the fat man said proudly. "Bob Popejoy is the name."

"Nice," said Remo in a tone that conveyed another impression entirely.

Inside, Bob Popejoy led Remo to a showroom and said, "Pick any casket from this room."

Then he took up the telephone, dialed a number and said, "Christine, this is Mr. Popejoy. I'd like a Jim Wilson fare."

"Who's Jim Wilson?" asked Remo.

Capping the mouthpiece, Popejoy whispered, "You are."

Ten minutes later, as Remo climbed into a spiffy cherry-wood number with plush scarlet lining and a bottle of mineral water supplied compliments of the Popejoy Funeral Home, the undertaker was explaining, "A 'Jim Wilson' is slang for any cadaver traveling by air. We get a special discount fare, of course. It will be cold in the cargo hold, but with frequent landings, you should be fine. Assuming you don't object to being a dead man." He smiled like a pleasant little cherub.

"I've been a dead man before," said Remo, climbing in as the Master of Sinanju dabbed at his eyes with a flapping sleeve.

"My son," he said in a choked voice.

"I'm not dead," Remo reminded.

"I am merely practicing my grief for the long voyage," the Master of Sinanju said.

THE FLIGHT WASN'T the most pleasant journey Remo had ever taken in his life, but when the casket was taken off the Aeroflot plane and loaded into a truck by workmen who sounded Russian to Remo's ears, he was happy to have arrived.

Considering his destination was Moscow, Russia, this was amazing in itself.

The baggage handlers were very considerate. They pried open the casket to let Remo out. One clutched a pair of pliers.

When the baggage handler in what turned out to be Bucharest, Romania, opened the casket clutching pliers, Remo had assumed he was in Moscow and they were customs agents.

Then he saw the gold teeth cupped in one man's hand and realized they were corpse robbers. Remo scared one dead when he sat up and slapped the man's jaw askew while the others fled into the night.

Remo pulled the casket lid back.

After a while, someone came along and loaded Remo's coffin in the transfer plane.

The gold thieves in the true Moscow were made of sterner stuff. They looked shocked, then one pulled out a Luger and decided that if their victim wasn't completely dead, he would finish the job right here and now in the bowels of Moscow's Sheremetevo II Airport.

Instead, Remo pinched his forefinger against his thumb, placed it a micrometer in front of the man's nose and let go. Ping.

The Russian stumbled back howling. The Moscow coroner cited the official cause of death as severe nosebleed. It would have made the newspapers except the dead man was found piled atop three others who died of acute undescended testicles, a condition that usually meant the testes had not dropped into the scrotum from the abdominal sac after birth. In this case, the testicles were kicked deep into the body cavities of their owners as if they were musket balls, not the other kind. But as this was physiologically improbable, not to mention a medically unrecognized condition, the Russian coroner fell back on a familiar term to mask the inexplicable.

Remo found the Master of Sinanju waiting for him in the Sheremetevo II Airport terminal. This time Chiun wasn't hovering over the luggage dump. He was realigning the fingers of a would-be pickpocket.

The man was on his knees howling as Chiun held his left wrist with his right hand while using his right hand to stretch the felon's fingers as far as the connecting cartilage would allow. Which was an extra inch on the long fingers and a quarter on the pinky. With a flourish, he popped the man's thumb out of its socket and left him clutching the broken ball of pain that was his fist.

"Russia was never like this," Chiun muttered as they claimed a battered green Zhiguli car whose checkerboard stripe denoted it as a local taxicab.

"There's a lot of crime in Russia these days," Remo admitted.

"The Russians need a good czar. Otherwise, they behave like children who do not get along with themselves or others."

En route to the heart of the city, they witnessed two broad-daylight knifings, as well as a man being methodically run over by a Mercedes SL. The man was being held down on the sidewalk by four other men as a fifth backed the car across his chest. Each time it passed over his chest, he expelled a *whoof!* and spasmed.

Remo asked the cab driver to stop, then sauntered over to assist. He assisted the four assailants out of the suddenly shattered, unworking sacks of bonemeal their healthy bodies had become. It was too late to save their victim, but it was better than nothing.

"What's happened to this place?" asked Remo as the taxi moved on through the gray streets that were choked with the filthy snow mounds of a recent storm.

"Democracy," the driver said. "Is it not wonderful?"

They saw American billboards emblazoned with Cyrillic logos. Remo quickly learned how to spell a wide variety of familiar U.S. products in the Russian alphabet by guessing what the letters meant.

Snow was piled as high as the second floors of buildings in some spots, and in contrast to his previous visits to the dreary city on the banks of the Moscow River, not a policeman or soldier walked the streets.

"Where's the law in this town?" Remo asked.

"The law of the jungle is the law now. It is wonderful. I make six times the rubles I made before the Soviet system went *pfui*."

"Good for you. Just get us to Gorky Street."

"It is coming up. But it is called Tverskaya Street now. What is your exact destination?"

"I don't have one."

"In that case, you will pay double the fare."

"Robber!" flared Chiun.

"Why is it double the fare?" asked Remo.

"I charge for unnecessary directing to a nonspecified destination," the cabbie said amiably.

"Well, it's only kopecks," said Remo.

The cabbie snorted. "Kopecks are valueless. Rubles rule Russia now."

They turned onto a long thoroughfare near a snow-burdened park where the familiar arches of McDonald's were a bright spot of color in an otherwise drab area. There was a line that stretched around the block to get into the fast-food restaurant.

"Gypsies buy Beeg Meks to resell in the park," the driver volunteered. "Is the new Russia not great?"

"It is not," snapped Chiun.

The driver lost his smile. "State your destination."

"Anywhere around here," said Remo.

"Oops. I now charge you triple."

"Triple? Why?"

"Imprecise directing of driver. It eats into my efficiency. Time is rubles. You are costing me rubles."

"Fine. See that gray stone building? Drop us in front."

The cabbie obliged by U-turning through blaring traffic and bumping up on the slushy sidewalk without regard for scattering pedestrians.

Turning in his seat, he began counting up the fare with the aid of his fingers.

"Let me see, fifty rubles for basic transportation. Double for misdirection and inefficiency, and a surcharge of ten percent for friendly conversation. Tip is extra, of course."

"You charge for conversation!" Remo exploded.

The cabbie beamed. "It is the American way, is it not?"

"No, it is not. U.S. cabbies don't charge for conversation."

"In this, I am mistaken. It is the Russian way."

"Let me show you the American way," offered Remo. "Here's your money, and here's a reminder of the old adage that says 'Be nice to tourists.'"

And reaching forward, Remo handed the man his steering wheel, which came off its column with a brittle snap.

They left the cabbie bellowing about the exorbitant price of spare parts in capitalist Russia.

Walking the slushy length of Tverskaya Street, Remo told Chiun, "See anything that looks suspicious to you?"

"Yes," said Chiun.

"Where?"

"That place," said the Master of Sinanju, pointing to a basement place of business with a faded-gilt sign over the glass door that said Iz Tsvetoka.

"What's that mean in English?"

"'From the little flowers.'"

"What's so funny about that?"

"In Italian it would be 'Del Floria.'"

Remo frowned. "Sounds familiar. But I don't see the connection."

"You will," said Chiun, turning abruptly to pad down the stone steps. The door chime tinkled when he padded in, Remo a half step behind him.

Pausing, Remo saw that it was a tailor shop. A frazzle-haired old man was bent over the steaming 1950s-style pants presser. He looked up querulously and said, *"Do'bree den."*

Chiun replied in a volley of fluent Russian, and the frazzle-haired old man suddenly pulled a pistol and tried to kill them.

Chiun ducked the first bullet and let Remo handle the second. Remo sidestepped it easily, flying across the scarred counter, disarming the old man with a casual slap that left the attacker clutching a hand seemingly turning scarlet from sunburn but which was actually hemorrhaging at every capillary.

"Sukin syn! Sukin syn!" the old man screamed.

"He is calling you an offspring of a female dog," Chiun said.

"I get the idea," Remo responded, rendering the old man unconscious with a neck squeeze. "Why the hell did he try to kill you?"

"Because I commanded him to take me to his leader."

"Leader. As in Martian?"

"As in the organization for which he maintains this flimsy blind."

"How do you know this is a blind? It looks like a regular tailor shop."

"Look around you. Is it not familiar, Remo?"

Remo glanced about. It was small, cluttered and smelled of steam and starch. In the back was a fitting room closed off by a red curtain. The curtain was the only splash of color in the dank little shop.

"Yeah. Now that you ask, it is."

"Unless I am mistaken, you will find a button concealed on the steaming device. Press it."

Remo checked out the pants presser. "I don't see anything..."

"Make steam," suggested the Master of Sinanju.

Reaching for the wooden knob atop the machine, Remo depressed it. The machine squeezed a pair of blue serge trousers and spurted steam. When he looked up, the Master of Sinanju was pushing the back wall of the fitting room around on a pivot as the red curtain finished falling back in place.

"Wait for me."

The steel panel clicked shut in Remo's face before he got to it. It resisted his touch, so Remo smacked it with a palm, and something snapped. After that, a fingertip sent the panel spinning freely.

Slipping through, Remo found himself in a reception area where a blonde in a maroon shirt and red turtleneck was bunkered down with an AK-47. She began spraying rounds in Remo's direction while flashing red wall lights and a warbling electric horn filled the area with noise and sensory confusion.

"She is yours," said Chiun, stepping out of the way so the bullet stream directed at his balding head snapped at Remo instead.

"Why is she mine?" Remo demanded.

"She is Russian, and you yearn for romance."

24

Harold W. Smith was trying to reassure the President of the United States in a calm voice.

It wasn't easy. The President seemed to be pulling in three directions at once.

"CIA is telling me they're checking with their cosmic bureau."

"Their psychics, you mean," Smith said dryly.

"The National Reconnaissance Office is trying to reconstruct the orbital situation over Cape Canaveral when the *Reliant* melted down. And the National Security Agency has just handed me a classified document assuring me that the letters in that damn photograph are Russian for 'Peace.'"

"I have confirmation that the Russian space station was nowhere over the *Reliant* or the BioBubble when they were destroyed," Smith said.

"So it's not the Russians."

"My people are looking into that angle."

"Then it *is* the Russians."

"I have no facts. I am following leads."

"I need results. What's next? This thing could hit the White House—or Congress." The President hesitated. "Actually that wouldn't be so bad. Melt it down and start over again."

"Mr. President," Smith said, clearing his throat.

"Just kidding," the President said sheepishly.

"I am tied into the U.S. Space Command's SPACETRACK system."

"What's that?"

"SPACETRACK tracks orbiting satellites and debris. It is part of the early-warning system against enemy ICBMs and performs the added function of safeguarding our shuttle fleet from orbital collision."

"There's a lot of space junk up there. Have they got anything new?"

"No, Mr. President. But their system shows conclusively that the Mir space station was not in a position to inflict the destruction we have witnessed thus far."

"So it's not the Russians."

"I am not saying that," Smith said carefully.

"Then what are you saying?" the President said, his hoarse voice exasperated.

"I am saying that we cannot and should not jump to any conclusions until we have sufficient facts."

"What happens if this thing strikes again?"

"If it is the intention of this unknown agency to strike again, we have no defense against it. But there is an upside."

"What's that?"

"A third strike will show us the pattern, if there is one."

"Someone's hammering our space program, Smith."

"Theory. And a theory is not a fact," Smith reminded him.

"Keep me informed."

"I suspect if there is another strike, you will know before I do," said Harold Smith.

"In that case," the President of the United States sighed, "I guess we have no choice but to keep watching the skies."

25

The chattering stream of bullets came at Remo Williams like a smoking, slow-motion squirt of water, but in reality the rounds were moving at supersonic speed. Remo's highly trained eyes read them in slow motion.

The first gleaming bullet floated toward his face. Smoking, its tip looked as smooth as a tiny lead skull.

Dropping under the stream, Remo allowed the rounds to flatten against the pivoting panel at his back. Under the hammering lead, it spun madly right, then left, then right again as the cursing receptionist swung her stuttering weapon from side to side.

There were many Sinanju techniques for dealing with hot lead. Chiun had taught Remo the basics, which had not changed since the days of the old Chinese muzzle-loaders. In response to the proliferation of automatic weapons, Remo had come up with a few innovations of his own.

The AK-47 carried thirty rounds in a clip, with another thirty in the backup clip duct-taped to the one in the receiver.

Remo counted the shots, and when the last one smacked into the jerking panel, the AK ran silent. The receptionist yanked out the old clip. She never got to flip it around and jam its mate in.

Remo was unexpectedly towering over her as he brought his palms together over the smoking muzzle.

The clap made the Russian girl blink. In that blink, Remo sidestepped so swiftly he seemed to vanish from sight.

She would have sought him out except that the AK was for some reason jittering in her hands as if attached to a working vibrator. She shook with it. Then, before her shaking eyes, the muzzle disintegrated.

She swore in venomous Russian.

Remo put her out of action with a tap to her forehead that made her brain bounce around the inside of her skull so hard it stopped functioning, a bruised, bloody sponge.

Reinforcements showed up in the form of a trio of Russians wearing dark suits enlivened by bright red ties.

"Cron!" one shouted.

Over the years, Remo had been attacked by enough Soviet agents that the Russian word for "stop" was as familiar to him as the English. He pretended to raise his hands in surrender.

"Anybody here speak English?" he asked.

No one volunteered that he did. Instead, they stepped forward with their Makarov and Tokarev pistols trained on his stomach. Remo decided the hell with it and jumped them.

His knees bent so imperceptibly there was no warning until his feet left the floor as if on springs.

Remo cleared the twenty feet between the reception desk and the trio of Russian agents before they could process the sensory information that they were under attack.

He might have teleported himself, except instead of materializing in their midst, he dropped down on them from above.

Landing in the splayed-spider position, Remo took out all three with short-armed punches and slap-kicks. Their guns clanked to the floor, unfired, dragging their dead owners down with them.

Dancing away, Remo turned to the patiently waiting Master of Sinanju and asked, "Aren't you going to help?"

"I found this place. I have earned a respite from this hectic assignment."

"There's nothing hectic about this assignment."

"You are making a great deal of noise for one whose task is yet to be completed."

As if to demonstrate Chiun's comment, another panel rolled aside to disgorge a pair of thick-skulled Russians wearing black uniforms stripped of any insignia.

"Point taken," said Remo. "I come in peace for all mankind," he told the pair, who clutched folding-stock Kalashnikov rifles.

They seemed to understand English because they hesitated.

One asked a harsh question: "What do you do here, *Amerikanski?* This is simple tailor shop."

"My mistake. I thought it was Shchit headquarters."

The pair exchanged glances, their eyes got sick and they mumbled unhappy excuses in a mix of English and Russian before taking their muzzles into their mouths and yanking back on the triggers.

Like watermelons under a chopping machine, their heads disintegrated and they fell dead.

"Check this out, Chiun," said Remo. "Guess I was right, after all. They liquidated themselves because their cover was blown."

Chiun floated to the panel and kicked it in, disclosing a long stainless-steel corridor marked by a ceiling-mounted security camera.

"They're going to see us coming," Remo warned.

Chiun nodded firmly. "This is good. It will encourage fear in their craven hearts."

"I wasn't thinking of that. Smitty'll have puppies if our faces are broadcast all over Moscow."

The Master of Sinanju considered.

"I will show you a trick you do not know, Remo," Chiun said thinly. He shook his head from side to side and kept shaking it until his pupil caught on.

Together, they crossed into the bowels of the organization that had ordered their destruction.

26

Colonel Radomir Rushenko was wolfing down a good proletarian lunch of red caviar on black bread chased down by a glass of warm *kvass* when the red light on his desk started to go *bap-bap-bap-bap.*

The light happened to be buried under a sheaf of telexes from his operatives scattered about Russia and abroad, so the blinking light went unnoticed. The *bapp*ing was muffled, and at first Rushenko didn't hear it through the meaty sounds he made while consuming the overflowing sandwich.

A telex from Kazakhstan, where a Shield operative watched over the Baikonur Cosmodrome, had his attention.

Unable to develop reliable information at this time on recent Mir activities. Station not believed to be testing weapon.

Another telex from his mole in Glavkosmos was more substantive:

Widely believed here that recent *Buran* launch, reported to be test of new Mir docking coupler, was subsidized by commercial fee. Kremlin disinformation suspected. Unknown what was launched, by whom or for what purpose.

Rushenko frowned heavily. This suggested a foreign contractor.

The insistent *bap-bap-bap* of the desk alarm penetrated his thinking processes, and he swept the telexes away, scowling.

It was the intruder alarm. It meant only one thing: a penetration.

And penetration here in the most secret stronghold in holy Russia could mean only one of two things: the traitorous Russian police. Or worse, local *mafiya biznesmeny* intent upon extracting ransom from what was outwardly a legitimate business. It was absurd how these hooligans operated in the new, licentious Russia. Twice in the past, it was necessary to liquidate *mafiya* interlopers selling "protection." Yet still they came. Such things were inconceivable in the good old days of Red rule.

Engaging his intercom, Rushenko got his chief of security.

"I have an alarm. What is happening?"

"Two men have penetrated the outermost circle, comrade Colonel."

"Only two?"

"We have six casualties. Reinforcements are on the way."

"I am on my way," Rushenko said, rising from his chair so hastily his sandwich toppled to the floor. His shoes crushed a glop of red caviar into the red rug, and he tracked it down the corridor, whose scarlet ceiling lights proclaimed a highest-urgency penetration, and stormed into the security room.

It was a nest of TV monitors and radio equipment in a very confined space. Even for Shield, Moscow floor space was at a premium.

A Ukrainian in the uniform of the old Red Army but without insignia of rank was punching up views of the reception area, the second line of defense. This was the first penetration of the tailor-shop cover.

Rushenko winced to see crack former Spetsnaz commandos lying in their own blood alongside the latest heroine of Mother Russia. There was no sign of their assailants.

"Where are they?" he demanded, his hands turning to fists.

The security man tapped a screen on the second tier of monitors. "There, comrade Colonel."

Rushenko squinted. Two men were moving down the corridor. No sooner had he laid eyes on them than they vanished from sight. A pointing finger directed his gaze to another monitor that picked them up as they walked into an ambush.

The ambush consisted of two Spetsnaz kneeling at either side of the corridor terminus.

Rushenko smiled grimly. "They will not get past the outer ring alive."

"They should not have gotten into the outer ring in the first place," the security chief said tightly.

"Where are their weapons?" Rushenko asked suddenly.

"They have none."

And Rushenko lifted an eyebrow thick as a woolly caterpillar. "What is wrong with this camera?"

"Nothing."

"Their faces are two blurs."

The security chief adjusted the monitor. Try as he might, the faces of the interlopers couldn't be clarified, though other details were quite sharp.

"It does not matter," Rushenko grunted. "They will be dead soon."

The faceless duo slipped up the corridor. The camera showed the two commandos lying in ambush, prepared to whip their weapons around the corner and spray the stainless-steel corridor in a withering cross fire.

"All that will be left is blood and bio-matter for disposal," the security chief agreed.

As the moment of truth neared, Colonel Rushenko and his security chief involuntarily tensed. The two strange ones walked along casually, as if entering a cafeteria. Had they no inkling of the danger? Or did they imagine this would be an easy penetration?

The instant the two commandos jerked around their positions, Rushenko breathed, "Now!"

The AKs erupted, spewing a cross fire, back and forth, back and forth, so that a ball bouncing randomly down the corridor would have been shot to pieces.

Unfortunately the exact moment of truth was the same moment the pair jumped over the kneeling commandos. They landed in perfect synchronization, on one foot only, while the other kicked backward with studied viciousness. Both feet caught an unwary commando at the back of his head.

And both commandos crumpled atop their quieting weapons. One fallen hero managed a last defiant trigger squeeze. Unfortunately all he got for his trouble was a burst through the soft tissues under his own chin, which made his face fall off like hard frosting from old cake.

The two interlopers vanished around another corner like a pair of blur-featured ghosts.

"Why are there only two?" Rushenko queried suddenly.

"Perhaps," the security chief returned thickly, "two are all that is necessary."

"Seal the passage."

"Da." A finger depressed a stud, and bulkhead doors dropped down on either end of approach corridor 4. They were almost into the middle ring. It was too dangerous to allow them to penetrate farther.

"It is done," said the security chief.

"Let them suffocate for lack of air."

A switch was thrown. Pumps began sucking up the corridor's already stuffy air.

The two seemed to understand their plight without consultation. They were very good. Just watching them, Rushenko realized they were trained agents.

"These are not *mafiya,*" he muttered.

"FSK?"

"If so, they are men who are worthy of Shield. Their loss is regrettable."

The intruders were at the inner steel door, touching it with their fingers, as if taking the metal's temperature.

The corridor was miked. The security chief turned up the volume.

He got an exchange of unfamiliar words.

"What language is that?"

Colonel Rushenko shook his head. It was not Russian. Nor American English. It was strange. The last thing he expected was a foreign agent. For if the Kremlin did not suspect the existence of Shield, what other nation could acquire that forbidden knowledge?

"I have changed my mind," he said. "They must be interrogated before liquidation. Open the inner door."

Before the order could be executed, the taller of the two punched the door at a point at the level of his head. The door rung out like a badly tuned gong. The entire installation shook for the briefest of moments.

It was very disquieting. A human fist should not affect steel that way.

Then, as the door shivered in the aftermath of the blow—clearly shivered—the tall one struck it again.

It jumped clear of its frame as if a great electronic magnet had repelled it.

"I am witnessing the impossible!" Rushenko blurted.

"I am activating the next line of defense, cómrade Colonel."

The next line of defense was deadly in its simplicity.

Floor vents began leaking kerosene, with its unmistakable odor. The ceiling water sprinklers suddenly ignited like upside-down hurricane lanterns.

One began to drop sparks. Soon, they were all dropping rags of flame that touched the steel floor without consequence. But the kerosene was spreading now....

Grabbing the microphone, Colonel Rushenko barked into it. "If you wish to live, throw up your hands in surrender!"

The two ignored his voice.

Rushenko turned to his security aide. "Is this getting through?"

"*Da*. Perhaps they do not speak Russian at all."

"Then what would be their purpose in penetrating this installation?"

"Perhaps they are lost tourists?"

Colonel Rushenko tried English next. He never finished his warning.

The two began turning off the ceiling lamps by the simple expedient of leaping up and squeezing the sprinklers shut. It was miraculous in its sheer simplicity. One went to one end of the corridor. The other stationed himself at its opposite end.

Methodically they reached up and took hold of each steel aperture in turn. The audible *crunk* of the metal surrendering to their crushing grips came back through the sound system.

Meeting in the middle, they closed off the last dripping flames just as the kerosene pool began meeting in the middle.

Nimbly, they leaped over these until they reached the innermost door. This time the shorter of the two breached the barrier. His method was to spin in place and lash out a foot that sent the door screaming from its frame to bang on the floor.

"They are not human," the security chief of Shield gasped.

"They are human," insisted Colonel Rushenko. "They merely require special deaths before they will consent to die."

"You no longer desire them alive?"

"I desire them very much alive. But I am no fool. They are unconquerable. We must concentrate on proving them not to be unkillable."

"The next corridor is a dead end," the security chief said.

"Thank you for that information," a squeaky voice said in perfect if old-fashioned Russian.

"Damn you! You left the connection open!" Rushenko roared as the two took the right branch, not the left.

"This is not good," the security chief said, cutting off the circuit. "That branch will take them to the inner circle."

Rushenko stood unmoving for nearly a minute, his dark Kazakh features working. "It was Korean," he muttered.

"What?"

"They spoke Korean," he said bitterly. "I should have known who they were before. But now I know. We must abandon this installation."

"We have countermeasures remaining in inventory."

"I am a fool. If these two have knowledge of us, however slim and imperfect, others do, too. We must evacuate. Give the command."

"Yes, comrade Colonel," said the shaking security chief as he broke a key from a neck chain and inserted it into a panel. He turned it with a harsh twist.

A Klaxon blared over and over.

"Come," said Colonel Rushenko, tearing from the room.

Racing deeper into the Shield installation, he returned to his office. The paper-strewn desk stood as it had before, its red light going *bap-bap-bap-bap* like a spitting thing.

Reaching into a desk drawer, Rushenko found a catch and yanked it. The desk lifted mechanically and rolled aside, disclosing a concrete well and immaculate pine steps going down into shadow.

"What about the others?"

"They have their secret exits," Rushenko hissed. "Or their cyanide pills. Come."

Rushenko led the other into the tunnel, and the desk began returning to its spot, dropping back into place, its shadow overwhelming them.

"Are there no lights?" the security chief complained.

"The tunnel goes in one direction. Just follow my voice."

From behind them came a fierce splintering, joined with the complaint of gears and machinery under terrible stress.

A crack of light appeared back the way they came.

Rushenko turned. The light elongated and began chasing them.

"Hurry!"

They ran. They didn't hear any pursuing footsteps, so when the security chief happened to look back over his shoulder, he was shocked to see a tall man, the blur of his face like a death's-head, just three paces behind.

A thick-wristed hand took him by the back of his neck and dissolved his eyes with a two-fingered blow that penetrated his brain.

Colonel Rushenko heard the ugly death thud and decided against looking back.

It didn't matter. A cool hand arrested him by squeezing the back of his neck. His still-running feet made futile whetting sounds, then stopped.

"I told you I'd be right with you," a cool voice said.

Colonel Rushenko reached for his side arm. He got it out, but it was snatched out of his clutches. He next reached for the cyanide pill in his inner blouse pocket.

A hand clamped his wrist, got the pill and powdered it before his disappointed eyes.

"Nice try," said the taller of the two interlopers. His face was still a blur. It made Rushenko's eyes hurt to look at it.

"What is wrong with your head?" he asked.

"Oh, sorry." And the man shook his head once. Miraculously the features cleared. Deep-set eyes looked at him without mercy.

Colonel Rushenko realized the truth then. The man had been vibrating his head somehow at a speed that defied the human eye and TV cameras to read it. It was wonderful technology, whatever it was.

"How did you know that was a poison pill?" Rushenko asked as the cyanide powder finished dropping from the man's open fist.

"That's where my superior keeps his."

"You are U.S. agent, obviously?"

"You are head of Shield."

Rushenko quailed inwardly. Shield was known!

"I do not know these Shield. It is an American word," Rushenko insisted.

"Suppose I say Shchit?"

"Then I would tell you you are a vulgar *Amerikanski*. We say *govno*."

The American gave Colonel Rushenko's cervical vertebrae a squeeze, and Rushenko found himself walking backward. His legs were moving involuntarily. No, that was not it. They were moving voluntarily.

But it wasn't of the colonel's own volition. It was the American's.

He was walked back like a puppet up the wooden steps to his ruin of an office. The desk was a shambles. Somehow the *bapp*ing light continued to signal its now-useless warning.

"This is the headquarters of Shield," the American said flatly.

"This is Radio Free Moscow. We are Communists."

Then the American began peeling Colonel Rushenko's fingernails off, one by one. He did it with casual cruelty.

"We want to know about the thing that hit our shuttle."

"I know nothing of this!" Colonel Rushenko sobbed, amazed at how swiftly he was reduced to blubbering.

"Kinga told a different story."

At that point, his left thumbnail came off. The false one. Under it was the real one, and under that his Shield tattoo. A tattoo that should have meant nothing to anyone who wasn't a Shield operative.

The other interloper stepped into the room then. Colonel Rushenko saw that he was Asian. His nationality was unclear. Dressed as he was, the man might have been from one of the former Asiatic republics. Remembering Kinga's last report, the colonel felt the saliva in his mouth dry like warm rain on a hot rock.

"You are the Master of Sinanju."

The little old man bowed serenely.

Rushenko addressed Remo. "And you are—what?"

"Tour guide. What about the thing that got our shuttle?"

"This was not our operation," Rushenko said with a trace of regret.

"Then whose was it?"

"This is unknown to us. We are investigating."

"Why would you investigate a U.S. problem?"

"Because someone is attempting to blame Mother Russia for this matter, of course. Why do you think?"

A finger and a thumb reached out and squeezed Colonel Rushenko's thumb. The tip turned red, then purple, then popped like a Concord grape. It was exceedingly painful to behold, never mind endure.

"Lose the attitude," the American agent requested.

"*Da*. It is gone," Ruskenko gasped.

"I want to hear about Shield."

"It does not exist," Colonel Rushenko said.

The squeezing fingers drew additional blood.

"It has no official existence, I meant to say," Rushenko gasped. "The Kremlin does not even know about us."

"That's better. Who sanctioned it?"

"No one. I created it."

The Master of Sinanju came up, his hazel eyes interested. "Why?"

"To safeguard Mother Russia until Soviet rule is restored."

"You could have a long wait," the American said dryly.

"But it will be worth it," said Colonel Rushenko fervently.

"Okay. Enough of Shield. We gotta get to the bottom of this thing."

"I agree. I have operatives at Glavkosmos and Baikonur looking into this even as we squabble."

"We will await these reports," said the Master of Sinanju.

And Colonel Rushenko found himself sitting back in his red leather chair, into a gooey mess that he belatedly realized was a puddle of red caviar. He was relieved. He thought he had soiled his trousers.

The old Korean sifted through the desk papers, reading classified telexes with a casual air before ripping them to shreds and wastebasketing them.

"How did you find this place?" Rushenko asked at one point. "Kinga did not know its location."

"We traced the e-mail back."

"It has no listed address."

"We got the street. After that, it was easy."

"How so?"

The American jerked a thumb at the preoccupied Korean. "He recognized the cover."

"I have watched American television, too," said the old Korean blandly.

"What show was that, by the way?" Remo asked.

"Ask Uncle Vanya."

Remo snapped his fingers. "I get it now. I never watched that one much. Too farfetched."

While they waited for incoming reports, the American with the thick wrists passed the time by stacking the bodies of defunct Shield agents about the room.

"What killed them?" Rushenko asked.

"Sloppiness," sniffed the Master of Sinanju.

And Colonel Rushenko understood. They were liquidated by the finest assassin of the modern world. It was no wonder his security levels were so ridiculously pregnable.

The calls poured in over the next two hours.

The American lifted the receiver to Colonel Rushenko's mouth each time, squeezing his neck threateningly with his free hand. Colonel Rushenko felt obliged to answer in his normal tone of voice.

"Comrade Colonel, there is news out of America."

"Yes?"

"Our mole in the American CIA reports that SPACETRACK has isolated the orbital device responsible for the strange accidents in America."

"Yes?"

"It is dubbed Object 617 in their catalog of objects in the near cosmos."

"Yes, yes."

"It went into orbit a month ago. The orbit is polar."

"Who launched this infernal thing?"

"We did."

"Again?"

"It was the payload of *Buran 2.*"

"The Kremlin launched this thing?" Rushenko roared.

"That is what the CIA believes."

Colonel Rushenko looked to the dead-eyed American with his own eyes going sick. "The fools in the Kremlin have gone mad. There is no reason for this, no logic."

"Tough. We got what we came for."

"And you have served your purpose," added the Master of Sinanju.

"If you kill me, I cannot help you," Rushenko said thickly.

"Who says we need your help, Russian?" said the Master of Sinanju.

"Your interests are my interests. I wish to get to the bottom of this affair, too."

The two U.S. agents exchanged glances. The old Korean nodded, and the pressure of death left the throat of Colonel Rushenko, who understood that if he was to live, it wouldn't be for long.

For the most deadly killers in all of humanity owned him like a dull puppet of wood and strings.

27

The call took ninety minutes using the Moscow phone system.

"It's the Russians," Remo told Harold Smith.

"I have checked with SPACETRACK. The orbits do not coincide with Mir."

"It's not Mir. It's something launched by the Russian shuttle. This is out of Shield."

"Then there *is* such an organization."

"Yeah. Unofficially. It's some kind of holdover from the Soviet period. The guy who runs it says the Kremlin doesn't even know it exists. Sound familiar, Smitty?"

"Who gave you this information?" Smith pressed.

"The guy who runs it. Say *dos vedanya* to—what's your name, by the way?"

"Colonel Radomir Eduardovitch Rushenko," said the colonel, between sucks of his wounded thumb.

"Better known as Uncle Vanya. Smitty, this info came by way of the CIA. *Our* CIA."

"They have a mole in the CIA!" Smith sputtered.

"You act surprised. Lower Slobovia probably has moles in the CIA these days."

Smith cleared his throat. "No intelligence coming out of the CIA is reliable these days," he said dismissively.

"According to the mole, SPACETRACK has a fix on this thing."

"If SPACETRACK has such a fix, why has this not been reported to the White House?" Smith countered.

"Maybe SPACETRACK knows a hot potato when they smell it," Remo suggested.

"Hold the line open."

"Good idea. If we get disconnected, it could be Valentine's Day before we can reestablish contact."

Harold Smith put them on hold, and Remo turned to Colonel Rushenko.

"My boss says hi."

Colonel Rushenko said nothing other than to grit his teeth. Then he remembered the mushy feeling in the seat of his pants.

"I am sitting in caviar," he said.

"Lucky you. Some people only fall into clover."

"I do not mean this metaphorically. I am sitting on my lunch."

"Enjoy it. Lots of Russians are starving these days."

"Yes. Thanks to the corrosive poison of capitalism."

"Your throwback opinion doesn't exactly count."

"Thank you for bringing this to my attention," Colonel Rushenko said acidly.

AT FOLCROFT SANITARIUM, Harold Smith called a major at SPACETRACK, representing himself as General Smith with the U.S. Space Command.

"Yes, General?" said the major at SPACE-TRACK.

"We have a rumor here that you people have something in inventory whose orbits coincide with the BioBubble and *Reliant* mishaps."

The man on the other end of the line made a brief choking sound, as if a chicken bone had just been expelled from his throat.

"I have nothing on that in this office, General Smith."

"Connect me with an office that has this information," Smith said tartly, recognizing a bureaucratic shuffle when he heard one.

"Just a sec."

The line clicked, buzzed, then went dead. When Smith redialed, it was busy. The busy signal was angry and insistent in its way.

Hanging up, Smith logged on to the SPACE-TRACK active data base, and got a real-time snapshot of what SPACETRACK had from its many ground-based radar stations. On his desktop monitor, the gigantic image was squeezed down too small to read. Smith blew up the different grids one by one until he found Object 617.

Smith knew little about celestial navigation. He recognized that the object had a polar orbit. This meant it executed a continuous loop from the North Pole to the South Pole and back again every ninety minutes. Since the earth rotated under it, it passed over virtually every spot on earth at one point or another, and if maneuverable, could be made to overfly any point on the globe. Usually this was a certain signature of a spy satellite.

Smith punched up the file on Object 617.

What he saw made him gasp.

It was logged in as having been inserted into orbit a month before, deployed by a *Buran* shuttle, classified by Space Command as a recon satellite of unknown purpose and marked for periodic observation.

Optical images taken by GEODSS—the Ground-based Electro-Optical Deep Space Surveillance element of the Air Force Maui Optical Station—showed a dark ball framed by struts painted a stealth gray.

If this was a spy satellite, it was of a configuration and purpose that baffled Harold Smith. For one thing, there were no observable lens apertures.

Logging off, Smith picked up the blue contact phone that connected him to Remo in Moscow.

"Remo, Object 617 exists. It's in the SPACE-TRACK inventory as a spy satellite. The Russian space shuttle did deploy it. That is confirmed."

"So I guess we need to talk to the Russian shuttle people."

"This will be difficult."

"Oh, I don't know," Remo said airily. "Our good friend Colonel Rushenko here has offered his help."

"Be certain to convert our new friend to a neutral posture at the end of this phase of the mission."

"Already thought of that," said Remo, hanging up.

"Thought of what?" Colonel Rushenko asked.

"Our boss just sent his regards."

"You cannot deceive me. I am to be liquidated because I know of you."

"Hey, you'd do the same for us. In fact, you tried pretty hard."

Rushenko made a fist with his fleshy face. "I have nothing more to say. Other than that, I have not finished my lunch and I am very hungry."

"No time," said Remo, picking him up by the scruff of his thick neck.

"There is candy in my desk."

Shrugging, the American rifled through the contents of the cherry-wood desk until he pulled out a brown wrapper. "This looks familiar," he said.

"It is a candy bar."

Remo showed the wrapper to the Master of Sinanju. Chiun squeezed his eyes at the red letters that spelled "Mapc."

"What's this say?" asked Remo.

"Where did you find this!" Chiun hissed.

"Belongs to Colonel Klink here."

"The word is the same as your 'Mars.'"

"No kidding." Remo looked to Colonel Rushenko. "This is a Russian Mars bar?"

"I normally detest American products, but Russian chocolate has seriously deteriorated since the collapse."

Remo stripped the wrapper, pocketed it as a souvenir and trashed the rest.

"I desired that," Colonel Rushenko protested.

"Might have been poison."

"Who would poison good chocolate?"

"The same manner of cretin who would consume fish while they are but eggs," said the Master of Sinanju in a distasteful tone.

And steely constricting fingers brought unwelcome unconsciousness to Colonel Rushenko's unhappy brain.

Not to mention his growling stomach.

28

Bartholomew Meech watched the computer screen in his sprawling lab where monitoring systems pulsed and beeped and the incessant rain made the windows swim, blocking out the oyster gray world beyond them.

He drained a cup of heavily sugared Starbucks black coffee and hoped the screen wouldn't beep. But he knew it would. Then it did, and flashed, "You have mail!"

Meech brought it up.

To: R&D@qnm.com
From: RM@qnm.com
Subject: I'm back
Just blew back into town. What's the latest?

Meech composed his reply with caffeine-shaky fingers.

To: RM@qnm.com
From: R&D@qnm.com
Subject: . . . .
I killed a man. The NASA crawler driver.

The reply hit the screen a moment later:

Not your problem. You're only a cog in the corporate machine. Go to confession on your own time. On company time, you do what the firm requires. What's Pagan saying now?

Meech replied:

He's talking up asteroids again. And ozone holes. But it's not what Pagan is saying. It's what the press is saying. They're blaming Russia now. We've ignited a global incident.

The response:

Great! We need to throw up more smoke, keep the Russians from figuring things out and throw the blame back on the Martians. Hit Baikonur. Hit it hard.

Bartholomew Meech shook and shook as he read the green glowing words. Then he composed his reply: "What about Russian casualties?"

He knew what the reply would be before it appeared: "They're only vodka-swilling peasants. This is our jobs. Go to it."

Bartholomew Meech came out of his chair heavily and prepared to fulfill his responsibilities to his employer. His glasses were as steamy as the windows that looked out over a fog in which a gigantic, saucer-shaped object ringed with illuminated windows seemed to float disembodied in a gray drizzle like the advance guard from another world.

29

For the head of Russia's most secret counterintelligence agency, Colonel Radomir Rushenko was very open.

"I myself did not prefer to call my modest ministry Shield," he was saying.

"We do not care," said Chiun as the Yak-90 airliner droned over Soviet central Asia en route to Kazakhstan.

"I wished to call it Rodina, which means 'Motherland.'"

Remo yawned elaborately.

"But there was already a television program by that name. I did not wish confusion. Nor did I like the program. In fact, I do not much like Russian programming these days."

"Let me guess," said Remo. "Too many American imports?"

"Yes. How did you know that?"

"It's the same thing the French and Canadians keep complaining about."

"They are quite correct in their complaints."

"Didn't stop you from ripping off 'The Man from U.N.C.L.E.,'" Remo contended.

"It was a very clever cover."

"Chiun caught on right off."

"Did *you?*" Rushenko asked Remo pointedly.

Remo changed the subject. "What's the real purpose of Shield?" he asked.

"As I have said, to preserve the union."

Remo blinked. "Union? What union?"

"The *Soviet* Union. What other union is of historical consequence?"

"We have a union in America, too, you know."

"Then you sympathize with the aims of Shield."

"Not really."

"But now we are on the same team. Like Solo and Kuryakin, *da?*"

"We are on the same team, *nyet,*" said Remo.

"Which organization do you belong to?" asked Rushenko.

"Who says we belong to anyone?" Remo retorted.

"It is obvious you are not CIA."

"Why is it obvious?"

This time Colonel Rushenko smiled elaborately. "Because if the CIA employed the House of Sinanju, FSK would know this. And what FSK knows, Shield knows, too."

"Who put those moles in the CIA?"

"I refuse to say categorically. But I will admit to having moles in the FSK."

Remo reached forward and took Colonel Rushenko by the back of his thick, black-stubbled neck.

"Let's try answering this question again, shall we?" he prompted.

"Yes, of course."

"Name names."

"I do not know these names."

Remo made a buzzer sound. "Wrong answer. Prepare to be defenestrated at thirty thousand feet."

And Remo jammed the Russian's face against a window so he could get a clear view of every foot of the deadly drop.

"I know code names," Rushenko sputtered. "For these moles were KGB moles we acquired. It was decided not to pry into personalities. Just accept intelligence reports."

"How do you know they weren't CIA double agents? Or FSK turncoats feeding you false information?"

"All information coming from the CIA is assumed to be false or unreliable," said Colonel Rushenko.

"Why's that?"

"They persist in using psychics."

"So why gather it?"

"It is useful to know what the CIA thinks it knows. As useful as knowing what it correctly knows."

"You know, I'm glad I'm just an assassin. This spy stuff sounds confusing."

"It is a man's game," Colonel Rushenko said with dignified satisfaction.

"It is foolishness," Chiun broke in. "Information does not matter. Only who rules, who lives and who dies."

Rushenko nodded heavily. "That, too, is important. But who rules in the modern world often depends upon intelligence."

"There has never been an intelligent Russian ruler," Chiun said pointedly as he watched the wing for signs of structural flaw. "Otherwise, Russia would never have fallen into such ruinous chaos time and time again."

"This democratic experiment will end soon. There will be a new regime. Just like the good old days."

"A czar will emerge if a strong man with Romanov blood can be located," Chiun countered.

"We are not speaking the same language," Colonel Rushenko said, deciding that it would be impossible to pry secrets from these two.

The copilot came back to announce that they were nearing their destination. "Leninsk is but twenty minutes away," he said in English because Remo had insisted all conversation take place in English so there would be no misunderstanding.

It had been like this since they had taken Colonel Rushenko to the Sheremetevo II Airport, woke him up and told him to use whatever pull he had to get them to Baikonur Cosmodrome.

Colonel Rushenko was so pleased to find himself still among the living that he complied by whistling up a Yak-90 by telephone. This was the third leg of their trek, and at every refueling stop the Shield colonel seemed to have ready agents willing to do his bidding.

They tightened their seat belts, which were simple hemp ropes.

Once again Colonel Rushenko apologized for this embarrassment but such was the state of post-Soviet Russia, or as he called it, "this regrettable interlude."

Below, the snow-dusted steppes of central Asia rose up to meet them and Colonel Rushenko once again waxed expansive. "I will give you a good example of disinformation. The copilot has told you we are approaching Leninsk."

"Yeah?" said Remo.

"But Leninsk is three hundred kilometers from Baikonur."

A slim nail touched Colonel Rushenko's carotid artery.

"Choose your next words with care," Chiun warned.

The colonel instantly broke out in a cold sweat. He found his voice after two swallows. "You misunderstand. This is no trap. I am merely making a point."

"Make it," suggested Remo.

"When Gagarin became the first man in space, TASS informed the world of the proud fact that he was launched from Baikonur Cosmodrome. This is what credulous Western media picked up. Ever since, the West has referred to the launch point as Baikonur Cosmodrome, but it is not in Baikonur at all, but near Leninsk, another place entirely."

"So?"

"This was never corrected. Which proves the West are a pack of fools."

"Spoken like a man clinging to a broken fantasy," said Remo.

"The Soviet Union will rise again."

"Not if a good czar rises first," said Chiun.

The Yak dropped lower, its engines straining. Remo took a second glance at the slipknot snugged against his midriff. In the flat distance, the most prominent landmark of Baikonur Cosmodrome showed—a gantry complex of squat, girdered towers. Support buildings ranging from broad hangars to white monoliths of blank sheet metal were arrayed around the gantry area. There were two runways—one very long and the other seemingly endless.

"Do you know that I am a Kazakh?" Rushenko asked Chiun as the noisy engine straining made the cabin rattle alarmingly.

"It is written on your brutish face."

"Thank you. Kazakhs belong to the same ethnic family as Turk and Mongols and Koreans. There may be some of your blood in my veins."

"I may search for it after I have slain you," said Chiun in a thin voice.

Colonel Rushenko shut up. He grabbed for his armrests. One broke off in his hand. He hid it under his seat in shame.

The plane was lifting on one wing as it banked into a steep approach turn for the extremely long Cosmodrome runway.

"We will be using the same runway the *Buran* uses," Rushenko said expansively. "For our shuttles land at the same place they are launched from—a feat the West is incapable of."

"At least our shuttles carry live people," said Remo.

"Which is unnecessary, for robots are capable of most shuttle operations."

A moment later, Rushenko's eyes were drawn to the western horizon.

"Look. A sun dog!"

Remo and Chiun jerked their heads to their respective windows, Chiun taking care to touch Colonel Rushenko's throat with a deadly fingernail in case this was some Russian trick.

In the high sky, a hot ball of yellow light burned.

"I do not recognize this," said Chiun.

Rushenko said, "It is what is called a sun dog. A reflection of the solar orb upon ice crystals high in the atmosphere. I have never seen one like this, however."

A column of intolerably incandescent light sizzled past their ship a second later. It struck the ground with a dull boom.

Buffeted by a blast of heat, the Yak actually turned over once. Only their seat belts kept them from bouncing off the ceiling.

The ship righted itself with agonizing slowness, then came level. The engines found their normal pitch after an uncertain blooping.

"What has happened?" muttered Rushenko, holding his throat.

"Looked like a big beam of light," said Remo.

"The breath of the sun dragon," said Chiun, his wrinkled face touching the window to peer below.

"You mean sun dog," said Colonel Rushenko.

"He means sun dragon. And don't ask."

"Proklyatye!" Colonel Rushenko exploded. "Look!"

Below, there was a round, smoking hole where a long blue hangar building had stood a moment before. Remo had been looking at the building before the sun dog appeared. Now it was thoroughly obliterated.

Smoke rose from the black patch, but not much. It was as if whatever had burned down from the daylight sky had so scorched the earth that there was almost no natural fuel left to give off smoke.

"I am without words," Colonel Rushenko said thickly.

"What was it?" asked Remo.

"Mother Russia has been attacked."

"This is Kazakhstan," Chiun reminded him.

"Yes. I am sorry. I forget. It is my home soil, but no longer part of Russia. Still, the impossible has happened. The United States have launched a terroristic strike at an ally of Russia. This can have one certain consequence. Total war. We are mortal enemies again. Not that we were not before.''

And Colonel Rushenko turned completely pale under the weathered Kazakh skin. He looked like a man no longer concerned about preserving his own life because no one's life had any value now.

30

There was an Mi-8 helicopter waiting with rotors turning slowly as the Yak-90 came to the end of its roll-out. The crew piled out as fast as they could and ducked under the fuselage, where they waited with chattering teeth and shivering limbs for another bolt from the endless blue sky of Kazakhstan.

Remo, Chiun and Colonel Rushenko stepped off casually, their eyes fixed on the same unthreatening sky.

"No clouds," said Remo. "Couldn't be lightning. Though it boomed like lightning."

"It was a sun dragon," said Chiun.

"I saw a sun dog," insisted Colonel Rushenko.

"A sun dog's never been known to burn a building down like that one," Remo argued.

"No," admitted Colonel Rushenko.

"Then shut up."

"It looked solar."

Remo looked at him. "What?"

"I said solar," repeated Rushenko. "A great but terrible beam of sunshine."

Remo's eyes went to the sun. It burned as it always had. "It's one theory," he admitted.

They were waved into the helicopter by a man in an insignialess Russian uniform. He had a side arm.

Remo relieved him of it by the simple expedient of yanking his belt off and throwing it and the holstered weapon as far as he could.

When it landed, a tiny puff of dust almost two miles west, the Russian soldier decided not to object to his uncavalier treatment. Meekly he climbed aboard, and the helicopter lifted off in a clattering halo of sound.

"What has happened here?" Colonel Rushenko asked the man.

"The shuttle complex is no more."

"Both shuttles?"

The man nodded grimly. "Nothing but burning dirt remains."

Colonel Rushenko looked to Remo and said, "I do not comprehend this."

"I do. Somebody's covering up."

"Nonsense. A cover-up would not require the destruction of the Russian shuttle fleet."

"Some fleet. They fly once and are mothballed forever."

"Overfly the site," ordered Colonel Rushenko.

"I will allow this," said Chiun.

The helicopter skimmed low. Emergency crews were moving toward the blast site with all speed. As they came to the zone of scorched area, they slowed, then slewed to a rolling stop.

"The ground must be real hot," said Remo.

"Of course it is hot," Rushenko flared. "Everything that stood upon it is now gone."

"I mean *really* hot. The tires on their trucks are melting."

Colonel Rushenko peered through the Plexiglas and saw the tendrils of gray smoke curling up from the front tires of the vehicles that had ventured into the charred zone. Soldiers were jumping from their trucks, running a few paces then hopping back, their boot soles smoking.

"Better not land," Remo warned. "Unless you want a serious hotfoot."

"We do not need to land. It is obvious what has happened here," Rushenko said tightly.

"Not to me."

"A solar weapon was used. Obviously the West is more advanced in their Star Wars technology than we dreamed."

"It wasn't us."

"You are the only superpower remaining. Except, of course, Russia. Who else would have the technology and the will to attack Russia?"

"Kazakhstan," corrected Chiun.

"Thank you. My question remains unanswered," said Colonel Rushenko.

"No way would we hit our own shuttle to test a superweapon," Remo said flatly.

"Hah! The contrary. It is a brilliant maneuver. A masterpiece of Western disinformation. No one would suspect Washington of complicity in its own disaster."

"You sound like an old Cold War rerun."

"I live for the next Cold War," Rushenko admitted.

"Don't count on seeing it," said Remo. "Put this thing down," he added.

Colonel Rushenko gave the order in Russian, which Chiun verified.

The helicopter dropped down at the edge of the charcoal zone. Remo got out, and the waves of residual heat brought sweat popping out on his face and bare forearms. No sooner had they broken through the skin than the same heat waves turned them to faint wisps of steam curling up lazily.

Feeling the body moisture draining from his body at an alarming rate, Remo retreated a few paces and, as the heat began to abate, he approached again.

The area of scorched earth was a perfect circle, the edge sharp as crop circles. Concrete lay fused and cracked, riddled with glass specks and bubbling patches of tar here and there.

There was no sign that a giant hangar had stood here, housing Russian's grounded shuttle fleet. People had died here. Remo could detect the faint smell like burned pork—only it had human constituents. Whoever had been burned, they left behind no bones and no mark of their passing other than a pungent vapor.

Returning to the helicopter, Remo said, "You know what this looks like?"

"What?" asked the Russian.

"Like a giant magnifying glass was focused right on this spot."

Colonel Rushenko laughed at the thought.

Chiun said, "And you scoff at sun dragons."

"Well, that's what it looks like to me," said Remo.

The helicopter carried them to the operations building, where Colonel Rushenko found the Kazakh official who nominally controlled the site. In fact, it was a joint Russian-Kazakh command now that the former Soviet Union had found itself in the embarrassing position of having their primary space center sitting in a foreign country.

The Russian representative refused to accept Colonel Rushenko's request for information. But the Kazakh was only too happy to cooperate with a fellow Kazakh national.

They were shown to a windowless, soundproof room, and Colonel Rushenko spoke urgently as Chiun monitored the exchange of Russian and Kazakh for dark glimmerings of impending treachery.

Colonel Rushenko asked fewer and fewer questions as the exchange wore on. He got noticeably paler, though.

"This is unbelievable," he said as he faced Remo.

"Spit it out."

"According to this man, the *Buran* payload was not a Russian or an American satellite, but the product of a third country entirely."

"What country?"

"Paraguay."

DR. HAROLD W. SMITH was shouting across more than a dozen international time zones.

"What?"

"Paraguay," shouted Remo.

"What did you say?"

"I said the Paraguayans hired the Russians to launch that thing up there!"

"What thing?"

"The space thing!" Remo shouted.

"Perhaps you should redial," Colonel Rushenko suggested helpfully.

"It took me an hour and a half to get this connection," Remo shouted back. "I'm sticking with it."

"Sticking with what?" Harold Smith yelled.

Remo bellowed, "Listen, Paraguay launched that thing!"

"Remo, you are breaking up."

"It melted the Soviet shuttle fleet."

Colonel Rushenko smiled nostalgically at the American's lapse.

Smith's voice grew shrill and nasal. "What?"

"The shuttles are all vaporized."

Harold Smith's reply was drowned in the cannonading boom that followed.

All eyes went to the nearest window.

Off to the north stood the spidery launch gantry, where the big Energia rockets lifted the *Buran* fleet aloft, approximately once every eight years.

The gantry stood in the column of searing light. It hurt the eye to look at it. The air made a dull boom, then the light seemed to withdraw back into the heavens.

There was no gantry on the spot where it had stood.

Instead, there was only a grayish haze of smoke that was being pushed outward by a spreading heat wave.

Even through the sealed window, they could feel the heat wave overtaking the operations building. Window panes crackled in their frames.

"That's never happened before," Remo said worriedly.

"What are you saying? It happened only ninety minutes ago," said Rushenko.

"It's happening twice in the same place. It's never happened twice before."

Chiun allowed a flicker of worry to touch his seamed visage. "This is not a good place to be. The dragon seems especially angry at us," he intoned.

"I do not accept the existence of dragons," said Colonel Rushenko bravely.

"Believe it or not, that thing up there is trying to wipe out all trace of Baikonur," said Remo.

"Leninsk. And I agree with you. We must go."

The helicopter shuttled them back to the Yak. The crew was back inside the aircraft, hiding in assorted lavatories.

Remo got them out and into their seats, and they took off into the sky ahead of a third white-hot column of sizzling heat from the sky. It was followed by another thundering boom that shook the aircraft.

Out the windows they could see what remained of the sprawl that was the Baikonur Cosmodrome complex.

There were three patches of blackness. All of identical size. In a staggered row.

"Almost makes you believe in angry Martians," said Remo.

"Perhaps they are spelling out a message," said Chiun.

"Get off it."

"I am only glad to be out of it," sniffed Chiun as the Yak screamed for higher altitude and more distance from the smoking cosmodrome.

They watched through the window as long as it was possible to watch.

There was no fourth cone of light. No one was disappointed.

"Sure hope Smith understood what I was saying," said Remo.

"Who is Smith?" asked Colonel Rushenko conversationally. "Your Mr. Waverly, perhaps?"

"Remind me to kill you later," said Remo.

Colonel Rushenko subsided. But he made a mental note of the name Smith. Probably an alias. But Americans were so devious it was best not to discount anything they said.

31

The destruction of the Baikonur Cosmodrome and the Russian shuttle fleet hit the Kremlin with all the force of a nuclear detonation.

In the old days, it would have led to the highest state of alert. The old Strategic Rocket Force would have been placed on alert, their SS-20 and Topol-M missile crews put on prelaunch posture.

But this was post-Soviet Russia.

It took an hour for the first report to reach the Kremlin. Another hour to bring the leadership up to speed. A third to argue over a response.

By that time, everyone from the president of Russia to his defense minister was thoroughly drunk.

"We must have someone to blame," the president said, pounding the table with his hammy fist.

"America!" an adviser bellowed.

"*Da*. America."

So it was decided America was to blame.

Then the call was put in to the Strategic Rocket Force to go to maximum alert and to be prepared to launch a retaliatory strike at an instant's notice.

"At whom?" the general in charge wanted to know.

"Who else? America!" the defense minister bellowed drunkenly.

"But they will strike back with overwhelming force, obliterating us all."

This was considered on an open line with another bottle of Stoli being the only casualty.

"You make a good point. Target a portion against China, too."

"Yes, General," the Strategic Rocket Force commander replied, gulping.

With that settled, the Russian leadership went back to drowning their sorrows. Somewhere in this, someone remembered to call Major-General Stankevitch at FSK.

"General Stankevitch, I regret to inform you that Baikonur Cosmodrome has been obliterated by the same superweapon that has struck America two times this week."

"Then the U.S. is not to blame."

"You are mistaken. There is no one else."

"What?"

"There is no one else to blame but the U.S. They have the technology. We do not. Your task is to prove this."

"What if it is a lie?" asked Stankevitch.

"Prove that, too. But you must hurry. The fate of mankind and the Motherland depend upon learning truth. Go now. Learn things. Assemble facts. Report immediately."

And to Major-General Stankevitch's utter horror, the phone went dead with an audible *bonk*. No one hung up. The handset had simply fallen from a drunken fist.

Quietly the General replaced the butter-colored receiver on his end and sank into his chair.

He had the most difficult decision of his life to make. And if he made the wrong one, mankind was doomed.

Clearly, he thought, reaching into the locked bottom drawer of his desk, it was time for a drink.

32

The President of the U.S. received the report from the National Reconnaissance Office of the National Security Agency by telephone.

"Sir, it appears that Baikonur Cosmodrome has been destroyed by the same power that obliterated our shuttle."

"Then it can't be the Russians," the President blurted.

"Sir?"

"The Russians wouldn't target their own space center, would they?"

"That's a jump we at NRO are not prepared to make," the NRO director said guardedly.

"Why not?"

"Could be a diversionary tactic."

"Explain."

"They hit two of our targets, then hit Baikonur to throw us off the scent."

"But their own space center?" the President asked incredulously.

"Why not? Except for Mir, Russia's space program is all but defunct."

"The cosmonauts up on Mir can't get home if there's no place to launch their Soyez ships from," the Chief Executive argued.

"They still have Krunishev."

"Didn't he die a long time ago?"

"You're thinking of Khrushchev, Mr. President. I was referring to the Krunishev Space Center."

"Oh, right."

"It's possible the Mir cosmonauts are on a suicide mission," the NRO director continued. "If they don't ever return to Earth, they can't tell what they know about the operation."

"I don't buy it," the President snapped.

"We only report what our satellites find, Mr. President."

The President called Harold Smith with the news. Smith listened carefully then said, "My people were at Baikonur when it happened," Smith said.

"And you didn't tell me first! I had to hear it from NRO?"

"I did not want to precipitate a crisis," Smith explained calmly.

"It's *already* a crisis!"

"Now that you have been officially informed, yes, it is. Your advisers are trying to convince you this is a Russian superweapon."

"It *could* be."

"Their counterparts in the Kremlin are doubtless telling your Russian counterpart it's a U.S. superweapon."

"Ridiculous!"

"Both theories are ridiculous. But the two nations are so used to pointing the finger of blame at one another, all it will take for a global face-off to commence is one man giving the launch order."

"My God! Could the Soviets be doing that now?"

"Probably. And they are no longer the Soviets."

"But they're still the Great Bear of the North. And that means I'd better get NORAD up to speed."

Harold Smith's lemony voice was resigned. "You would be derelict in your duty if you did not, Mr. President."

The Chief Executive's naturally hoarse voice turned to gravel. "When I took the oath of office, I thanked my lucky stars that I had become President in the post-Cold War period."

"There are no eras that are not dangerous, Mr. President."

"Keep me abreast. I mean it this time. I have to make a painful call."

"Good luck, Mr. President," said Harold Smith.

WITHIN THE HOUR, America's nuclear arsenal was placed on the highest state of readiness: Defcon One.

This was not lost on the Kremlin, who then ordered their Strategic Rocket Force to go to the next state of readiness. High Red.

When informed that there was no higher or redder state of readiness above the one in which they had already been placed, the president of Russia belched and said, "I will get back to you on this quandary...."

And the planet Earth spun on while, orbiting it, a closed ball of stealth-colored material waited for the next signal from its unknown master.

33

When they landed at Sheremetevo II Airport in Moscow, Remo Williams told Colonel Radomir Rushenko, "Have this thing refueled and ready."

"Ready for what?"

"The flight back to the States."

"You are going back to the States? This is impossible. It will not be permitted."

"You're our insurance that it will be," warned Remo, leaving his seat.

The Master of Sinanju accompanied Colonel Rushenko to make the arrangements while Remo fed kopecks into an airport pay phone. After a half hour of trying, he failed to get through to America.

Returning to the aircraft, he informed Chiun of this unhappy fact.

"We will call from a city possessing a telephone that works," Chiun said, eyeing Colonel Rushenko unhappily.

"We should have never become friends," Rushenko lamented. "When we were enemies, we had motivation. Our phones worked. Our armies were feared and our space program was the envy of the entire world."

"The Communist world," said Remo.

"The entire world."

"Who went to the moon and who didn't?" countered Remo.

"The moon is only a rock. We had our eyes upon Mars."

"Why Mars?"

"It is the Red planet, is it not?"

"No," interjected Chiun. "In my language, it is Hwa-Song, the Fire Planet."

Colonel Rushenko shrugged. "It is the same thing. I can tell you this now because the world may soon end, and if it does not, Russians will not be going to Mars without space vehicles anyway. But when the U.S. achieved the moon landing, a twenty-year plan was drawn up to claim Mars for USSR. It would have been the ultimate expression of Soviet technological superiority. Anyone can land on the barren moon only three days away. But Mars, it is an authentic planet. We would have seized it, controlled the cosmic high ground and mocked you from its red glory."

"What happened to this twenty-year plan?" asked Chiun.

Rushenko shrugged. "What always happens. The quotas were not achieved, and it became a thirty-year plan, a forty and so on until it was forgotten."

"You can have Mars, too. I'm sick of Mars," Remo growled.

"No one will go to Mars now. It is a pity. All our dreams are rust and dust. Yours as well as mine."

"Save it for the funeral," said Remo.

"Whose?"

"Yours if you don't get off the subject."

Colonel Rushenko subsided. The Yak took off, heading west to Europe and the first refueling stop that had a working telephone.

34

Dr. Cosmo Pagan was in his element. For some, that element was the earth. Others, the sky. Still others, the oceans of the world.

Cosmo Pagan's element was nothing less than the media.

The phones would not stop ringing. It didn't seem to matter to anyone that he gave confused and contradictory theories to the strange events that were troubling the blue earth.

It certainly didn't matter to Cosmo Pagan. People read only one newspaper a day these days—if that. And they watched only one newscast a day. Since most people were creatures of habit, they stuck with what they liked.

Thus, Cosmo Pagan was simultaneously informing newspaper readers and TV viewers that the inexplicable events dominating the headlines were a direct consequence of ozone depletion, random asteroid strikes and the possible impact of cometary fragments from a hitherto-undiscovered invisible comet bypassing Earth.

The comet theory seemed to go over biggest. At least, Pagan got the most media requests to tell the world about the dangers of passing comets.

He got other calls, too. A zillion lecture offers. A bunch of new book offers. PBS was on the horn, too. They wanted to do a special on life on other planets. It was Cosmo Pagan's favorite topic. He had become an exobiologist chiefly because until proof of actual extraterrestrial life came along, he could just make stuff up. He didn't even need factoids.

Cosmo accepted all offers. Except one.

"Dr. Pagan," an anxious man asked. "I can't identify myself or my employer, but we're looking for a man just like you. You'd be our in-house consultant and company spokesman."

Cosmo Pagan didn't need to know the who or the what. He had only one concern. "How much?"

"A million a year."

"I *love* that number! It's a deal."

"Great," the suddenly relieved voice said. "But understand this will be an exclusive. You couldn't speak publicly on any subject in your field. In fact, we insist that you immediately halt all public statements on any subject until the contract is drawn up. Especially this asteroid and ozone scare-talk."

"Out of the question. I don't do exclusives. Goodbye."

The man kept calling back, upping his offer. But Cosmo Pagan was no fool. If his face wasn't before the public, he had no public. No public, no publicity. No publicity, no career. He stopped taking the nameless man's calls and got down to the serious business of informing his public.

This time Pagan asked that his wife, Venus, interview him for CNN. In fact, he demanded it. The last guy had asked hard questions. And since Venus Pa-

gan was still pretty sharp looking for her age, it was
nice to show her off once in a while.

The interview was conducted in his private observatory by satellite hookup. Cut down on commuting
costs that way.

"Dr. Pagan..."

"Call me Cosmo. After all, we *are* man and satellite."

Venus Pagan smiled with professional coolness. "In
your view, are comets dangerous?"

"When Halley came around in 1910, a lot of people thought so. They threw end-of-the-world-comet
parties. Spectrographic analyses of the comet's com-
position showed traces of cyanogen gas, and for a
while people worried our planet would be gassed to
death when it passed through Halley's tail. Gas-mask
sales boomed. But long-period comets like Halley and
Hale-Bopp don't come very close to earth spacially
speaking."

It was in the middle of his dissertation that the first
satellite images of the Baikonur Cosmodrome disaster were broadcast. It was supposed to be a military
secret. But in the post-Cold War world, commercial
satellites had the same global overviews as spy satellites. The brief bidding war for the pictures was won
by CNN. The photos were rushed to the hot studio in
midtelecast.

"Dr. Pagan. I mean, Cosmo."

"Call me honey, angel."

"We've just been handed satellite images taken of
Baikonur Cosmodrome in Russian Kazakhstan. It's
been scorched in three places. These images resemble
satellite photos we've seen of the BioBubble and *Re-*

liant catastrophes. Can you shed any light on this latest event?"

Dr. Pagan accepted the photos, which were also broadcast in a floating graphic insert beside his head. He got very pale very fast.

"I might be mistaken," he said, "but there appear to be three impact sites—if that is what they are—which suggests to me cometary fragments. Asteroids don't travel in packs."

"No comet fragments were found here in the U.S.," Venus probed gently.

"This may be a broken-comet phenomenon we are witnessing. Understand that Earth is always revolving. As was the case with Jupiter when those fragments struck. Though they entered the Jovian atmosphere in a straight line, they impacted in a string along the planet's surface because Jupiter moved between each impact. A similar string of eight ancient impact craters across the Plains states has recently come to light. They're lakes now."

"If this is a broken comet falling to earth, could other pieces be speeding toward us now?"

"Yes," Dr. Pagan admitted unhappily, "they could. And there's no telling where they could impact. Even on me."

He looked sick at the very thought, and his fear was not lost on the American public he sought to reassure.

"Did you know that the number of scientists scanning the heavens for deadly asteroids is about the size of the staff of a McDonald's restaurant?" he added in an uneasy voice.

AT FOLCROFT, Dr. Harold W. Smith was baffled. He was running on sheer nerve and Maalox as he grappled with the threat that seemed now to be directed at the space programs of two nations.

He had told the President that the third strike would suggest a pattern. It did. One that suggested a rival space-faring nation.

That left the Japanese, the French and the Chinese. Of these possibilities, the Chinese seemed the most likely culprits. But the technology—whatever it was—seemed beyond Chinese capabilities. This, in turn, made Smith flash on the Japanese. They were working on a space-shuttle program of their own. The first test flight had ended with the HYFLEX prototype sinking into the Sea of Japan. It was possible that that failure caused Nippon Space to turn to Russia's shuttle fleet for lift.

But what would their motive for attacking the U.S. be?

Smith was reconsidering French Ariane involvement when Remo called from Budapest with a possible answer.

"Have you looked into the Paraguay thing yet?" he asked.

"What Paraguay thing?" countered Smith.

"People at Baikonur told us a Paraguay company hired that last Russian shuttle flight."

"Paraguay?"

"Want me to spell it?" asked Remo.

"No, and why are you shouting?"

"Habit," said Remo, lowering his voice. "The company is called ParaSol. One word. Capital *P* as in 'Paraguay.' Capital *S-o-l*. That's all I know."

Smith attacked his keyboard. "I am researching it now."

Remo's voice took on an awed quality. "Smitty, we were on ground zero when that thing hit three times."

"What did you see?"

"A hot time. Looked like a giant magnifying glass scorched the ground."

Smith paused. "You think it was solar?"

"We saw a sun dog before it struck."

"Solar..." said Smith.

"Mean anything to you?"

"A breakthrough in solar power could explain such a thing. The extreme, concentrated heat. The relatively compact size of the orbital device. If it takes its energy from the sun, it would need little in the way of on-board power."

"My money's on solar."

On Smith's screen, up popped a block of data.

"I have something on ParaSol," he said.

"What's it say?"

Harold Smith's voice sank. "The data is in Spanish. I will have to have it translated."

"Get to it."

"Hold the line, please," Smith replied, trying to type while cradling the blue handset against his shoulder and right arm. His rimless glasses slid off his patrician nose, and he miskeyed something, erasing his entire screen.

"Damn."

"What now?" asked Remo. "I gotta go soon. They're about done refueling the Yak."

"Where is your next refueling stop?"

"Wherever they'll let us set down. We're not particular."

"Call me from there."

"Will do," said Remo, hanging up.

Smith went to work recovering the data. In the middle of the automatic translation, his system alerted him of another broadcast of consequence. It came on automatically as Smith had programmed it to.

He found himself watching Dr. Cosmo Pagan lecturing the nation on comets.

"All comets come from a stellar marvel called the Oort Cloud way beyond our solar system. Our sun's gravitational pull yanks them toward it, and they slingshot around back into deep space. As they approach the orb of day, the pressure of solar winds on these dirty snowballs—as we astronomers like to classify them—creates the long ghostly tail that is so wondrous to behold. Hale-Bopp's tail promises to be the most spectacular of the century once it reemerges from its solar sleep. We are living in very interesting times, galactically speaking, with all these near-Earth objects booming by and falling to Earth."

Smith was logging off when the camera went to the woman interviewing Pagan.

She was an attractive, fortyish brunette. But Smith's bleary gray eyes weren't on her face, but on the identifying chyron at the bottom of the screen.

It read Venus Mango-Pagan.

The name Venus Mango rang a clear bell in Smith's steel-trap mind. Returning to his system, he punched in the name and hit Search.

He got his answer immediately. The name Venus Mango had surfaced on the phone records of Bio-Bubble director Amos Bulla a number of times. All incoming calls. None outgoing. Many calls over a period of four years.

Smith brought up the file with precise finger pecks.

The calls went back to the time the BioBubble had changed from a prototype Mars colony to its later, ecological-research incarnation. Exactly.

Smith's earlier search had revealed that Venus Mango was a CNN science correspondent. That simple fact had eliminated her as a possible BioBubble backer. Journalists are not usually wealthy people.

With a frown, Smith saw that he had been too hasty in his judgment. He had not delved deeply enough to learn that Venus Mango was the latest wife of Dr. Cosmo Pagan.

Energized by his discovery, Smith went in search of Dr. Pagan's financial records.

He found a flock of bank accounts, one of which showed large wire transfers going back to the Bio-Bubble change of ownership. All to BioBubble Inc. The name on the account was Ruber Mavors Limited. Red Mars.

"Dr. Cosmo Pagan controls the BioBubble now," said Harold Smith in a voice of dead-level certainty.

He called back the CNN report.

Dr. Pagan was saying, "Of course I don't yet rule out a floating ozone hole. I'm an exobiologist, not a prophet. As for the Martian theory, I'm not partial to it because I like to believe that if there are Martians, they'd be friendly toward us Earthlings. Are we not going through the same eco-crisis that ravaged their beautiful world eons ago?"

Pagan smiled like a man in love.

"Still, you can never tell. In the interest of covering all permutations, I would like to share some interesting Martian trivia, if I may. The Soviets were the first to attempt to soft-land a probe on Mars. Their

Mars 3 and *Mars 6* spacecraft both mysteriously stopped transmitting before touching down on the Martian landscape. No one knows why. At the time, some thought mischievous Martians were responsible. *Viking I* transmitted back pictures of a Martian boulder that seemed to have the Roman letter *B* chiseled into it. Since then, we've captured some very puzzling images, including pyramids and what looked like a great Sphinx-like stone face looking coldly at us from the stark Martian surface.''

"Do you yourself believe in Martians, sweetie?"

"If there are sentient beings on the Red Planet," Cosmo Pagan said solemnly, "they may have been driven underground by some great cataclysm such as an asteroid strike or the depletion of their own ozone shield. And these mysterious letters being reported in the sky may be a friendly warning to us Earth men. One day soon, we should get up there and find out."

"He's trying to throw America off the track," said Smith. "And whatever he's up to, it's pushing the planet toward nuclear confrontation. And this fool does not even suspect it."

Smith watched the segment to the bitter end, wishing he could drive his bony fist into Pagan's smirking face.

He was not normally subject to such violent impulses, but there was nothing he could do until Remo checked in again.

One positive thing had emerged. He now had a direction to point his Destroyer in. And a target.

35

Over Paris, they were refused clearance to land, and while they loitered over Orly International, French Mirage fighters chased them away.

Madrid wouldn't take them.

Nor would Lisbon.

Finally, as a humanitarian gesture, the British cleared the Russian Yak-90 to land at London's Gatwick Airport.

The landing gear touched the tarmac just as the fuel-starved engines went cold. They rolled to an unpowered stop and were instantly surrounded by crack SAS commandos and ordered to evacuate the aircraft, for they were all being detained by the crown.

This prospect raised Colonel Rushenko's lagging spirits considerably. "Do you hear? We are being detained!"

"Don't think it doesn't mean you're not going to the boneyard of history," Remo warned.

"If you kill me here, you will be arrested for a capital crime on British soil. I have done nothing to you."

"You ordered us liquidated," reminded Chiun, looking out at the emergency vehicles, behind which crouched the dark-bereted SAS with their Sterlings and their flat pistols.

"Did you know that the British have a very secret agency called the Source?" Rushenko offered.

"They can't thread a needle without sticking themselves," Remo said dismissively.

"Oh. You did know . . ."

"For years."

"What is your secret agency called?"

"It's not called anything. It doesn't have a name."

"That is a very smart agency. I only wish I had realized this option sooner, then you would never have found me."

Remo was going from window to window, looking outside over each wing. Challenger tanks were now blocking the Yak's nose and tail so it couldn't move in any direction.

"I'm not getting off this plane," Remo said after sizing up the situation.

"Someone must tell these cretins that we are charged with saving the world," said Chiun.

"That, too," said Remo. "But I was thinking that once we're off this plane, the only way home is on another plane. One with stewardesses. I'm not going through *that* again."

"What is wrong with stewardesses?" asked Colonel Rushenko.

"They're going through a phase right now."

"Phase?"

"They want to pop my buttons."

"That is a very peculiar phase."

Remo and Chiun huddled, and when they returned to the seat where Colonel Rushenko crouched so his head was not a target for SAS marksmen, Remo announced, "You're surrendering."

"I am not to be killed?"

"That's between you and the Brits. You're surrendering, taking the blame and telling the British all they need to hear so they let us fly on."

"What could I possibly tell them that would convince them to do this?" Rushenko wondered aloud.

Remo cocked a thumb at the Master of Sinanju standing behind him wearing a satisfied expression.

"That *he's* a passenger."

"I see," said Colonel Rushenko. "Of course, the British know the Master of Sinanju works for America. That may very well impress these people, who are not easily impressed."

Chiun smiled thinly. "This was my idea. For it is said that the highest master is he who does not need to fight."

"It is a brilliant solution," Rushenko said, visibly relieved.

"You're only saying that because you think you'll live," said Remo.

"The British will not kill me, for I will remind them that we are now ideological friends."

"You may tell them what you wish," said Chiun, stepping aside so that the Russian could scuttle to the main exit.

Remo slapped Colonel Rushenko on the back between the shoulder blades so hard that Rushenko's breath was knocked out of his lungs. He had to clutch the air-stairs rail going down. He managed to make it to the ground, hands held high, while he waited for SAS commandos to jump him.

Which they did with typical British reserve. They slapped him to the tarmac, chipping a front tooth. His hands were pinned behind his back, and he was handcuffed and dragged to the shadow of an armored BMP.

There, he gave in to interrogation so quickly that he wasn't believed.

"I am telling you I am in the company of the Master of Sinanju, who works for America, as I know you know."

"Likely story," a brush-mustached SAS major clipped.

"It is the truth."

A decision was made to storm the plane. Four commandos. They went up the air-stairs, paused at the cabin door, which was still hanging open, and tossed in flash grenades.

They went in firing.

And they came out flying, minus their weapons and wearing their birthday suits, to tumble all the way back to the ground in complete humiliation.

"I told you I spoke true," Colonel Rushenko said after the commandos were retrieved by armored car. "Do you believe me now?"

Reluctantly the SAS major did. The tanks were ordered off the runway, and the Yak was refueled.

It returned to the skies approximately the time Colonel Rushenko breathed a sigh of relief that kept on going, much to his growing astonishment. He couldn't stop exhaling, for some reason. He felt lightheaded. His vision darkened.

By the time his captors realized he had succumbed to heart failure, there was nothing anyone could do for him. He was quite blue. And then quite dead. Quite.

OVER THE ATLANTIC, Remo snapped his fingers.

"Forgot to phone Smith."

"Emperor Smith may wait. It will gladden his heart that we have returned to safeguard his beleaguered shores."

"Hope he dug up something useful, or we went a long way for nothing."

"Smith's oracles are almost infallible."

"Speaking of failure, Colonel Rushenko should be worm food about now."

"If you struck the Blow of Delayed Peace correctly..."

"Right between the shoulder blades. He'll never know what snuffed him."

"It serves him right for ordering my death," Chiun sniffed. "It was inconsiderate, not to mention foolhardy."

"Wake me up when we're on the ground." And Remo dropped off to catch some much-needed rest.

Somewhere over the dark Atlantic, he awoke to find the Master of Sinanju looking out into the night sky.

"Star gazing?" he asked.

"I am watching for the sun dragon."

"Feel free."

"Sun dragons and arrow stars are harbingers of disaster, Remo."

"Show me a time when there weren't disasters. Comets don't affect events on earth. That's as squirrelly as astrology."

"Spoken like a true Virgo," sniffed Chiun. His nose was to the glass, his hazel eyes questing.

A thin line of light against the night caused his eyes to open up. Then they subsided.

"What was that?" asked Remo.

"Only a dung star."

"A what?"

"You would call it a meteor."

"Why is it called a dung star?"

"Because it is known to Koreans that so-called meteors are but the falling dung of true stars. And not to be confused with sun dragons."

"Korean astronomy sounds as screwy as astrology."

"You will speak differently should you confront the sun dragon."

"Never happen."

Chiun's eyes became reflective. "Remo, you asked me if there were any legends attending the reign of Master Salbyol. There was one."

"I'm listening."

"It was prophesied that when the sun dragon next returned, the Master at that time would ascend into the Void to do battle with the awesome beast."

"Reigning Master or just Master?" asked Remo.

"The prophecy omitted that stipulation. But obviously Salbyol had to have meant Reigning Master. For he is the more important of the two."

"So you figure you're going to climb into the Void to fight a comet?" said Remo.

"Sun dragon. But that is not what worries me. For those who enter the Void, as you know, do not return to the living." Chiun's voice was hollow. "Remo, I am not yet prepared to die."

"How did Salbyol come up with this prediction?"

"How else? By consulting the stars."

Remo snorted. "If Korean astrology is anything like Korean astronomy, you don't have a thing to worry about."

Chiun grew deep of voice. "You are wrong. For I have felt the hot breath of the sun dragon, and you have felt it, too,'' said the Master of Sinanju, padding off the the rear of the cabin to be alone with his unspoken thoughts.

Remo let him be. He figured they'd both cross that bridge when it presented itself to them.

36

At the SPACETRACK nerve center in Cheyenne Mountain, Colorado, all eyes, electronic or otherwise, were on Object 617, which was just sweeping down from the North Pole on its periodic polar path.

This time its orbit would take it over western Europe. Its last two orbits had covered the flat heart of the Asian republics on Russia's eastern flank, where SPACETRACK had no ground cameras and NATO had no eyes.

It was while Object 617 was approaching France that its radar signature abruptly shifted.

"Major, it's moving," a radar technician said.

Any eye that wasn't on Object 617 now shifted to track it on the giant projection screen with its Mercator projection of Earth's orbital envelope. Over eight thousand objects, ranging from one yard in size to space junk as small as a pea, each tagged by a green ID number, were displayed and accounted for. Object 617 had been designated a highest priority, and its radar blip was flashing red.

Amid the sea of phosphor green objects, it stood out like a bloodshot eye.

Object 617 was changing position. Its path was taking it toward the U.S. Eastern Seaboard.

"That thing is maneuverable," the major growled.

"It's also coming into GEODSS acquisition range, sir."

GEODSS was the ground-camera backup to SPACETRACK's radar net. Grabbing a dedicated line, the major put in a call to his counterpart at GEODSS.

"See if you can grab it," the SPACTRACK major told the GEODSS major.

"Will do, Major."

At GEODSS headquarters, secure international phone lines were worked until the word came back.

"Finland has it, Major. The picture is coming in now."

GEODSS had its own giant screen, and the feed displayed the mysterious orbital object as it shifted over the Atlantic.

"Will it pass over the continental U.S.?" the GEODSS major barked.

A technician shook his head. "Not this orbit. But on the next, for sure."

"How long?"

"Give it ninety minutes."

"I gotta tell the President," said the GEODSS major, grabbing another dedicated line whose plastic contours felt slick under his perspiring palm.

THE CALL FROM GEODSS did not go directly to the White House. It had to go through channels. After twenty minutes, an Air Force general at the Pentagon told the secretary of the air force, who called the secretary of defense, who took the intelligence to the President personally. Getting through District of Columbia traffic ate another twenty precious minutes.

The President sat heavily in his chair in the Oval Office at the end of the defense secretary's grim recitation.

"Will it pass over Washington?" he croaked.

"It can."

"Do we know what it is yet?"

"No. It's just a dark ball. But in its present orbital orientation, we can see only the Earth-facing side of it."

"We're going to have to shoot it down," said the President. "We can't wait for it to strike again. We have to shoot it down."

"We can't," snapped the secretary of defense.

"What do you mean, can't?"

"Not without starting a war with the Russians."

"If it's a Russian satellite, the war has already started."

"We don't know that."

"If it's not Russian, then why should they care?"

The secretary of defense wore the face of a man who has discovered himself trapped in an inescapable box.

"The technology exists. We have an antisatellite missile that can be rigged up for launching from a high-flying F-15. Or maybe it's an F-16. We just have to attach a special launch rack. But deployment of weapons in space is specifically prohibited by the START treaty."

"It is?"

"Absolutely. The Russians are cosignatories on that treaty. If we violate it, all of space may be militarized. And given the shifting geopolitical sands over there, don't think there aren't a pack of Kremlin hard-liners only too happy to start a new arms race in space."

"Maybe that's it," the President breathed.

"Sir?"

"Maybe they want to provoke us into attacking this doomsday satellite. To get us to violate START so they can militarize space."

"It's a theory...."

The President took his graying head in his hands and hung it in agony. "All we have is theories. And the doomsday clock is ticking. What if they're out to attack Washington?"

"If they are, we're sitting ducks here. There's no defense except a preemptive strike." The secretary of defense paused and in a voice made thick by controlled emotion, asked, "Mr. President, are you ordering such a strike at this time?"

The President of the United States stared at his own dazed reflection in the desk surface a very long time before he opened his mouth to answer.

IN MOSCOW, Major-General Iyona Stankevitch of the FSK put down his third glass of vodka and buzzed his secretary.

"Bring me the Cosmic Secret file. At once."

Then he downed another stiff belt. He intended to drink all the vodka possible in the few short hours he and the world had left to enjoy.

37

LaGuardia wouldn't take the Yak-90. Nor would Kennedy International Airport.

"Divert to Boston," Remo told the nervous Russian pilot.

"We have barely the fuel to make it to Boston," he protested.

"Perfect."

"Why is that perfect, crazy one?"

"Once you tell them we're out of fuel, they've gotta let us land," explained Remo.

"They could force us to circle until we crash."

"You're thinking of the Russian response. This is America."

Over Logan International Airport, they orbited for what seemed to be an eternity.

"Look Remo, there is our home!" Chiun squeaked.

Remo looked out the window. Below, Quincy Bay sat gray and flat under overcast skies.

"I don't see it," said Remo, not really wanting to.

"See the very blue house?"

"How could I miss it? It's Superman blue."

"Follow the winding road north."

Remo did. And there was the fieldstone monster Chiun had dubbed Castle Sinanju.

"Too bad we can't parachute out," he said.

"We will be out of fuel soon," Chiun remarked.

The number-two engine stalled out at exactly that point.

Remo rushed to the cabin. "What's going on?"

"We are out of fuel," the pilot reported.

"You were supposed to tell the tower before we ran out, not after."

"I am dizzy from all this circling. I forgot."

"Can you put us down okay?"

"If the other engine does not conk."

In the next moment it did.

"What do I do now?" the pilot moaned.

"Can this lame duck glide in?"

"It is a jet. It glides exactly like a brick. Not at all."

"Then ditch," said Remo, flinging himself back into the cabin.

They came down in Quincy Bay with flaps down and the Russian pilot praying as the choppy water skimmed under their settling wings.

Remo had moved to the cabin's rear, knowing that a nose-in landing would demolish the front of the plane but not necessarily the rear. Chiun stood with him, expectant.

It was a good theory. In practice, the Yak pulled up at the last minute and pancaked, breaking the fuselage exactly in the middle like a loaf of Italian bread.

Cold seawater rushed in. Remo and Chiun let it slosh over them. Not that they had much choice. G-forces kept them from moving.

The Yak's tail sank first. They let the water take them in its cold, unforgiving grasp. The shock to their systems was like being seized by a clamping vise of ice.

The tail struck the seafloor, creating a cloud of dark sediment. They swam out, finding the Russian pilot kicking and flailing aimlessly.

Remo pulled him to the surface, where all three men treaded water for as long as it took them to recharge their lungs with cold oxygen.

The Russian looked around with stunned eyes. "I am in America?"

"Congratulations," said Remo.

"Does this mean I am not to die?"

"No," said Chiun. "We have to kill you."

"Yes," said Remo. "You got us here alive. You get to live. Just keep your nose clean."

"Right now I am only concerned with keeping it warm. The rest of me, too."

Chiun struck out for the shore. Remo tugged the Russian along and, once on the ice-crusted beach, sent him on his way with a shove.

"Remember, you never saw us," Remo warned.

"I care only about filling my belly with chizburgers and registering for warfare."

"It's called welfare," Remo said wearily.

TEN MINUTES LATER, Remo and Chiun were entering Castle Sinanju.

"Good thing I talked you out of taking your steamer trunks, huh, Little Father?" Remo said to Chiun as he stripped off his icy T-shirt.

"I was very wise to make the correct decision. Your counsel had nothing to do with it," returned Chiun before he disappeared into another room to change.

Remo had the kitchen telephone and was putting in a call to Folcroft.

Harold Smith answered breathlessly. "Where are you?"

"Home," Remo said casually.

"Home?"

"You'll read about it in the morning paper. We had to ditch in Quincy Bay."

Smith made a strangled sound. "I have made progress," he said after regaining his composure.

"Good."

"But not on the Paraguay angle. On ParaSol, a shell company, which shut down only two days ago. I have a search spider tracing its parent company through international data links. In the meantime, I have discovered who was funding the BioBubble."

"Yeah?"

"Dr. Cosmo Pagan."

Remo kicked ice off his toes. "How does he figure into this?"

"That is your assignment, Remo. I have correlated Pagan's theories. No matter what he predicts, he always returns to the Martian hypothesis. It is clear to me he is generating a media smoke screen for reasons of his own."

"Think Pagan's controlling it?"

"Until I have a firm lead on the ParaSol connection, it is the only avenue open to us. Remo, go to Tucson and interrogate Pagan. The BioBubble has been in financial difficulty since he took control. He may have had it destroyed for insurance reasons."

"Doesn't explain the *Reliant*," Remo challenged.

"Pagan is antishuttle."

"Okay," Remo said slowly. "That doesn't explain Baikonur."

"The Russian space-shuttle fleet was hangared there."

"How antishuttle can a guy be?"

"Pagan believes in a Mars mission, Remo. My information is that he suffers from a rare form of bone cancer. His days are numbered. It may be he wanted to accelerate a Mars mission. In some warped way, Pagan could see a Mars landing as his final professional achievement and his cosmic legacy."

"Sounds wacky."

"Move quickly. Moscow has placed its nuclear forces on the highest state of alert. And Washington is responding in kind."

"You know, this reminds me a lot of that trouble a few years back when the ozone layer was getting holes knocked in it and the Russians thought it was us trying to fry their missiles."

"I had that same thought. It is another example of how dangerous technological breakthroughs can be in the nuclear age."

"We're on our way to Tucson," said Remo, then hung up.

The Master of Sinanju came down from upstairs, wearing a splendid bone white kimono with black piping.

"Nice traveling outfit," Remo complimented.

"It is not for travel," said Chiun.

"Then you'd better change. It's back to Arizona for us."

"Smith has work?"

"Cosmo Pagan is Ruber Mavors. Smith wants us to shake him until something falls out."

"At least it will be warm in Arizona," said Chiun.

"Let's hope it doesn't get *too* warm," Remo responded.

38

Dr. Cosmo Pagan had friends in high places. And not only the stars and the comets of the galaxy.

He had friends in NASA, despite his critical opinions. As well as in the Air Force and other organizations where the heavens and what went on in them was of professional interest.

Someone at Cheyenne Mountain called to whisper, "There's a mystery object in low Earth orbit."

"Is it cometary?"

"No. Man-made."

"Oh," said Dr. Pagan, who only cared about man-made space objects if they were going some place interesting. Earth orbit was like taking a cruise to nowhere. Literally.

"It'll pass over the continental U.S. tonight. If it stays on its current path, it will overfly your area."

"Why should I care?" asked Dr. Pagan in a bored voice.

"Because SPACETRACK thinks this is the thing that hit the *Reliant*."

The bored quality dropped from Pagan's manner like clothes falling off a hooker.

"Can you slip me coordinates?"

The coordinates came over the line in a hushed voice, and then the line went as dead as outer space.

Dr. Pagan rushed to his thirty-inch Schmidt-Cassegrain refractor, punched the right ascension and declination into the on-board guidance computer, hit the "Go-to" command and waited patiently while the control motor toiled as it oriented the tube toward the northern quadrant of the night sky, the observatory dome rotating so the slit lined up with the scope.

He was very interested in seeing what had caused the BioBubble to collapse into viscous glass and steel. Very.

While he waited, he pulled a candy bar from one of his jacket pockets without looking. Absently he bit the wrapper off and chewed off a hunk of chocolate, caramel and nougat.

"Nothing like a Mars bar," he murmured. "Unless it's a Milky Way."

39

Finding Dr. Cosmo Pagan's Tucson home was easier than Remo had ever imagined. Harold Smith told him it was, on a secluded hill off Route 10, south of the city.

The house was shielded from view by ponderosa pine and cottonwoods. But the private observatory showed clearly on the hill. It was as red as Mars, and it was crisscrossed by black lines suggesting Martian canals.

"If this isn't the place, I'll eat my hat," said Remo.

"You do not wear a hat," said Chiun.

"Good point. Boy, if there were Martians living among us, I'd expect them to live in a creepy place just like this," said Remo as they pulled into the long circular driveway.

They got out. Lights burned throughout the house. It was painted a very sedate maroon that looked almost brown in the dark. A carport protected a red Saturn and a vintage Mercury Cougar.

"Front approach works for me," said Remo.

Chiun girded his jet black kimono skirts, saying, "I fear no Martians."

At the door, they simply rang the bell.

Mrs. Pagan answered, took one look at Remo's FBI ID and said, "He's in the observatory. Quarter mile back in the woods on the hill. You can't miss it."

"You got that right," said Remo.

As they got back into the car, Mrs. Pagan called out, "Will you tell him those people from QNM keep calling?"

"Sure."

"Tell him they doubled the consulting fee again."

"Sure thing," said Remo.

The observatory looked even more like the planet Mars as they walked toward it. Its scarlet hue glowed under the light of the moon. The top was a bluish white, like a polar icecap.

"This guy worships Mars like the ancient Greeks," said Remo.

"The Greek did not call it Mars, but Ares," Chiun said.

"What did the Koreans call it again?"

"Hwa-Song. The Fire Planet."

"Good name."

"It is also considered an ill omen when in the sky."

"I'll keep that in mind," Remo muttered as they picked their way through a stand of cottonwoods.

The shuttered slit was open in the great red dome, and they could see the black end of the big telescope peering up at the night sky.

"Looks like Pagan is Mars gazing. I say we just walk in."

"You may walk in. I will enter another way," said Chiun.

"Be my guest."

With that, Chiun was absorbed by the surrounding murk.

The door, Remo discovered, was not locked. It gave at his touch.

Carefully Remo eased into the cool, dark dome, all his senses alert. He sensed only one presence. That made it simple.

Letting his eyes adjust to the dim interior, Remo saw the long telescope tube resolve itself first. Then the man seated on a tall stool at the narrow end of the telescope.

Remo was approaching when, without warning, Dr. Pagan suddenly recoiled from the eyepiece of his telescope.

The stool upset. Remo moved in, caught man and stool, righting them while Dr. Cosmo Pagan flailed his corduroy-clad arms wildly.

"Easy," said Remo.

Pagan grabbed his chest and pumped air into his lungs. "I just saw—saw—"

"What?"

A squeaky voice from above said, "Me."

Remo looked up. "What are you doing way up there, Chiun?"

"Looking down."

And the Master of Sinanju leaped from the open aperture and slid down the telescope tube on both feet to alight with the ease and grace of a settling black moth.

"I thought a space alien was looking back at me," Cosmo Pagan muttered as he dusted off his arms. "Who are you two?"

"FBI," said Remo.

"What does the FBI want with me?" Pagan said, frowning.

Remo peered through the eyepiece. "I don't see Mars."

"I don't always look at the Red Planet, you know. And you're both trespassing. Please leave. I don't do autographs. It's beneath me."

Taking his eyes from the scope, Remo looked Pagan dead in the eye and said, "We know you're Ruber Mavors."

Pagan swallowed hard and said, "That's Latin for 'Red Planet.'"

"It's the name you go by when you're pumping money into the BioBubble. We need to know why."

"I don't have to tell you anything."

"Wrong answer," said Remo. And the Master of Sinanju reached up to take Pagan by the back of his neck. Chiun constricted his bony, long-nailed fingers.

Cosmo Pagan sank to his knees before Remo, his face contorting and turning red as a beet. "I'm a world-renowned astronomer and exobiologist," he gasped.

"Right now," Remo said, "you're doing a pretty good impersonation of a Martian."

Pagan's features turned rubbery. "You can't do this to me."

"Why not?"

"It's un-American. I'm a cultural icon. I have tenure."

"Why'd you take over the BioBubble? Let's start there."

"Someone had to. They were jettisoning the Mars-colony phase of the project. It was the only thing keeping Mars before the public eye. I had to save it."

"The Mars-colony idea went south when the Russian space program cratered," Remo countered.

"You're thinking in human terms. In geologic time, a Mars landing is just around the corner. It's just that we twentieth-century molecule machines won't live to see it.''

"Speak for yourself, white," said Chiun, relenting enough that Pagan returned to a pinkish complexion.

"I got behind it to keep the dream alive. No matter what it took."

"Including pumping in oxygen and hot pizza?" said Remo.

"Whatever it takes. It was my project and my money."

"And when it became a laughingstock, you just fried it."

"That wasn't me!"

"Prove it."

"I don't have the kind of money and technology to put that thing up there," Pagan protested.

"What thing?" asked Chiun thinly.

Pagan swallowed.

"Hah!" said Chiun, squeezing harder. "The truth, Man of Mars."

Pagan got even redder. His veins began to pop until his face started to display an unmistakable Martian cast. A Mars bar fell out of his pocket.

"That is the truth," he gurgled. "All I know about the thing up there is what a friend at SPACETRACK told me. NORAD thinks it's an enemy satellite of some kind."

Remo looked past Dr. Pagan's reddening features to Chiun's severe ones, and they both came to the same conclusion based on a reading of Pagan's hammering vital signs and inability to withstand pain.

"He's telling the truth," said Remo.

"Of course I'm telling the truth. Why would I destroy my own dream?"

"We heard a Paraguayan company paid to have that thing launched through the Russian shuttle. Know anything about that?"

"Did you know *Buran* really means 'blizzard'?" said Dr. Pagan.

"What does that have to do with anything?" Remo growled.

"I get paid heavy consulting fees for spouting neat factoids like that," said Pagan, retrieving the fallen Mars bar and pocketing it.

"Not interested," said Remo. "Let him go, Little Father."

"Thank you," said Dr. Pagan, adjusting his corduroy jacket and giving his red turtleneck a shake.

Remo eyed the jersey and remembered the Shield secretary in Moscow who'd tried to kill him with an AK-47.

"Ever hear of Shield?" he asked.

"No. I've heard of the ozone shield, though."

"How about Shchit?" asked Chiun.

"Who hasn't? Although I personally shun language like that."

"He never heard of Shield," said Remo.

"If that's all you two want, I want to see that orbital device for myself. It's due to fly by pretty soon."

"Be our guest. We have better things to do."

"Up Uranus," muttered Dr. Pagan, climbing atop his stool and planting his right eye to the telescope eyepiece. By the time Remo and Chiun reached the door, he was all but oblivious to his surroundings.

"By the way," Remo called from the open door, "your wife asked us to give you a message."

"What's that?" Pagan asked absently.

"The QNM people keep calling. They doubled your fee again."

"Tell them I'm not interested."

"You tell them. We're FBI, not messengers," said Remo, shutting the door.

They walked back to the car in silence and got into it.

On the way back to the highway, Remo said to Chiun, "Everywhere we go, we hit a dead end."

"We should be looking for Martians."

"If this keeps up, I might start agreeing with you. But I still think we're dealing with something solar."

"When are you ever correct?"

"Some of the time," Remo said as they pulled onto the highway and raced back toward Tucson and a flight he wasn't looking forward to.

40

At SPACETRACK headquarters in Cheyenne Mountain, they watched Object 617 skim over the Eastern Seaboard in silence. And then gave a collective sigh of relief.

No one's sigh was greater than the U.S. President's slow, hot exhalation of released tension.

He had been about to have the thing shot down when CURE Director Smith had called to reveal that he now suspected Dr. Cosmo Pagan of being the mind behind the device.

"Pagan? I can't believe it!" the President had said.

"It is unproven. But my people are on the way to deal with him."

"They won't kill him, will they?"

"His survival depends upon his complicity."

"He's a very popular guy. I read all his books."

"I will keep you informed, Mr. President."

Leaving the Lincoln Bedroom, the President had returned to the Oval Office and his defense secretary. "We stand down. For now."

"I can't disagree with that decision," the defense secretary said, visibly relieved.

Object 617 passed harmlessly overhead, and World War III was placed on temporary hold. Even if the planet never suspected it.

When it came back on its next orbital sweep, it had shifted again. Farther west this time. It was overflying the American West now.

All who were privy to this intelligence relaxed even more. The area it was passing over was relatively unpopulated. Montana to Arizona. There were missile silos there, all in sparsely settled areas. Most were slated for dismantling anyway.

"We may get a break," the secretary of defense reported to the President. And they waited.

BARTHOLOMEW MEECH WATCHED his monitors, his face the exact color of sun-bleached oatmeal, as he moved the small joysticks controlling nitrogen thrusters far, far above his ground station.

Behind him, his computer screen displayed a message.

To: R&D@qnm.com
From: RM@qnm.com
Subject: No call back
The SOB can't be bought and won't shut up. It's up to you.

AT GEODSS, THEY WERE getting real-time optical feeds on the object. It showed as a dark ball, half in eclipse, the other half illuminated by the stark, high-contrast moonlight of space.

But as it swooped low over Salt Lake City, abruptly it flowered.

The dark struts that embraced the black ball of unknown material extended like a spider awakening. Hardly visible in its stealth mode, when it was partially open the inner core shone bright as a new-minted quarter.

"What in God's name is that?"

No one could venture a guess.

Then the stealth sphere unfurled into a great disk.

And in the center of the disk, three sharp-edged black letters showed clearly: "МИр." ·

Then the overhead screen filled with such intolerable white light that the technicians were forced to pinch their eyes shut and look away.

41

It was Chiun who spotted the letters in the sky first.

"Remo! Behold!"

Remo braked and got out.

He saw the three letters that meant 'peace' in the Russian language, and then he was dropping to the ground covering his head and eyes because he knew what was coming next. Chiun followed suit.

They heard the boom as the world turned bright through their pinched-shut eyes, and they remained on the ground as a sizzling pressure wave rolled over them, scorching and wilting nearby foliage as if touched by a demonic exhalation.

"Stay low, Little Father," Remo warned.

"It has passed," said Chiun.

"There may be a second hit."

There wasn't. Remo and Chiun jumped up at the same time. They looked back down the road and saw the up-curling smoke from the hill on which Cosmo Pagan had been. The hill was still there, but not the trees and observatory. It looked like a smoking compost heap.

"It got Pagan," said Remo.

"Why?"

"That," said Remo, "is the question of the hour."

They drove back as far as they could. A circumference of about a sixteenth of a mile had been turned into black burned sand and earth. Glass had formed in smoking lumps. A few surviving old-growth tree stumps smoked like cauldrons. It was very hot. They couldn't get as close as they wanted.

But they got close enough to know that Dr. Cosmo Pagan, his house, his observatory and his wife had all been turned to mingled smoke and fumes that was now rushing up to meet the stars.

Overhead, a tiny dot of light hurtled past. The three ironic Cyrillic letters seemed to dwindle and shrink. Then they were gone, and so was the fleeting dot of light.

In the hot silence of the Arizona night, Remo Williams mumbled words he never expected himself to speak. "Maybe Martians *are* behind this after all," he muttered.

"You have just taken the first path to wisdom," intoned Chiun.

"Which is?"

"Agreeing with me," said the Master of Sinanju.

42

Dr. Harold W. Smith took the news well, given the extraordinary circumstances.

"Pagan is dead?" he blurted.

"Zapped," said Remo.

Smith's mouth turned to metal as he absorbed the import of Remo's telephone report. He had a paper cup brimming with water at his elbow. He swallowed it in one gulp. Then, as an afterthought, took two generic-brand painkillers with one extrastrength Alka-Seltzer.

His stomach bubbled and fizzed as he groped for a response. "Pagan must be connected to Object 617."

"He swore he wasn't, and believe me, if he was, Chiun and I would have wrung it out of him."

"Why would the power behind the device seek to kill him?"

"Your guess is as good as mine, Smitty. But we're at another dead end."

"We cannot accept defeat. We are dealing with a man-made phenomenon. It must have a solution."

"Unless it's Martian-made," said Remo.

"There are no Martians."

"We know it's not the Russians or Pagan or the Pentagon. And I'll bet the ranch it's not the Paraguayans—or whatever they're called."

"Perhaps Pagan was silenced because he was getting too close to the truth," Smith said slowly.

"Earlier you were saying he was behind it because his theories were all over the sky."

"Hmm," said Smith.

"It is not the Russians," declared Chiun.

"We already know that, Little Father," Remo said.

"Russians would know how to spell 'peace' correctly," added Chiun.

"What is that?" asked Smith.

"Nothing. Just Chiun putting in his two cents."

"The word in the sky is not Russian," said Chiun. "Tell Smith this."

"You hear that, Smitty?" asked Remo.

"Yes."

"He heard, Chiun. Now leave it alone. Smitty's trying to think."

"Put Chiun on," Smith said in a suddenly urgent voice.

"Why?"

"I want to hear what he has to say," said Smith.

Shrugging, Remo surrendered the line to the Master of Sinanju.

"Repeat what you just said, Master Chiun," asked Smith.

"I saw the letters in the sky. They did not spell 'peace.'"

"What do they spell?"

"Nonsense. The *P* was not a Greek *P.*"

"What was it?"

"It looked like a *P.* But an inferior *p.* The others were capital letters. The *P* was not. Its tail hung too low."

Remo said nothing. His face was a frown with cheekbones.

"The *P* is definitely lowercase," Harold Smith acknowledged.

"Big deal," said Remo. "Chiun found a typo. What does that prove?"

"Please stand by," said Smith.

"We are instructed to stand by," Chiun told Remo. Remo pretended to be interested in the low-hanging planet Mars.

AT FOLCROFT, Harold Smith purged his mind of all assumptions. He'd learned a long time ago that a fresh view could sometimes solve an otherwise intractable problem.

Three letters. Capitals *M, N* and lowercase *p*. Two of them seemed straightforward. That was an assumption, he realized. He frowned. What if the Cyrillic *N* was not what it seemed? What if it was exactly what it first appeared to be—a backward *N*?

Smith was looking at a digitized image of the photos the missing Travis Rust had taken seconds before the *Reliant* was destroyed. He had programs for everything. He initiated one that flopped the digitized image.

Instead of the Cyrillic letters meaning "peace," he got three ordinary English initials: "qNM"

It looked for all the word like a chemical formula. He wondered why the *q* would be lowercased like that.

Recalling that he had an open line to Remo and Chiun, Smith said, "I have flopped the image."

"Is that good or bad?" Remo wanted to know.

"It comes out *qNM*, but the *q* is lowercased."

"Makes sense. If it was a lowercase *p* before, it's a lowercase *q* now."

"I do not know what qNM could mean," said Smith. "It makes even less sense than 'Mir.'"

"You got me."

"But not me," said Chiun, taking the phone from his pupil's hand so swiftly Remo could still feel it even though it was no longer there.

"Emperor, before Pagan was liquidated, we carried to his ears a message from his wife."

"Yes?"

"An entity called QNM had called to increase his fee."

"QNM? Did she say what it was?"

"No, only that QNM had been calling incessantly."

Remo added, "She said it was over a consulting fee."

"Consulting! That means either media or a commercial firm," Smith said tensely. "One moment."

He was not silent very long.

"Remo."

"I am here," said Chiun, turning so Remo could not seize the phone.

"Listen," said Smith. "I have pulled up several QNMs. None are media outlets. But among the corporate names there is a company called Quantum Neutrino Mechanics. Their company logo is unusual. It features a lowercase *q*."

"Why would it do that?" Remo asked.

"Trademark-registration concerns," Smith said flatly.

"Bingo!"

"qNM headquarters is in Seattle, Washington. Go there. Now. Remain in touch by telephone. I will dig deeper."

"On our way," said Remo, hanging up so hard the receiver cracked like an ice sculpture.

"Looks like we're back in the game," he told Chiun.

"That is not enough. We must be ahead of the game."

"Right now I just want to stay one step ahead of the next flock of stewardesses I meet," said Remo.

43

It was a long way from sunny Massachusetts to rainy Seattle.

For Reemer Murgatroyd Bolt, of Quantum Neutrino Mechanics, it was almost exactly eleven years, three thousand miles and four career changes ago.

It had almost come to a crashing halt back at Chemical Concepts of Massachusetts on Route 128, the symbol of the Massachusetts Miracle. The Massachusetts Miracle had gone south somewhere around the time of the 1988 presidential elections, taking a certain Greek governor, the Bay State and America's Technology Highway with it, as Route 128 was known back then.

The DataGen and GenData and General Data Systems that had dotted 128 back in the booming eighties were gone now. As was Chemical Concepts of Massachusetts. As was Director of Marketing Reemer Bolt, who got out before the sky fell and it all came crashing down.

For a while, the entire world almost ended. And now history seemed to be repeating itself.

In his office, with the eternal rain pattering at the Thermopane windows that kept out the winter chill, Reemer Bolt shuddered as his mind went careening back to those heady days in which the planet Earth came perilously close to being incinerated. All because Reemer Bolt had charge of a product whose utility at first eluded even a marketing genius like himself.

It was called the Fluorocarbon Gun. It shot fluorocarbons, chemicals that had been banned by most industrialized nations because they ate away at the ozone shield high in the atmosphere. Holes in the ozone allowed dangerous solar radiation to penetrate. One hole accidentally knocked out a Russian missile battery, precipitating an international incident that almost ended the world—and Reemer Bolt's promising corporate career.

It was a huge marketing debacle. The biggest since the Edsel. ChemCon was forced into strategic bankruptcy.

Through it all, Bolt remained unscathed. In fact, his corporate future improved. On the strength of a new résumé that showed he had been in charge of a fifty-million-dollar project with global ramifications, Bolt moved from director of marketing of ChemCon to president of Web Tech. He knew nothing about Web Tech and, when he left to become COO of Quantum Neutrino Mechanics three years later, he knew even less about Web Tech. It didn't matter. No one ever got fired or laid off or punished for screwing up a billion-dollar corporation. They were handed golden parachutes, stock options and golden handshakes and wished well by anxious stockholders delighted to be rid of them.

It was middle managers and workers who invariably ate failure in corporate America. Not the Reemer Bolts. No matter how high the tides rose, their necks always stretched farther and their chins always lifted over the lung-quenching flood.

It was true that the corporate-downsizing mania threatened even the Reemer Bolts of the world. Somehow he got himself involved in the military-industrial complex. He didn't realize it for several weeks until he walked in on a Web Tech management research-and-development conference and saw the scale-model tank.

"Who brought that toy in here? This is a place of business," he snarled, knowing that no one ever snapped back at a snarling executive, never mind questioned him. They were petrified for their jobs.

"It's our next project," he was told by a more than brave technician.

"Scrap it," Bolt told him.

"Why? The Pentagon has accepted it."

Bolt froze inwardly. This was in 1991. He knew that if there was one thing an executive never did, it was reverse a decision. No matter how disastrous. He had been caught. He could not retreat. To retreat showed weakness. Worse, it showed a complete and unforgivable ignorance of the product line. That simply would not do. Not in corporate America, where smiling, two-legged sharks circled the office water cooler hoping to take a bite out of an unwary co-worker's ass.

"It has Failure written all over it," said Reemer Bolt. "Scrap it."

No one questioned the decision. It saved Reemer Bolt's high-six-figure salary and perks for three years, while Web Tech, six million dollars in development costs and a fat government contract down the drain, stumbled aimlessly until Reemer Bolt could smell the stench of decay seeping into his air-conditioned office and hired a head-hunting agency to find him a safer hole.

At first, the interview with Quantum Neutrino Mechanics didn't go well. Then the interviewer noticed the blank spot in the résumé.

"The years 1984 to 1987 are blank."

"Yes," Reemer Bolt said, knowing that he could not deny the obvious.

"Were you employed at that time?"

"Yes."

"In what position?"

"I cannot answer that," Bolt said in his most firm and sincere tone.

The interviewer blinked. "Say again, Mr. Bolt?"

Bolt cleared his throat and made it deeper. Much deeper. "I am contractually forbidden from, and cannot answer, that question."

The man blinked again. This was unusual. Even in corporate America.

"Was this government work?"

"I cannot confirm that," Bolt said truthfully.

"Did it—can you at least whisper something, Mr. Bolt? A blank spot does not look good."

Bolt shook his head. Here was the difficult part. He knew that some résumé blank spots reflected alcohol or cocaine addictions. If they jumped to either conclusion, he was dead.

The interviewer looked around furtively. "Did this position by chance have anything to do with national security?" he breathed.

It was a wild guess, and Reemer Bolt answered, not entirely untruthfully, "I can neither confirm nor deny that assertion."

The interviewer relaxed. He leaned back in his chair. His entire face softened. "Mr. Bolt, I think I can say you've moved to the top of the list. Quantum Neutrino Mechanics is looking for a man like you."

Bolt smiled. He was the kind of man who had progressed in life from his mother's breast to one easy teat after another. He knew the scent of fresh milk. He was smelling it now.

The trouble was, the milk was running out for the defense industry, and since Quantum Neutrino Mechanics was courting Reemer Bolt, he never bothered to look into their product line. Only his personal package.

"Congress is backing away from Star Wars," Reemer was told one day a year or two after the Berlin Wall fell and he had been with qNM long enough to feel he could bluff his way through any meeting on any level of the company. He had all the latest buzzwords down. This year *synergy* and *outsourcing* were in vogue.

"I have no problem with that," said Bolt in a brusque, take-no-prisoners-and-suffer-no-fools voice.

The managers seated around the boat-shaped fumed-oak conference table hesitated. One finally gathered the strength to speak up. "It leaves us out in the cold."

"Build a fire," Bolt said.

"With what?"

"Rub two sticks together. Or try a magnifying glass."

Reemer Bolt forgot that last comment as soon as the meeting was adjourned. It was only an aphorism. Now known as R. M. Bolt because he thought the initials commanded more respect than being called Mr. Bolt, he was into managing by aphorism. He had good, imaginative people working under him. All they needed was the right kind of push.

He remembered telling them to build a fire but forgot about the magnifying glass until R&D presented him with the scale model.

"Who left this disco ball in here?" Bolt snarled, pointing at the blackish gray ball sitting under the high-intensity lamps.

"It's our future."

"Disco is dead," Bolt said.

"If you'd indulge us, R.M.," R&D head engineer Bartholomew Meech said.

Bolt went with the flow. Some days you pushed. Others you pulled. He was in a pulling mood that day. So he nodded.

The presentation involved overhead slides, an animated videotape that had Walt Disney Corporation fingerprints all over the production values, while six different white-smocked technicians pointed out features with their red laser pointers. All spiced with impressive-sounding technical terms like *aluminized mylar* and *photovoltaic panels*.

In the end, R. M. Bolt understood none of it. He found himself glowering at the disco ball to keep the dull lack of comprehension off his face.

"Take it again from the top," he instructed. "So my grandmother would understand it."

And they did.

"It's solar-powered."

"Orbiting continuously above the earth."

"Where it will do the job America needs done."

Reemer frowned. He wasn't getting it yet. Then someone said the word that touched his marketer's heart.

"And it will promote the heck out of qNM," said Bartholomew Meech.

"I like it," Bolt said.

Smiles all around. Grins. Beaming ones.

"One question," Bolt asked after the second impenetrable presentation.

"R.M.?"

"Will this have any effect on the ozone layer?"

"Not unless we want it to."

"I *definitely* do not want it to," Bolt declared with precise enunciation so that everyone understood.

"Then it won't."

"See that it goes right into production," said R. M. Bolt, leaving the room without understanding anything except that Quantum Neutrino Mechanics was still in business because now he had something to tell the stockholders.

The memos coming back from R&D were encouraging.

Production was on schedule.

Project was ahead of schedule.

Ahead of schedule and under budget.

Magic words, all of them. Each memo added an extra quarter to the period of Reemer Bolt's tenure at qNM.

Finally Meech came and said proudly, "We're ready to launch it."

"Go ahead," said Bolt, thinking of a marketing launch, not the other kind.

Meech and his engineers looked momentarily confused. "We don't have a launch vehicle."

"Find one," said Bolt, his marketer's instincts thinking that with television channels exploding exponentially, how hard could it be to secure advertising time?

They came back with a six-page report—a marvel of business writing because they could have added a ream to the page count and increased their employment contracts by a solid year—outlining launch plans. That told Bolt one of two things: either they were fools or they were extremely enthusiastic about the project.

That also told R. M. Bolt he should start exercising his stock options—qNM was here to stay. At least through the turn of the millennium—or whatever they were going to call it.

The gist of the report was given to Bolt orally, relieving him of the tiresome responsibility of reading it.

"The Chinese have the best price," Meech said enthusiastically. "The Japanese are too expensive. The French are impossible to deal with. And the Americans, of course, are out."

"Of course," Bolt said, having no clue as to what the conversation was about. But he had given the staff affirmation, and the affirmation was coming back in the form of approving nods.

"That leaves the Russians," finished Meech.

"Doesn't it always?" said Reemer Bolt.

Another nod. A short one. Bolt decided not to push his luck any more and just listen.

"Their reusable launch vehicle is for rent. In fact, we could buy if it we wanted to sink a billion into it."

"Why buy when you can rent?" said Bolt, quoting a local TV ad for a company that rented furniture to people with bad credit.

"Exactly," Meech said as if having his view of reality reaffirmed.

"The Russians are so hard up for cash we think we can negotiate them down," another engineer chimed in.

"Do we have a budget for this?" Bolt asked calmly.

"It's not in the current budget."

"I'll authorize it."

Everyone beamed. It was so infectious, R. M. Bolt beamed back. It was like love. There was no understanding it, no analyzing it and no denying it. But when it was happening, it was best to just accept it and return it, because it always came back with interest.

Then came the catch.

Bolt asked an obvious question. "What is our market?"

They looked at him with dull, blank expressions.

"R.M?"

"Market," Bolt snapped. "Who can we sell this to?"

Meech adjusted his taped-together glasses and shuffled his sneakered feet. "We explained all that."

"Refresh my memory," Bolt ordered.

"The Pentagon's not underwriting SDI R&D, but if we launch a working prototype, we have their attention in a way never before seen. It's viable, and a PR coup that will put qNM in the forefront of planetary defense, which we feel will be the cutting edge for the new century, technological-application-wise."

Bolt stared blankly.

"And best of all, the energy is free!" Meech added.

Reemer Bolt's scowl broke like the sun breaking through thunderheads.

"You spoke the magic words." Then his voice darkened again. "Just make damn sure the Pentagon will buy it."

"Oh, they'll buy it," Meech promised.

"Make certain. It's our jobs."

"I guess we can program it for planetary interventions. Not just defense."

Some of the engineers went pale at that. Bolt ignored the not very subtle warning sign. "Do it."

"No problem, R.M. We're on it."

They started to return to their labs when Bolt stopped them. "Wait!"

They hesitated.

"Aren't you forgetting something? It needs a name."

"We're calling it the Paraguay Project because that's where we assembled the components. It was cheap and offered the best security, patent-wise," said Meech.

Bolt shook his head firmly. "'The Paraguay Project' won't cut it."

"How about the Solar Harnesser?"

"Sounds horsey."

"The Sun Tamer, then?"

"Reminds me of a cheap Western."

"I know," offered a nameless engineer. "We can call it the ParaSol 2001."

"What does *that* mean?" demanded Bolt.

"Nothing, really. But people respect numbers. Especially big ones attached to futuristic-sounding words. I think it has something to do with math anxiety."

Reemer Bolt's close-shaved face wavered between a scowl and a mere frown. Eventually realizing they were running into lunch, he said, "Makes sense to me. Go with it."

And with that, Reemer Bolt turned his back on the project.

It was many months later that he finally pieced together the bits of data that explained what the ParaSol 2001 actually was. He did this by pink-slipping an engineer and debriefing him while the man blubbered behind closed doors. That way, no one was the wiser.

Bolt had to explain it to the board of directors; otherwise, he would never have bothered.

"The ParaSol 2001 is designed to repel planet-threatening threats," Reemer Bolt said proudly as he stood before a wall chart that showed threat quantities and their H-bomb equivalents. It was a very frightening display. It even scared him.

The board, as usual, cut right to the heart of the thing.

"Who in their right mind is going to pay to defend the planet against external threats?" CEO Ralph Gaunt asked.

"They'll pay if we're the only game in orbit."

"Knowing the Pentagon generals, they'll appeal to our patriotism and expect us to do the job gratis to save our own butts," Gaunt scoffed. "No profit in saving the world, Bolt."

"Already thought of that. It can be directed earthward to zap any military target on earth. No other Earth-based weapon has that feature."

The board stared stonily. Bolt sweated.

"And best of all," he added quickly, "it's the most gigantic advertising billboard in human history."

With that, Bolt pressed a remote switch, and the scale-model ParaSol 2001 opened up like a dark, unfolding flower to reveal the qNM logo in neat black letters right down to the lowercase *q* which had been the first-year suggestion that earned Reemer Bolt his initial salary hike. He was very proud of it.

"Our logo. Twice as big as the moon in the evening sky. The PR value will be stunning."

This won over the board. They had just one question.

"Will it hurt the ozone layer?"

"Don't worry. I already thought of that," said Reemer Bolt, who felt an old, cold fear trickle down the gully of his back. After all, he was directly responsible for the 1987 Montreal Protocol Treaty, which called for reducing fluorocarbon emissions by the year 2000. Even if he couldn't exactly put in on his résumé.

Now, many months later, that sweat was back and it was very very hot. The board was screaming. They didn't care anymore about planetary defense or the global marketing footprint or Pentagon generals. They wanted Reemer Bolt. And they wanted answers. Was that thing up there ours or Russia's?

Working his desktop system, Bolt checked his e-mail.

To: RM@qnm.com
From: RalphGaunt@qnm.com
Subject: Where are you?
Am in Cancun. Hotel says you checked out. Urgent we meet. Where are you?

Bolt typed out a reply:

To: RalphGaunt@qnm.com
From: RM@qnm.com
Subject: Whereabouts
Sorry. Did not receive sent message. Had to fly to Paraguay to debug ParaSol 2001. Will return to States in forty-eight hours. All will be explained.

The reply came back almost instantaneously: "Remain in Paraguay. En route."

"Perfect," Bolt said, "I didn't get that message, either."

Then he settled down to do the final damage control. It was pretty bad out there. The press was full of Martian fever and war-scare talk with Russia. As long as the Martian fever stayed hot, maybe the Russians would remain cool. But he couldn't trust to fate. He had to take action—smart executive action. If Reemer Bolt could save the planet, it might be possible to salvage his career.

As he started pounding out a message to Meech down in R&D, he muttered, "This is almost as bad as that ozone mess back in '85. Why does this crap keep happening to me?"

44

Seattle was wreathed in an early-morning fog when the jetliner descended toward the airport. A steady winter drizzle drummed on the fuselage as their landing wheels whined out of their wells.

In coach, the Master of Sinanju stared out of the window, unable to see the wingtips in the fog.

Then, in the near distance, a great saucer of steel and glass became visible, floating above the fog.

"We are too late, Remo," he squeaked.

"What?" asked Remo, returning to his seat after having just locked a hysterical stewardess in the rear rest room.

"The star chariots of the Martian invader have landed. Behold the certain sign of their arrival on earth."

Ducking his head, Remo looked past the Master of Sinanju's concerned face. "Oh, that." He sat down.

"Do not dismiss the evidence of your eyes. It is a flying saucer."

"It's the freaking Space Needle, Chiun."

"And a more fearful spectacle I have never seen. See how it hovers over the vanquished city? Note its chilly grandeur, its utter fearlessness from attack. Tell the pilot to turn around. We will not land in occupied Seattle, lest we, too, fall into Martian hands."

"The Space Needle is a building. You just can't see the part that's holding up the saucer in all this fog."

"It is a trick," said Chiun.

"No trick. Now settle down. We have to hit the ground running."

"Never fear. Our foe is doomed."

"That's the problem," said Remo. "We still don't know who we're supposed to doom."

"We will leave no one standing."

"That could take all day, and there's no telling what that thing up there could hit next."

HAROLD SMITH HAD breached the firewalls protecting the computer links for Quantum Neutrino Mechanics. The difficulty was, there was nothing on the qNM local-area network that referenced the thing in orbit, or ParaSol.

Smith refused to accept defeat. There had already been too many dead ends in this situation.

Downloading the entire qNM file system from hard drives to the magnetic-tape records, he initiated a massive unerase program.

It would take time to process. There was no guessing what it might or might not uncover. But if a corporate cover-up was already under way, this was the only way to unlock it.

THE 747 TOUCHED DOWN. Once they reached the terminal, Remo checked in with Harold Smith by pay phone. By mistake, he fed it a kopeck and had to move on to the next booth when it refused U.S. coin.

Smith's voice was urgent. "Remo. I have uncovered e-mail files that explain much. The man you want goes by the initials R.M. That is all I have. He signs his e-mail 'RM,' but I find no one owning those initials in the qNM personnel files."

"So how do I find him?"

"He interfaces with R&D. That would be 'Research and Development.' Start there."

"Sounds like we're cooking."

Hanging up, Remo told a waiting Chiun, "We're looking for someone initialed 'R.M.'"

"Ruber Mavors."

"Coincidence. I hope."

"We shall see," said the Master of Sinanju.

They ran for a taxi and were soon being whisked through the eternal Seattle rain.

BARTHOLOMEW MEECH WAS sweating bullets. It had been three days of no rest, no sleep and too many paper cups of Starbucks coffee.

On the research-and-development floor of Quantum Neutrino Mechanics, he moved from console to console, monitor to monitor, tracking the ParaSol 2001. It was approaching the South Pole now. He wished it would just crash there.

A beep yanked his thin face to the interoffice computer system.

"You have mail!" the system flashed.

And deep inside, Bartholomew Meech groaned.

Accessing the file, he brought up another communication from his immediate superior:

To: R&D@qnm.com
From: RM@qnm.com
Subject: Project termination.

CNN is reporting Pagan fried. Now is the pru-

dent time to shut down the project before Gaunt
gets back from Paraguay.

Here are your instructions:

Target French, Chinese and Japanese space
centers, then shut down the project.

Furiously Meech pecked out a reply.

To: RM@qnm.com
From: R&D@qnm.com
Subject: Are you insane?
We're getting in deeper. More people are going to
die. When does this stop?

To: R&D@qnm.com
From: RM@qnm.com
Subject: Shut up!
It stops after you've programmed in the next target string. Then destroy the controller array and
get your résumé in order, just as I'm doing with
mine. There are greener pastures out there. And
once Gaunt parachutes in, you're dead at qNM
anyway.

Remember—the corporate shield protects us.
If anyone lands on the corporation, it won't be
for months. We'll be elsewhere. New guys will
take the heat.

Bartholomew Meech stared at the screen.

"God damn," he muttered. He hated the way this
was turning out. There was no way he could score a
benefits package as generous as qNM's ever again.

He hit the key that erased the e-mail message and
turned to do his corporate duty.

Meech felt the cold shadow on his back before he actually faced the two silent presences.

One was a tall thin man with wrists like I-beams. The other was a short Asian in native costume and very old. Both looked as if they were having a bad day and looking for someone to blame.

The tall one asked, "Who's R.M.?"

"Don't know what you're talking about. Where are your access badges?" asked Meech, pushing his glasses back on his nose.

"Lobby guards wouldn't give me one," said the tall man.

"Why not?"

"Because," answered the short Asian, "they did not want us to enter this place."

"So how did you get past them?"

"We went over their heads," said the tall one.

"Those we did not break over our knees," added the other.

There was something in the cold eyes of the duo that made Bartholomew Meech feel creepily cold in the brightly lit R&D room of Quantum Neutrino Mechanics world headquarters.

"So where do we find R.M.?" asked the tall one, flashing FBI ID. When Meech hesitated, he shoved it in his face, saying, "Hurry up. We have a lot of bones to splinter."

"I want immunity," Meech blurted.

"Earn it."

"R.M. is two floors up on eleven."

"Then why is he talking to you by computer?" asked the tall thin one.

"Deniability."

The Asian slipped behind him and asked, "What is your role in this matter?"

"I'm technical project manager of the solar mirror."

"I was right. It was solar."

The old Asian nodded with grim satisfaction. "Yes. A sun dragon."

"We call it a Soletta. It's a gigantic mirror of aluminized mylar. It collects solar energy, focusing and beaming it out as a superconcentrated ray of heat."

"To kill people," said the tall one.

"No! That wasn't it at all. It was for the good of mankind we built it. And for the publicity."

"How does frying patches of the planet translate to 'for the good of mankind'?" asked the tall thin one.

"It's not supposed to fry terra firma. It's designed to hit rogue asteroids threatening Earth."

"Huh?"

"It's true. The planet stands stark naked against an incoming asteroid. Look at what happened to Jupiter. Or the dinosaurs. The ParaSol 2001 was designed to lock on to an incoming asteroid and zap it. Small impactors would be vaporized to nothing. Big extinctors we figured could be deflected from Earth-harming trajectory by vaporizing parts of them. The jets of escaping gases and metal would act like propulsion rockets, redirecting their path."

"Sounds like a giant magnifying glass."

"Exactly."

And the tall one gave the short one a see-I-told-you-so smile that the short Asian pointedly ignored.

"It would have worked except we got tripped up by feature creep. We wanted it to point to Earth in case the Pentagon needed to rent it as a weapon in some future war. Some idiot vendor sold us a defective computer chip, and it was installed in the guidance system, screwing up the orbital orientation. It ended up pointing Earthward, not spaceward. Useless for the original mission. And to make things worse, the company logo was displayed backward.''

''So why hit the BioBubble?''

''We didn't know it was pointed backward. We just test-fired blindly, figuring we wouldn't hit anything important up there.''

''What about the *Reliant* and Baikonur?''

''The *shuttle* was melted to feed Pagan's Martian theory. Then, by some fluke, the qNM logo came out spelling 'Mir' in Russian, and we hit Baikonur so the U.S. wouldn't attack the Russians by mistake and the Russians who launched the ParaSol wouldn't give us up to Washington.''

Meech wiped his perspiring brow and licked his sweaty palm clean. He closed his eyes like a man in pain. ''After that, it was all we could do to cover our asses between corporate and the media and that damn Cosmo Pagan.''

''You hit him to shut him up?''

''Yeah. I mean, no. That was R.M. Everything was him. He gave the orders. I only executed them.''

''Like a good little corporate Nazi.''

''That's not fair. I never shoved anyone into an oven.''

''No. You just fried them where they stood,'' said Remo.

And suddenly Bartholomew Meech felt a sharp pain in his back. ''Did I just get stabbed in the back?'' he asked, afraid to turn around.

"Why does that surprise you?" asked the squeaky voice of the little Asian. "Have you not betrayed your own country?"

"I just did what the corporation said."

"And now you get to die for it," said Remo.

"I don't feel like I'm dying...."

"It'll catch up. I have a final question."

"What?" Meech asked dazedly. He weaved on his sneakered feet.

"Which of these things shuts the mirror down?"

"I have to do it myself."

"You don't have time."

"Whatever you do, don't—" And eyes rolling up to show white, Bartholomew Meech fell over dead. *Schlump!*

"Damn," said Remo.

Chiun fluttered fingernails about the room. "It does not matter. We will destroy the good machines with the bad."

"He said there was something we shouldn't do," Remo said worriedly, gazing around the instrument-packed confines.

"And whatever it is, we will not do it. We will merely break everything in sight."

Remo considered this, shrugged and said, "Can't cause any more trouble than we already have."

And they went to town. Their hands and feet flashed from console to mainframe to devices they didn't even recognize. Metal and plastic fractured and caved in. Wires came sputtering out like aroused vipers, hissing blue-green sparks.

With a grim ferocity, they transformed the big room into a litter of glass and transistors and circuit boards and shattered, inert machines.

"That's done," Remo said firmly. "Next stop. The eleventh floor."

ON THE ELEVENTH FLOOR, Reemer Murgatroyd Bolt was told by his secretary, "Two men to see you, Mr. Bolt."

"What men?"

"I don't recognize them. They asked for R.M., as if they know you. Mr. Bolt, they're not wearing qNM employee badges."

"Ask them what they want," said Reemer Bolt as he was clearing out his desk.

"They said you're the last loose end."

"Loose end of what?"

"They refuse to say, Mr. Bolt."

"Tell them to make an appointment, Evelyn."

"Yes, sir."

A moment later, Evelyn's screaming came through the door, then the door came off its hinges to impress itself into the opposite wall, knocking assorted framed Maxfield Parrish prints off their hooks.

Reemer Bolt came out from behind his desk, paling. "Who are you?" he blurted.

"Exterminators," a man with unusually thick wrists said.

"Exter—"

"We do maggots, silverfish and cockroaches."

"This office is clean."

The tall one looked to the old Asian and asked, "This guy look roachy to you?"

The Asian shook his head. "No, he is a maggot."

Reemer Bolt got a very bad feeling in the pit of his stomach. Exactly the same feeling had come over him the last time he was terminated.

"I can't imagine what this is about," he said lamely.

A pair of glasses landed on his desk. Bolt looked at them quickly. They looked exactly like Meech's glasses, down to the broken bridge repaired by white tape.

"He told us everything."

"The mindless nerd. I explained how the corporate shield protects him."

"Not against us."

"Nonsense. Everything that happened was an accident. A combination of product failure, feature creep and defective chips supplied by outside vendors. In fact, I've memoed the board that we sue the chip supplier. This is all their fault. It's not the firm's. I will testify to this in court."

"The e-mail's been unerased. We have the whole story."

"You do?"

The tall one nodded. "We do."

"In that case, you will have to take the matter up with legal. They are on the thirteenth floor. This is their department. I'm only management."

"Sorry. We work outside the law."

Reemer Bolt was surrounded now. There were only two of them, but he felt exactly as though he were surrounded by twenty-two.

"You are forgetting the corporate shield. It protects men like me."

"Show us this shield," asked the ancient Asian.

"Show? It's not a tangible shield. It's a—a..."

"A what?"

Bolt snapped his fingers. "A concept."

The tall one with the dead-looking eyes shook his head in a very final way. "Too bad. We work with our hands. You want to hide behind a shield, it's gotta be real.''

"It *is* real. Ask legal. They will fill you in. I'll call them up right now."

Reemer Bolt reached for the desk telephone, and the one with the wrists reached out ahead of him.

He said, "Uh-uh." It was a very serious uh-uh. Dead serious.

And the one with the nails inserted Bolt's forearm into a desk drawer he had been in the process of clearing out.

A natural question occurred to Reemer Bolt. "Am I being terminated?"

"Bingo!"

"I'll go quietly," Bolt said hastily. "I just have to finish collecting my personal effects."

"That's nice of you, but you won't need them," the tall one said in a very reasonable tone of voice.

What happened next was so bizarre, so incredible, and happened so fast that Reemer Bolt found himself watching it with a sick fascination that gave way to a growing concern much too late to reverse the procedure.

The one with the wrists shoved Reemer's arm all the way into the open drawer. Of course, it wouldn't fit. It was too long. So he folded it at the elbow joint. Unfortunately he folded it the wrong way.

Crunch. Then he hammered Bolt's shoulder into the drawer. It didn't fit, either, so the other one laid two hands on the shoulder while Bolt vainly tried to keep his face from smushing into the desk's very hard edge.

The shoulder collapsed into suet under kneading fingers.

Then they took hold of his legs and bent them around so viciously he could feel a splintery cracking in the vicinity of his pelvis.

Reemer Bolt found himself staring out the window as the pair systematically pulverized his lean musculature and healthy bone into pockets of flesh-covered bonemeal and hamburger.

In the reflection of his office window, Bolt could see what was happening to him.

It was if he were a master contortionist and were fitting himself into a space too small for an ordinary human. Except that Reemer Bolt had absolutely nothing to do with what was happening to him. It was like having an out-of-body experience. Only it was more of a body-into-drawer experience.

He saw his torso, accompanied by the grinding of shattering ribs, slide in and then he was looking at his head sticking out of the drawer with its stunned-face reflection just as the one with the wrists laid a cold hand on his hair and began forcing it into the drawer.

That was about the time Bolt snapped out of his fascinated daze and mustered the presence of mind to scream.

The trouble was his lungs were the consistency of dead liver and there was nothing to scream with.

His eyes saw their own reflection, then they were swallowed by the desk drawer and the drawer was slammed shut with a finality that failed to register on Reemer Murgatroyd Bolt's dead, squashed brain.

REMO LOCKED THE DRAWER and told Chiun, "Assignment done. Time to call Smith."

Harold Smith sounded relieved. "You are positive the device is inoperative?"

"We got R.M., his technician and everything that looked electronic."

"I have finished reading the e-mail files. This is a rogue operation. qNM is not corporately responsible. Exit quietly."

"Will do," said Remo.

Then Smith's voice turned sharp. "One moment." Smith's voice became raw. "Remo, I am looking at a real-time-feed visual of the device. It is opening again."

"So? Maybe that means it's dying. Don't animals relax when they die?"

"This is a machine. It was in shutdown mode. Now it is unfolding again."

Remo said to Chiun, "Uh-oh."

"What is that?" asked Smith.

"Nothing," said Remo.

Then Smith said, "It is deploying."

Silence made the line hum.

Then Harold Smith said hoarsely, "Remo, it just emitted another burst of concentrated heat. Stand by."

It was the longest twenty minutes of Remo's life.

Smith came back on the line. "Remo, it has struck Baldar Mountain in the Asgard Range."

Remo groaned. "There goes Norway."

"No. Antarctica. We were fortunate. It is uninhabited. Thousands of pounds of ice are now steam. That is all. But the ParaSol 2001 is not folding up. It's still tracking. It may strike again."

"Probably a last gasp," Remo said hopefully.

But it wasn't.

"Another burst!" groaned Smith. "It is out of control."

"Well, just shoot it down."

"That is the problem. We cannot fire missiles into space."

"Well, you can't just let it run amok."

"I must contact the President at once."

Chiun spoke up. "There is another way."

"What's that?" asked Remo and Smith at the same tine.

"A Master of Sinanju must ascend into the Void to deal with this scourge that is a sun dragon. So Salbyol foresaw."

"You volunteering?" asked Remo.

"Yes!" cried Chiun. "I will be the first Korean in space."

"You're on," said Remo.

45

Commander Dirk McSweeny couldn't believe his ears.

"Launch? Today!"

"The *Atlantis* is on the pad. The countdown's started. You go up in an hour," said the NASA flight controller in a breathless tone. He looked serious. And sane. But he couldn't be either. Space shuttles were not launched on short notice.

"What about the mission? The package isn't ready."

"Scrubbed. You have a new mission and a new payload."

"What is it?"

"Classified. You take the orbiter up. And deploy the payload."

"You know it doesn't work that way. We have to train for a new payload."

"Not this time. This time you're flying a glorified delivery truck."

"What about payload-deployment procedures?"

"Don't worry about them. It's self-deploying."

"Self—"

"You heard me."

Within an hour, Commander McSweeny was being suited up, along with his mission specialists and what he saw was a severely reduced crew of five. That meant a military mission.

"What the hell is going on here?" he yelled as they dropped his helmet over his confused face.

"Just relax. It's a short mission. Up and back down the same day."

As they were being escorted to the vehicle, lugging their portable oxygen tanks, McSweeny asked his flight controller, "Can you at least tell me what the payload is?"

"Sorry. This run you're just a stick jockey."

In Moscow, FSK Major-General Stankevitch sat with the Cosmic Secret file sitting on his desk like a time bomb, his stomach burning with half a bottle of vodka. Upon his shoulders rested the fate of the world.

"Get me the Kremlin," he told his secretary, and reached for the bottle. Very soon there would be no more vodka, no more air, no more water. For anyone.

The Master of Sinanju was beside himself with rage.

"Never!"

"You gotta," pleaded Remo.

They were in an all-white ready room at the Kennedy Space Center.

"Never! I will not shear off my nails. It is bad enough that I am bereft of one. But to willingly abandon the others! My ancestors would be ashamed of me. They would shun me in the Void when my time came."

And he inserted one hand into a white gauntlet. The long nails popped through like daggers.

"Tough," said Remo. "You volunteered. You can't go up without a space suit, and they don't come with extralong fingers."

Chiun folded his arms. "Have them sewn. I will wait."

"That mirror just zapped a piece of the South Atlantic. Nobody got hurt, but it's all ready to power up for another burst. It's only a matter of time before it hits a populated place."

"I cannot." Chiun looked up at Remo with imploring eyes. "Remo, you must go in my stead."

"Me?"

"It has been prophesied that a Master of Sinanju would battle the returning sun dragon. I can see now that it is not destined to be me. Therefore, it must be you."

"I didn't volunteer."

"I have volunteered the House. Since I am constrained by circumstances beyond my power to alter, you must go and uphold the honor of the House. Not to mention save precious humanity from this scourge."

"Look, the countdown's starting. One of you has to go!" the flight controller implored.

"One of us will," Chiun said. And he pointed his jade nail protector at Remo. "You. You will go."

"I'll do it," said Remo angrily. "But you owe me, Chiun."

Support personnel helped Remo into an atmosphere suit.

"We need to brief you on how to go to the bathroom in space," the flight controller said anxiously.

Remo shook his head. "No time. I'll hold it."

"How to eat."

"Give me a fistful of cold rice, and I'll be fine."

"Emergency procedures."

"That's up to the crew. I'm cargo."

"At least try to understand MMU operations for your EVA."

"If I can't understand what you just said," Remo shot back, "how can I understand what I'm supposed to understand? Just suit me up. I'll wing it."

Support personnel blinked dazedly.

"Just get him in the suit," the flight controller said resignedly.

Remo eyed the Master of Sinanju. "Did Master Salbyol say how this would turn out?"

"No," admitted Chiun.

"Figures," said Remo as the gloves were snapped on.

The last thing to go on was the helmet. The visor was blacked out so that Remo could see out but no one could see his face.

Then he was being led to the huge white transport van.

"This is a proud day. My son, the star voyager," said Chiun.

"It's 'astronaut,'" grumbled Remo.

"What do you think the word means, ignorant one?"

"I just hope someone checked the O-rings on this thing," Remo muttered hollowly.

Commander McSweeny was still cursing under his breath when the countdown reached zero and the thunder of the shuttle's multiple engines slammed at his tense spine and the sensation of leaving his stomach behind overtook everything. He had a big bird to fly. And if that was all NASA wanted this trip, they were going to get the best shuttle pilot who ever flew.

MAJOR-GENERAL STANKEVITCH received the news with a weird mixture of anger and relief.

"All lines to the Kremlin are tied up," his secretary reported.

"These damn phones!" he exploded.

"It is not the phone system. All lines are in use. There is something up."

"Keep trying. The Motherland depends upon us. I will keep drinking."

ONCE IN SPACE, Commander McSweeny was fed his instructions by ground control.

"You are to locate and overtake solar mirror approximately a sixteenth of a mile in diameter."

"That won't be hard to miss," McSweeny grunted.

Maneuvering the orbiter, he found it.

"Is that a qNM logo?" he muttered.

"It is. They make great avionics."

"Okay, what do we do now?" McSweeny asked Houston.

"Pace it."

The *Atlantis* fell in beside the slowly turning mirror.

"Houston, *Atlantis* is flying right next to it."

"Okay, *Atlantis*. Open payload bay doors."

"Opening doors." A minute later it was, "Doors open."

"Stand by, *Atlantis*. Your cargo is self-deploying."

"What the hell kind of cargo is self—?"

Then an astronaut who was not a member of the *Atlantis* crew came floating out on an EVA line. He carried no MMU thrust-pack. Only on a flexible tether, but somehow he gravitated toward the big solar mirror as if he were swimming through space. That, of course, was impossible. No one could swim through space. Not unless he could somehow glide along on the solar winds.

As McSweeny and his crew watched with utter fascination, the astronaut with the blackout visor moved unerringly toward the solar mirror that dwarfed them all into insignificance.

In space, it should have been impossible.

But there it was.

WHEN HIS SECRETARY came back with the word that the Kremlin was still incommunicado, Major-General Stankevitch grabbed up the fateful file and announced, ''I will take the file to them personally.''

On the way out, he grabbed a fresh bottle of vodka, too.

REMO WILLIAMS HAD NO EYES for the beauty of the blue earth 120 miles below him. The stark starlight held no fascination, either. His dark eyes were fixed on the gigantic ParaSol 2001 slowly spinning before him.

He felt like a fly trying to catch a spiderweb.

The moment the great shuttle cargo doors had split open, Remo launched himself with a two-footed kick. He was amazed at his own lightness in zero gravity. But he had no time to enjoy the sensations of weightlessness.

The looming ParaSol was filling his field of vision. It gleamed like a plate made of soft aluminum foil, except for the gigantic black areas that spelled out three letters that had reignited the Cold War: "МИр."

And in his helmet earphone, a familiar lemony voice intruded.

"Destroyer."

"Here," said Remo, acknowledging Smith's use of his rarely spoken code name.

"You are looking at a disk of aluminized Mylar on a folding-strut frame. Do you see the focusing lens?"

"Yeah."

"That is your target. According to my estimates, it has been collecting solar radiation from its rear collectors and discharging energy every twenty-eight minutes. It is due to fire again in four minutes, twenty-eight seconds."

"What's the situation on the ground?" asked Remo.

"A mile-wide circular section of the Sahara has been turned to glass. No known casualties."

"Our luck can't hold."

"The President is on the hot line to Moscow, explaining the situation. The Russian leadership is wary but willing to listen. They are tracking the ParaSol, too. They expect results."

"I'm floating as fast as I can."

"Listen carefully. Its present orbit will take it over Russia, Iran and Saudi Arabia. You must disable it before any of those nations are struck."

"Almost there," said Remo as the great disk all but enveloped him in its shadow. It billowed and rippled like silvery Saran Wrap.

"I am watching you in real time through my GEODSS link."

As the tumbling mirror came within reach, Remo lifted his white-gloved hands to catch it. They grazed Mylar. Remo made two fists and began tearing the tough metallic fabric.

It refused to tear. And momentum took Remo into the rippling fabric itself.

He bounced back, reached out a hand and grabbed a handy strut. Using it for leverage, he swung his sluggish body around.

This time he popped through the fabric. He kept going. The obverse side came into view, showing the qNM corporate logo.

Reaching back, Remo grabbed his tether, hauling himself back with both hands.

"Be careful!" Smith said sharply.

"I'm not exactly trained for this kind of work," Remo shot back as he regained the mirror.

And Remo started in on the Mylar envelope. With an open tear to work with, it was easy to make the rip wider. Silver Mylar fragments began floating away. Remo used the support strut as a kick point and launched himself toward the center, where the big lens sat like the spider in the mylar web. It was pointing down at the North Pole. Soon they would be over Siberia.

"Estimated burn in two minutes, twelve seconds," Harold Smith was saying.

Remo ripped methodically as he made his way along. All he was accomplishing was to inhibit the ParaSol from collecting future solar energy. The only way to disable it was to nail the lens.

"One minute, three seconds," Smith said, his voice tinny in the space-suit helmet.

Remo tried to shake a strut loose, but he had no leverage. His strength worked against him. The mirror orbited on.

"Twenty-two seconds . . ."

The lens began to flash.

Smith's voice became raw. "Target confirmed as industrial city of Magnitogorsk. You must not fail."

"Damn," said Remo. Gathering up coils of loose tether, he pulled in two directions. The cable snapped silently. And Remo whipped it around.

The broken end snaked around like a tentacle. It moved with agonizing slowness, while Harold Smith, useful as a Greek chorus, counted down the seconds to nuclear Armageddon.

"Ten seconds, nine, eight, seven . . ."

The lens shattered at four seconds to doomsday. There was no sound, of course, only glassy fragments tumbling in all directions. Some pierced the mylar web. Others spun toward Remo, catching starlight, reflecting it brilliantly.

"Good news and bad news," Remo said thinly.

"Yes?"

"ParaSol is dead. But I'm adrift."

"The shuttle will retrieve you."

"Glad to hear it."

Without warning, the ParaSol detonated.

Again there was no sound. Other than Remo's surprised curse.

"What is it?" Smith asked anxiously.

"It blew up! I gotta get out of here."

Reflexes kicked in. Remo tried to swim but he was in space. There was nothing to push against. The explosive wave radiated toward him like a metallic dandelion coming apart under a giant's breath.

Eerily tumbling shards of glass and metal and mylar foil billowed outward in all directions of space. As they came at Remo in a dense cloud of space-age shrapnel, he had only one cold thought: *I'm dead.*

Then Harold Smith was saying, "Remo, I am watching you. The debris will spread and expand outward the farther it gets from the point of detonation. Your primary survival tactic is simple. Dodge all debris. First, curl yourself in a ball."

Remo oriented himself toward the explosion.

Pieces of material arrowed at him. Very quickly, they were only inches from his vulnerable space suit.

In a way, it was easier than dodging bullets. He had six directions to dodge in. But nothing to work against.

The mylar he ignored. It was the metal struts that had the ability to pierce his space suit and expose him to the hostile environment of space.

But the metal was another thing. Remo moved his arms and lifted his legs to avoid tumbling shards. A chunk of strut came within reach. Remo grabbed it. It pulled him along, actually carrying him ahead of the oncoming storm. By redirecting its trajectory, he used it to bat away other threats like a ball player suspended on a string.

After a while, the last of the widening storm of shrapnel had passed by. Remo floated in a harmless sea of shining mylar.

When he was in the clear, Remo looked around and blurted, "Where's the shuttle?"

"Retreated to a lower orbit," Smith supplied.

"What about me?"

"There are no rescue procedures for an astronaut adrift amid so much dangerous space junk," Harold

Smith said with a tinny flatness. "The *Atlantis* could be imperiled."

"That's it? No procedures? So end of story?" Remo asked incredulously.

"You knew you were expendable from the day you joined CURE."

A cold sensation settled in Remo's stomach.

"Smitty, you aren't going to leave me up here to die...."

"I have no choice."

"Think of what Chiun will say."

Smith was silent.

"Think of what he'll *do,*" Remo added.

"I am thinking...."

"Think fast," warned Remo. "It's not getting any closer."

Then Smith said, "Can you see the *Atlantis?*"

"Yeah."

"Listen carefully. The mylar is composed of the same material that is used for solar sails. They catch the solar winds. One day man may be able to pilot spacecraft with gigantic solar sails as auxiliary propulsion. Can you reach a larger section?"

"I can try. There's a ton of it around here."

Actually it was more of a matter of waiting until a large enough piece floated to within grabbing range. Remo grasped and released two before he caught one that looked big enough.

Taking one end in both hands, he lifted it over his helmet. His feet found a rip on the lower end and dug in. By stretching, Remo made the fabric taut.

"Point yourself toward the sun," Smith instructed.

Remo did. Not that it was easy. He felt like a moth riding a leaf.

"Now what?"

"Wait. You will not feel the push. But I can direct the shuttle to orient itself with its payload bay ready to catch you."

"I can't see where I'm going."

"Trust the shuttle commander."

An eternity seemed to pass. Remo saw only the fabric before his face and occasional glimpses of stars. He had no sensation of movement. No sensation of time. He was using almost no energy, so he cut his air intake to six careful sips a minute. Enough to sustain life in this state.

In the air-conditioned suit, he began to perspire.

Remo knew he was safe when a dark shadow enveloped him.

"I'm in!" he cried.

"Incredible!" said Smith.

"Hey," Remo said in a suddenly cocky voice. "We're all pros up here."

"No," returned Smith. "You should have run out of oxygen seven minutes ago."

Grabbing at the folded remote manipulator arm of the shuttle, Remo found an oxygen-supply port and plugged his suit in. Air began to flow into his suit.

"Tell them to close the payload doors and light this thing up," he shouted down to Harold Smith. "And tell Chiun I'm coming home."

A relieved Harold Smith said, "Roger," and the com link was terminated as the darkness created by the closing clamshell doors swallowed Remo Williams.

A thought struck him for the first time.

"Hey! I'm an astronaut now. How about that?"

WHEN MAJOR-GENERAL Iyona Stankevitch presented himself, the Cosmic Secret KGB file and his
bottle of vodka to the defense minister of Russia, the
general took both, started to read one and sampled the
other as he read.

When he was done, he looked up from his desk with
glowering eyes.

"You are to be congratulated, Stankevitch."

"Thank you. But this is no time for such pleasant-
ries. I have performed my duty, and now you must
perform yours."

Nodding, the defense minister buzzed his guards,
who appeared instantly.

"Take this dolt out and have him shot."

Through a bleary haze, Stankevitch heard the harsh
words and actually comprehended them.

"What? Why?" he sputtered.

"Had you brought this to me earlier, we would all
be dead now. It is fortunate that it lands upon my desk
after the crisis has passed, and not before."

"But—but Zemyatin gave clear instructions if this
superweapon was ever deployed again...."

"The crisis is over. And so is your life."

As he was dragged out of the Kremlin office, the
defense minister's mocking words followed Iyona
Stankevitch. "And thank you for the vodka. It was
very thoughtful."

Stankevitch realized in that cold moment that the
old Red Russia still lived. In a curious way, it pleased
him to know this just before the people's bullets punished his vital organs....

46

It was a week later, and the Master of Sinanju was seated in the bell tower of Castle Sinanju, goose quill poised over a parchment scroll weighted to the floor with four jade buttons.

"Describe the beast's eyes, my son. Were they fearsome?"

"It didn't have eyes. It looked like a giant aluminum umbrella."

"ParaSol. We know this. But future generations will be ignorant of the mundanity of the menace. Salbyol prophesied a sun dragon. I must describe a sun dragon for the edification of future Masters."

"It didn't have eyes or a tail. And I'm sick of talking about it."

"Then I will employ my awesome imagination to full effect," said Chiun, touching quill to parchment.

"You do that," said Remo.

The taboret phone rang. Remo ignored it.

"It is Smith," said Chiun, redipping his quill.

"I'm not talking to him. He hung me out to dry."

"He is still your emperor. You must speak with him."

"He can kiss my asteroid."

Finally, after 378 consecutive rings, Remo relented.

"If you're selling something, or are named Smith, cross your legs or risk the family jewels."

"Remo, I have discovered something interesting."

"Lose it."

"I have completed my deep background search on Reemer Bolt."

"So what?"

"Eleven years ago, Bolt was employed by Chemical Concepts of Massachusetts, the company that developed the fluorocarbon gun that nearly brought the planet to the brink last time."

"You're kidding!"

"My information is that he was marketing director. When I dealt with the ChemCon employees responsible for the ozone crisis of 1985, I overlooked him. It would appear that history repeated itself."

"So he really was a loose end?"

"No longer," said Smith.

Remo grunted. "Anything else?"

"There are reports out of Russia of a shadowy group of disgruntled ex-KGB operatives attempting to consolidate power."

"Shield?"

"They are being called Felix by ITAR-TASS. The name derives from Felix Dzerzhinsky, the founder of the Soviet secret-police apparatus."

"More loose ends," Remo groaned.

"We will watch them closely."

"Before you go, and you *are* going," said Remo, "whatever happened to that photographer who was dragged off by men in black on TV?"

"Travis Rust has been released unharmed."

"Who had him?"

"FORTEC."

"Why'd they snatch him?" asked Remo.

"Recall that Chiun slew one of their investigators at the BioBubble site. When the body was discovered, FORTEC thought they had a serious alien threat on their hands."

"They did. They just didn't know it. So long, Smith."

And Remo hung up. "How's it coming?" he asked Chiun, who was busily scratching out slashing characters on his scroll.

"I have decided the sun dragon possesses smooth silver skin, and not scales."

"It *was* silver."

"And three thousand years from now, it will trouble the House no more because the Reigning Master of Sinanju slew it without mercy," added Chiun.

"Wait a minute! I was the guy who risked his neck up there."

Chiun smiled thinly. "And I am the Master who is inscribing the truth for the Master who will carry on three thousand years hence."

With that, the Master of Sinanju signed the scroll with his name and sat back, his face serene with the knowledge that he would one day be remembered as the first Master to venture into the Void and return alive. As well as the first Korean in space.

All rumors to the contrary.

TAKE 'EM FREE

4 action-packed novels plus a mystery bonus

NO RISK

NO OBLIGATION TO BUY

A new warrior breed blazes
a trail to an uncertain future.

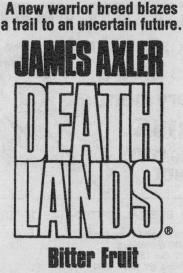

JAMES AXLER
DEATH LANDS®

Bitter Fruit

In the nuclear-storm devastated Deathlands a warrior survivalist
deals with the serpent in a remote Garden of Eden.

Nature rules in the Deathlands, but man still destroys.